LOVER'S BITE

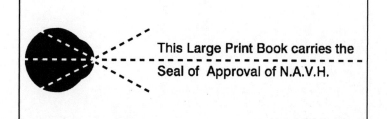

This Large Print Book carries the
Seal of Approval of N.A.V.H.

LOVER'S BITE

MAGGIE SHAYNE

WHEELER PUBLISHING
A part of Gale, Cengage Learning

GALE
CENGAGE Learning™

Detroit • New York • San Francisco • New Haven, Conn • Waterville, Maine • London

GALE
CENGAGE Learning

LIBRARY OF CONGRESS CATALOGING-IN-PUBLICATION DATA

Shayne, Maggie.
   Lover's bite / by Maggie Shayne.
      p. cm. — (Wings in the night series ; #2)
   ISBN-13: 978-1-59722-803-9 (alk. paper)
   ISBN-10: 1-59722-803-6 (alk. paper)
   1. Vampires—Fiction. 2. Large type books. I. Title.
PS3619.H399L68 2008
813'.6—dc22
                                                   2008018571

Published in 2008 by arrangement with Harlequin Books S. A.

Printed in the United States of America
1 2 3 4 5 6 7 12 11 10 09 08

LOVER'S BITE

1

Mirabella DuFrane exited the beachfront adobe mansion as if she were floating, rather than walking. The skintight gown — paisley print, plunging halter neckline, slit up to her slender hip — clung to every perfect curve, despite the fact that she'd given birth only three months ago. No one would have known it to look at her.

Speculation about the identity of her baby girl's father was rampant, but no one except Mirabella knew for sure. And Mirabella wasn't saying. It just added to the mysterious allure of Hollywood's brightest star.

She was the silver screen's flavor of the year. An exotic blend of Italian and Spanish, with copper skin, almond eyes, a figure most women would die for and many men would kill for — she was the ideal. And that she was so elusive — never married, and promising that she never would be — only added to her massive appeal. She was fond of telling the press that she was too free a spirit to ever be tied down, that no man could ever own her, possess her, or even hold her for very long. She would never be tamed. The tabloids were constantly pairing her with one man or another. Politicians, businessmen, actors. Any photo of her with a male was fodder for gossip in the rags. She never denied or confirmed any of it, just smiled her mysterious smile and answered questions with more questions when the reporters cast their lines into her waters on their fishing expeditions.

That was Mirabella.

And yet, there was something else about her. Something frail and otherworldly that rarely showed. It lingered beneath the surface, like a fragile seashell resting on the ocean floor and hoping no rough currents stirred it up to the surface.

Mirabella floated toward the black stretch limousine that waited at the curb, her gown's hemline skimming just above the sidewalk, creating that airborne illusion she so loved. Paparazzi swarmed, held at a distance by Bella's ever-present bodyguards.

Once it had been unusual for the press to be in Santa Luna in such droves, but this small coastal town, twenty-five miles south of Los Angeles, had become a haven for the rich and the famous. Too expensive for common folk, too remote for fans, it had become the hot spot for celebrity getaways — quick ones, when there was no time to go on a real trip. Mirabella had been a guest at an exclusive party at the mansion known as Avalon. Its fanciful and somewhat pretentious name had been thought up by its former owners, a Hollywood pair who'd peaked in the fifties before retiring here. The Avalon Ball had become an annual event, and Hollywood's elite hungered to see their names on the guest list. Because being invited was such a coup, no one complained too much about the press.

Cameras flashed in the night as Mirabella made her way along the clear path to the waiting car, smiling and waving all the way.

Then there were different kinds of flashes. Three of them. Bella's smile froze in place as her body jerked in perfect synch with those bright eruptions. Her milk-chocolate eyes fluttered, lashes lowering as she looked down. Blood flowers blossomed in slow motion like a Hollywood depiction of an acid trip over the front of her designer gown. She lifted her head, the huge gold hoops in her ears jangling. One hand rose, as if reaching out for help, and then Mirabella's heavily lined eyes fell closed, and she folded over herself and sank to the sidewalk, graceful, even with three bullets in her abdomen.

The press swarmed as her bodyguards fought to hold them off. Police on crowd control duty closed in to help, and within a minute, sirens could be heard as more police and an ambulance arrived.

"It was too late to save Mirabella DuFrane," a vaguely familiar male voice said.

It was some retired news anchor, Jack Heart thought, hired to narrate documentaries once he was replaced by a younger model at the news desk. He couldn't remember the guy's name.

"She died in the hospital that very night. But that's far from where this story ends. The starlet's body was stolen from the hospital morgue, and to this day, it has never been found, leading to numerous reported sightings in the years since. And her murder? Never solved."

There was a knock at the motel room door. Jack looked up, irritated at the interruption. Then he sensed who was on the other side. Topaz.

Jumping to his feet, he popped the DVD out of his portable player, returned it to its case — a case that bore Mirabella's image, and the title *DEATH OF A GODDESS: The*

Mirabella DuFrane Story — and closed the lid. "Just a minute." He quickly stuffed the documentary into his backpack, zipped it closed and tossed it into the closet. "Come in, Topaz," he said as he opened the door to greet her.

She stepped inside, and for just an instant, Jack's gaze was stuck fast on her face. The resemblance was subtle, but it was there in the delicate bone structure, the cheekbones, the jawline, even the eyebrows. Her skin wasn't as dark, and her ethnicity wasn't as obvious as it had been in her mother. But she was every bit as stunning.

No. More so.

"What are *you* staring at?"

"I was just thinking it's a shame your insides don't match your outsides."

"Oh, *I'm* the one who's not what I pretend to be? As I recall, you're the one who professed your undying devotion right up until you vanished with a half million of my hard-earned dollars."

"Inheriting is not earning."

"It was in my case." She narrowed her eyes. "And how do you know I inherited it, anyway?"

He averted his eyes. Topaz was under the impression that none of her vampiric friends knew who she had been in life. And maybe

11

none of them did — other than him. But he knew. Now.

"Lucky guess," he muttered.

"Yeah, well. I don't suppose the other half of my money appeared to you in your sleep, did it?"

"I gave you back the half I had. I told you, Gregor has the rest. I'll get it from him somehow, as soon as we track him down. I promise."

"Sadly, I know just how much your promises are worth, Jack." She shrugged. "And I'm pretty sure we've reached a dead end when it comes to tracking your former boss down."

"What do you mean?"

"I mean he got away. Reaper's calling a meeting in an hour. I'm pretty sure he's going to disband the gang — send us all our separate ways. At least until he can get a line on Gregor again."

He let his gaze move down her body as she spoke, barely listening to her words and instead tracing her curves with his eyes. Tight jeans, tiny silk blouse, her breasts straining against the fabric. Even while he stared at them, her nipples stiffened, as if they could feel his gaze like a physical touch. He got up and walked toward her.

She tensed, her brown eyes wary, watchful, but she wouldn't back away. No, she was too proud for that.

Jack traced her cheek with a fingertip. "I kept some of my promises — when I promised to make you scream, to play your body like no one ever had or ever would. I didn't break any of those vows, Topaz."

Her eyes fell closed, and her breath slipped from her lips in a slow, soft sigh.

He bent his head until his lips were only a breath away from hers, and he whispered, "If you stick around a little while, I'll keep them all over again."

He felt her body respond. Felt it tugging at his, felt her yearning, her desire. Even heard it in the breathy quality of her wavering reply, saw it in the way her lips trembled as she gave it, while his eyes fell closed and he swayed closer, about to kiss her.

"I could do that. Or you could just eat shit and die," she whispered.

He frowned and opened his eyes.

Hers were coated in a sheet of solid ice — one that concealed a riot of emotions, he was certain.

"I hate you, Jack."

"You want me," he said, straightening away from her.

"One doesn't negate the other."

"Okay. Fine. I'll be ready for Reaper's

meeting."

He backed away a few more inches, mostly to give himself relief. Yes, she was just a mark, albeit the only one he'd ever regretted. But he wanted her like he'd never wanted another woman. And he was determined to get her out of his system once and for all.

"Why are you here, Topaz?"

"To give you this." She fished a slip of paper from her jeans pocket and handed it to him. "And to say goodbye."

He opened it, glimpsing an address, then quickly refocused on her. "You're going somewhere?"

"I'm going *there*." She nodded at the paper in his hand.

"And you couldn't leave without coming to say goodbye, letting me know where you would be, in case —"

"In case you manage to keep a promise for the first time in your life and get me back the rest of my money. I wanted you to know where to send it. And you'd *better,* Jack. Because if you haven't repaid me by the time I finish my business in California, I'm gonna track you down, and I'm gonna hurt you. And *not* in the good way."

She turned on her heel, reached for the doorknob.

Jack gripped her shoulder and spun her back around to face him. "That's bullshit and you know it. You couldn't leave without saying goodbye to me, because you still have feelings for me." His arm slid around her waist, hand cupping her ass, and he jerked her against him. "Admit it."

"Oh, I have feelings for you, all right," she snapped. "Contempt. Disgust. Fury."

"Lust. Passion. Desire."

"Desire to do murder, at least," she agreed.

He ground his hips against her, and she closed her eyes, unable to suppress the shiver that passed through her. "Back off, Jack."

He released her, staring into her face in search of confirmation that she still felt the things he did — the physical things that made sense, not the other ones. Before he could find it, she was out the door, slamming it behind her.

Sighing, Jack pushed a hand through his hair in utter frustration. But then reason returned, and he lunged toward the door and peered through the peephole.

Topaz was standing on the other side, her hands pressed to her bowed head. She looked as if she wanted to scream.

He just wasn't sure whether it was with

anger or desire. Hell.

Jack wondered why she was really leaving. To get away from him, he would wager. But why go all the way to Califor—

He turned slowly, gazing at the closet door, but seeing, in his mind's eye, snippets of the film he'd just been watching, hearing echoes of the narrator's voice. He gazed down at the piece of paper she'd given him.

Avalon Mansion.

Santa Luna, California.

Good God, she was going to the very place where her mother had been killed. She was going to try to solve Hollywood's most compelling mystery.

It could be dangerous.

Maybe he should tag along. If only he could think of a plausible excuse. Reaching for his backpack, he unzipped it and reached inside. The bag full of money he'd claimed he didn't have was still there, still intact. He might need to give it back to her sooner or later, he supposed, as a way of convincing her of his sincerity and good intentions. The very reasons he'd given her back the first half. It hadn't worked entirely, but it *had* seemed to knock a chink or two in that brick wall she'd erected around her heart to keep him out.

He might need to return the rest to win

her trust.

He probably shouldn't waste his time. But then again, he had to stick closely to one of the members of the gang, because he had bigger fish to fry this time around, and having access to Reaper would be crucial. Sticking like glue to the big guy would be too obvious, though. And since the gang was splitting up, for the moment, he was going to have to pick one member to latch onto. Why not Topaz?

And so what if he had to give her back the rest of her money? He was pretty sure there was a lot more than 500 K to be made this time.

He fingered the manila envelope that rested inside the bag with the cash and the DVD. It was stamped with the words *CLASSIFIED: PROPERTY OF THE U.S. CENTRAL INTELLIGENCE AGENCY.* He'd found it in his former boss's safe, along with Gregor's half of Topaz's money.

Maybe — just maybe, if he played his cards right — Jack could make whatever there was to be made of what he'd found in that envelope *and* keep half of what he'd conned from Topaz.

That notion made his collar feel a little tight, his stomach a little queasy. He cleared his throat and shook off the unaccustomed sensations. Guilt was nothing but wasted energy.

He pulled out the DVD and told himself he really ought to slip it back into Topaz's belongings before she discovered it was missing. If she found out that he had been snooping through her stuff, she would really be unhappy to see him when he showed up on her oceanfront doorstep.

After she left Jack's room, Topaz held her head in her hands and waited for the hunger that had suffused her veins to ease, for the trembling that had possessed her body to stop. She wanted him. God, she wanted him so badly it was like an addiction.

She knew he was no good. And yet she wanted him. No good for her, and no good, period. And yet she ached for him. He was a con man. And yet she hungered for his kiss. If she fell back into those strong arms again, knowing what she knew about him, then she was the most pathetic, self-destructive, stupid woman on the planet. And she was determined to be none of those things.

"You okay?"

She lifted her head and met Roxy's eyes. Roxy. The wild, irreverent, redheaded mortal whose age was fathomless. The belladonna antigen in her blood, the hallmark of the only humans with the potential to become vampires, made it unlikely she would live nearly as long as she already had, but she showed no signs of slowing down. Roxy. The most trusted mortal Topaz could imagine. One of the sexiest, most beautiful women of any age she'd ever seen. And easily the wisest.

"You still love that asshole, don't you?" Roxy asked, coming to a stop very close to her in the hallway.

"That would make me a complete idiot, and I'm not an idiot, Roxy."

"No, you're not. But we can't always help how we feel."

"I can. I'm the least likely person in the world to fall for a con in the first place, much less twice by the same person. No way."

"Well, good. Don't let him con you again." Roxy shrugged. "Doesn't mean you can't enjoy him, though." She glanced toward Jack's closed door. "Hell, if I didn't know you were into him, I might give him a tumble myself. 'Course, that would spoil him for all other women, but you know, some things can't be helped." She winked at Topaz.

Topaz smiled, grateful for Roxy's always

uplifting influence. "Is everyone else in the van already?"

"Vixen and Seth are — probably making out in the back, if I know those two. Raphael's on his way. The devil only knows about Briar. I haven't told Ilyana about the meeting yet. On my way to do that right now, actually."

"Let's tell her together."

Roxy nodded, and the two of them strolled down the hall of the Super 8 Motel, toward the room the newcomer, Ilyana, had taken. They'd found the mortal — one of the Chosen, like Roxy, though far younger — locked in a cage in Gregor's suite during their latest encounter with the rogue vampire. They'd rescued her, but she was afraid of them, and no wonder, if that monster had been her only experience with the undead. She'd told them almost nothing. Not why he'd held her captive, nor for how long. Topaz could only imagine what she might have suffered while in Gregor's care, though she bore no illusions that it had been less than horrific.

Roxy tapped on the door. "Ilyana, it's Roxy."

The door opened and the mortal, with her pixie-short platinum-blond hair and striking blue eyes, stared out at the two of them.

Her eyes were warm and welcoming on Roxy's, but when they fell upon Topaz, they cooled considerably. "What do you want?" she asked.

"Group meeting," Roxy told her. "We're gathering in the van."

Ilyana searched Roxy's face, her gaze occasionally darting past it to Topaz's, but never lingering there. She was still wary. "Are we giving up the search for Gregor?" she asked at length.

"Taking a break, maybe. Giving up? No way. Raphael is way too stubborn for that," Roxy said.

Nodding, Ilyana turned. "I'll gather my things. Give me a few minutes."

"That's fine." Roxy pulled the door closed, and linked arms with Topaz. "You know, he's got it just as badly as you do."

"Who's got what?" Topaz asked, pretending she didn't know exactly what Roxy was trying to say.

"He —" Roxy pointed toward Jack's room *"— has got it —"* she pumped her fists at her sides and thrust her hips a couple of times *"— for you."* She poked Topaz in the chest with a forefinger. "Just as badly as *you —"* poke *"— have it —"* thrust *"— for him."*

"Okay, okay. I get it. Enough with the pantomime already. It's creepy."

Roxy frowned. "Men usually find it more sexy than creepy, but I suppose being a straight girl —"

"And you're wrong. He doesn't feel a damn thing for me."

"Not even . . ." Roxy pumped her hips again, more subtly this time, though.

"Well, sure, *that*. I mean, who wouldn't?"

"Exactly."

"But that's physical. He'd jump my bones if I'd let him. He'd also just as soon take my money and run again as look at me."

"Then why do you suppose he's here?" Roxy stared into Topaz's eyes for a long moment, almost as if she expected an answer to what she had to know was an impossible question. "He already took the money," she went on. "So why hasn't he run?"

"He only came back to me when it looked like our gang was going to kick his gang's ass."

"He could have gone anywhere to get away from Gregor and the rogues, Topaz. He didn't have to join up with us. I think you should keep that in mind."

"Probably figured I had a few bucks left in the bank he hadn't scammed yet. Or maybe he's planning to run a con on one of you."

Roxy lifted her brows and looked over her

shoulder toward his room. "Hot damn, it would be worth it. I wonder how much is in my IRA by now?"

"Fuck you, Roxy."

Roxy grinned from ear to ear. "I don't swing that way, Topaz. Though I compliment you on your taste in women."

Topaz felt her frown dissolve as she elbowed Roxy lightly in the rib cage, and the two of them laughed together as they made their way across the dark motel parking lot toward a canary-yellow conversion van named Shirley.

Jack waited until everyone else had headed out to the van to slip out of his room and down the hall to Topaz's. He picked the locks with the power of his mind, hand on the knob, ear to the door, willing the tumblers to, well, tumble. When they did, he opened the door and walked inside.

Her things were packed and her cases stacked. A half dozen of them, at least. Designer luggage, all of it matching, made by Coach. He thought they only made handbags and shoes. And those cost a fortune. What must an entire set of Coach *luggage* have set her back?

Damn, he must have left too much of her money behind if she could still afford to blow it like this.

Sighing, he gazed at the rumpled blankets, and his throat closed up. She hadn't made her bed — left that for the maid, along with a hefty tip on the nightstand to thank her for her trouble. The covers were untidy and thrown back to reveal the faint outline of her body on the mattress, the imprint of her head on the pillow.

Damn.

Before he could stop himself, Jack was crawling onto that bed, pressing his face to the place where she'd rested, inhaling her scent, and wishing it were her flesh he was lying on and not just her bed.

Intoxicating, the essence of Topaz that lingered there.

He sat up, put his hands in his hair and tousled it vigorously. "Snap out of it, Jack."

It was easier said than done, but he did manage to roll over and get off her bed and onto his feet. He reminded himself of his reason for being there, and the fact that the others were probably waiting for him in the van and might send someone looking for him at any moment. Okay, then. He slid the DVD into one of her bags and exited the room, making sure the door locked behind him.

He stiffened his spine, hoped his yearning

didn't show on his face, and then thought, so what if it did? He wanted her, that was all. It was physical. Sexual. Lustual, if that was a word. And if it wasn't, it should be, because it described to a T what he felt for the luscious, lovely Topaz-formerly-known-as-Tanya DuFrane, daughter of a movie star.

A dead movie star.

He headed along the hall to the exit, crossed the parking lot and joined the others in the van, climbing in through the already open side door and giving the interior a quick visual sweep. The back row of seats held Vixen and Seth, sitting so close together you could have fit a lumberjack on either side of them, but instead only Ilyana sat there. In the front seat, Reaper sat on the passenger side, Roxy behind the wheel, just like always. The middle row was host to Briar, who sat there with the same brooding, inwardly focused expression she'd been wearing since they pried Gregor's shock collar off her neck. Prior to that she'd been wild, fighting them every step of the way, hissing and scratching at every opportunity like a feral cat. She'd been dangerous, untrustworthy and probably bad right to her soul. And frankly, he had preferred that to this . . . this shell.

He supposed she would snap out of it

sooner or later. And he would lay odds they would all be wishing her back to this state of silent brooding once she did.

Beside Briar sat the object of his desire. Topaz. He met her eyes briefly, just to remind her that she felt it, too — this longing, this hunger — that she felt it and he knew it, and she knew he knew it. No use tiptoeing around the facts.

Finally he lowered himself onto the seat between the two women.

"About time," Topaz muttered.

Briar said nothing. She'd had very little to say since they'd rescued her from Gregor, who'd been torturing her the same way she'd personally helped him to torture Vixen. Reversal of fortune, big-time. It tended to mix a girl up, he bet.

Her eyes were haunted.

He couldn't help but chuck her under the chin just a little. "Don't look so glum, wildcat. Gregor had us both fooled."

She lifted her black eyes to his, but they never locked on. "He never fooled you," she said. Her voice was dull. A monotone that echoed from lack of emotion, the way an empty room echoed from lack of furniture. "You knew what he was the whole time. You were just playing him."

He shrugged. "Well, I've been around

longer than you have. You live and learn, you know." Then, uncomfortable with the turmoil swirling just beneath the surface of her eyes, he shifted his focus to Reaper. "What's up? We throwing in the towel?"

"Only temporarily. Until I get a handle on where Gregor has headed, there's no point in us all staying together."

"Nor any particular point," Seth cut in, leaning forward in the rear seat, "in us splitting up." He looked around the van. "Is there?"

Just as the others were muttering in agreement, Reaper said, "There is, actually. I, um . . . I believe I'm being followed."

Jack gasped louder than any of them. Hell. Probably overkill. Topaz cut him a narrow-eyed look, but he pretended not to notice. "By whom?" he demanded.

"I don't know for sure, but they seem awfully familiar to me."

"You think they're spooks?" Seth asked.

"No one says 'spooks' anymore, kid." Reaper swallowed hard, then nodded. "But yeah. I think they're Agency. They can be dangerous, and there's no point in all of us being at risk."

Roxy smacked the steering wheel. "Right. You'll just send us on our merry way while you take the heat alone," she snapped.

"And if you get your ass killed, then no great loss."

He glanced her way, and his eyes softened. "Rox, I'm not gonna get my ass killed. I'll drop out of sight for a while. Lay low until the heat's off. And it'll be a hell of a lot easier for me to do that without a half dozen soldiers, no matter how loyal, marching along behind me. Don't you think?"

She sighed — probably, Jack thought, in frustration that she couldn't argue with his logic.

"So you're not going to continue tracking Gregor?" The question came from Ilyana, who sat close behind Jack.

"Oh, I'm going to. Just quietly and discreetly. I might lie low for a few days before I put forth too much effort, though, just to try to shake these agents off my tail."

Everyone looked at him, Ilyana, waiting, as if she didn't think he was finished. He hesitated, then went on. "Look, Gregor admitted he was working for the CIA. His rogue activities had a purpose. He and his gang have been murdering and feeding on the innocent with the full knowledge, approval and support of the Agency, all just to lure me in. Everyone knew I was the one the vampires would send to shut him down, to take him out."

"Because you were an assassin when you worked for them," Ilyana said, her voice soft. "Before you became a vampire."

"Yes. And because they're aware I've continued in that role, when necessary, ever since," Reaper told her. "Gregor was supposed to capture me and hand me over to my former employers. But he got greedy, decided to try to drain me and take my power instead, then kill me."

Jack nodded. "I picked up on that much before I switched teams," he said. "Gregor developed a real lust for killing, for taking whatever he wants without remorse or repercussions. And he's been gathering money along the way. You feed on the wealthy, you tend to make a profit in the process. He's been raking it in, pillaging, really. And I think he's drunk on his power. All he wants is more."

"Absolute power corrupts absolutely," Reaper quoted softly.

"What do you think the CIA intends to do with you, if they ever do get you back?" Jack asked him. "What the hell do they want with you now that you're a vamp?"

"I was the best assassin they ever trained, Jack. Imagine how much better I'd be now that I'm a vampire. And they've already mucked up my mind to the point that they

29

can control me by dropping a single word. You've seen the results of that."

"They probably think of you as a valuable secret weapon," Roxy whispered.

Jack lowered his head, unable to look any of them in the eye for a moment.

"They'll stop at nothing to get me back," Reaper said. "And that includes kidnapping or even torturing any one of you. I can't have that on my conscience. I'd have to turn myself in if that happened. So do me a favor and take off, so I won't have to."

That, too, was impossible to argue with, Jack realized. Reaper was good.

"I'm willing to go off on my own," Ilyana said softly. "But I intend to continue the search for Gregor. If you like, I can contact you when I find him."

Every eye in the van focused on her. She had only just joined them and had no reason to be so invested in their mission.

"Is it vengeance you seek?" Vixen asked.

Ilyana shot her a look.

Vixen seemed to shrink a bit more deeply into her long copper hair and began playing with the ends, as she tended to do when nervous. "I mean, he held and tortured me, too. But . . . honestly, for your own sake, it's better if you can look ahead, rather than behind you."

"I don't want vengeance," Ilyana said softly.

"Then why —"

"He has something of mine. That's as much as I'm going to say. I won't rest until I get it back. So if any of you want me to call you once I find him — and I *will* find him — then give me a means of reaching you before I leave."

Topaz dipped into her pocket, scribbled a number on a scrap of paper and handed it to her. Roxy did the same.

"I intend to stick with you, Reaper," Seth said from the backseat.

"Not this time." Reaper quickly looked over at Roxy. "Or you, either. Come on, guys, cut me some slack here. Just for a little while. Scatter and wait. I'll call you back when things cool off. It won't be long."

They all sighed. Topaz finally spoke. "I actually have some personal business to attend to. I'll be in California. Jack has my contact info."

"Can you get me a copy, hon, before you go?" Roxy asked. "I'll make sure everyone else gets it, too."

Topaz slanted him a look, and he returned a sheepish shrug. "They don't trust me any more than you do, I guess."

"Can't say I blame them."

"Here," Roxy said, reaching past Reaper to open the glove compartment. "Why don't we all just jot down some info? A cell phone, a friend, an address, an e-mail, anything. As long as we each have one means of communication that we can commit to checking often and not changing." As she spoke, she pulled out a small notepad and a couple of pens, and passed them around the van.

"If you know how to reach me, they'll still have reason to come after you," Reaper said.

Jack shook his head. "They'd have no way of knowing we had your number. They could just as easily assume we do, even if we don't."

Reaper hesitated, then sighed and nodded. "You're right. Okay, then."

Everyone jotted and passed, until they all had copies of each other's info. Then, finally, Seth said, "Can I take the Mustang?"

"Yep," Reaper said. "And Roxy will keep Shirley. She and I can drop the rest of you wherever you want. But let's get on it. I want us scattered to the winds before dawn. Okay?"

"Not exactly," Jack said. And he shifted his gaze from Reaper to Briar, who sat beside him in silence. "I think Briar should stay with someone."

"I can take care of myself," she said softly.

"I know you can. No one said you couldn't. But, uh . . . well, you can't be trusted on your own, can you? Like the rest of us, you know the word that can be used to turn our friend Reaper here into a whirling dervish of death. Unlike the rest of us, we can't just have you running around all alone."

She narrowed her eyes on him. "I could kill you as easily as looking at you."

Jack actually felt his lips pull at the corners, though he didn't exactly smile. "There you are," he whispered. "Where have you been, Briar?"

She crossed her arms over her chest, quickly covering the flash of anger with her new expression of bland disinterest. "You can assign me any babysitter you like. I'll stay until I want to leave. And when I want to leave, nothing's going to stop me."

"She stays with me," Reaper said.

Briar's studied expression showed a hint, a very brief hint, of panic.

2

The adobe-style mansion sprawled beneath the stars, with countless arches and a clay-red pottery roof, bright red doors and bright green trim. The front walkway was made of flagstones that had been in place so long they appeared to be part of the ground. The drive was paved and curved inward toward the house, then away from it, forming a giant, gentle S as it looped toward a massive garage that could easily house six vehicles. The apartment above the garage was larger than many people's houses.

Topaz stood beside the taxi, her back to the cab, her eyes on the house. The lawns rolled, the grass far from lush but rather spotty, with bare spots and red rock peering through. Cacti of every type filled the spaces in between, some of them flowering, some small and compact, while others stood with their arms raised above their heads like the stereotypical "reach for the sky" cacti in countless Western films.

Sand crept up to the very edges of the lawn, invading every time a breeze came up. Beyond the villa, ocean waves filled the night with their song, a chorus of harmonic whispers, growing louder, more insistent, but never becoming shouts. Not even when the waves broke and tumbled over the sand, then retreated in the closest sound there could be to silence. *Shuuuuushhhhhhh.* And then there was the fragrance those waves left in their wake — freshly laundered sunshine, brine and the sea.

Her mother had died here, Topaz thought. Right here, while that massive ocean looked on, never missing a step in its endless soft shoe.

For a moment Topaz stood there, staring at Avalon's front door, and then suddenly she was swept back in time, her imagination fed by the DVD she'd finally viewed. Why now, after all these years? Why? Why was she suddenly so driven to know everything about her mother when she'd deliberately avoided any of the stories and tales, the gossip and legends, the conspiracy theories and police reports, up until now?

But it didn't really matter why. It was here. *She* was here. And she had to know everything.

In her mind's eye, it all played out again, this time with even more detail, supplied by some inner knowing, perhaps, or maybe she was making it all up.

The stunning superstar, Mirabella, smiling, waving, laughing as she stepped out the door — that door, right there. It was red and wooden and arched at the top. She walked toward the road, moving so gracefully that she seemed to float over the flagstone walkway. She'd been wearing heels. Four-inch-high chunky heels with platforms underneath the front — very seventies. Strappy on top, open toes. Her toenails had been done, too — a minty green shade that matched one of the colors in that long dress, along with the color of her fingernails, her designer bag and her eyeshadow. Thick black liner, pale, pale shadow. Frosted lipstick. Big hair.

And yet she was gorgeous. Absolutely stunning. Her beauty had been so real, so deep, so natural, that it suffused every hint of mod she'd tried to use to enhance it. Most women would look back at that period and wonder what they'd been thinking. Mirabella might have, too, but it wouldn't have mattered. She was just as beautiful in a dress the same pattern as the *Scooby-Doo* Mystery Van as she would have been completely naked. Her eyes were too powerful to be disguised by heavy makeup. She was Mirabella, no last name needed, at the time or now. Everyone knew who she was.

The black limo pulled up closer, and the driver got out to open the door. A throng of paparazzi snapped shots from a distance, but they were kept from getting too close by the discreet bodyguards, posted at intervals a few yards away from the starlet.

And then the shots rang out. Three of them.

The beautiful actress's flawless smile froze on her lips even as it fled from her eyes. Topaz could see this part so clearly. She'd memorized the expressions as they had crossed her mother's face, one behind the other. She wasn't sure if she was glad someone had been filming or not. Part of her thought she might have been able to visualize every nuance even without the film.

Trembling, Mirabella looked down to where her hands had flown to her body, then drew her palms away slowly to see the blood that coated them. Shivering, Topaz found her own hands echoing the same motions, her own eyes looking downward, her own mind slightly surprised that there was no blood on her hands.

Mirabella's gaze lifted, her eyes calling out

for help in stunned silence. Pleading for help from someone, *anyone.* And then her knees just folded, and she sank to the ground like a flower that had been cut. Her thick black lashes lowered like velvet curtains on the world's most vibrant stage. Her eyes fell closed, and she took her final bow.

Topaz stood there, staring down at the flagstone walkway, straining her senses. Was this the very spot, then? It was close. As close as she could make out from the footage that had been taken that night.

She sank to her knees, pressing her palms to the cool stone, as if by some fluke she would still be able to feel some trace of her mother's energy. Her life force. Even her blood. Was that it there, discoloring the stones? Or was that nothing but a pattern in the rock?

The sound of a motor jerked her attention back to the present, and she rose, blinking away hot tears and turning just in time to see the taxi rolling out of sight, kicking up a cloud of dust in its wake. Her suitcases were stacked, none-too-neatly, on the curb.

She'd handed the guy two twenties for a twenty-five-dollar fare. She guessed he thought the rest was his tip. And it would have been deserved, if he'd carried the cases to the door for her. Bastard.

Anger was good. She could be furious over fifteen bucks and no service, and distract herself from the real feelings trying to overwhelm her. Feelings of grief and sadness, a sense of loss, for the mother she'd never known and never really mourned. Was it long-overdue pain? Or was she indulging in self-pity? Or maybe just diving headlong into anything, no matter how painful, that would remove her attention from Jack Heart?

Didn't matter. She was here; she was doing this.

Squaring her shoulders, Topaz marched up the walkway to the front door and reached out to ring the bell. But in the wire flower basket beside the door, an envelope caught her eye — probably because it had her name on it — stopping her hand in midair.

She tugged the envelope out of the basket and opened it, and a key spilled out into her palm. There was a note besides, scrawled on Avalon Mansion stationery, with the address and phone number at the top.

Topaz,
The place is all yours. Since you've paid for every room, there will be no other guests, and as you requested, my

husband and I have moved into the garage apartment and will give you all the privacy you require. Unless you call to request it, we'll stay out of your way for the duration of your seven-day stay. Feel free to call if you need anything. Enjoy your vacation.

Kimber Argent, Owner
Santa Luna

Topaz sighed. "Great. I thought they'd at least be here to say hi and schlep the freaking bags up to my room."

"Could be you were a bit too convincing when you told them you wanted to be left alone, hmm?"

She whirled, stunned. *No one* crept up on a vampire. Well, not usually. She'd been distracted. And now she was . . . gaping like an air-starved goldfish. She clapped her jaw shut.

"You *did* tell them you wanted to be left alone, didn't you, Topaz?" Jack asked from the sidewalk.

She tried to answer, then settled for nodding instead, as she fought to suck in some air, clear her throat, control the stupid, stupid, *stupid* impulse to run back down that walkway to him and throw her arms around his neck.

"Surprised to see me?"

"Surprised. Dismayed. Irritated." Good, good. She was speaking. Real words. And not welcoming ones, even. Great.

"And a little bit glad?" He was standing right beside the massive pile of luggage. Before she could answer, he scooped up half of it and strode up the walkway. "If nothing more, at least be glad there's someone to carry your bags."

She didn't move. Just stood there, with the key in one hand, the note and envelope in the other. There was a car behind him on the curb, one she'd been too absorbed in her own thoughts to hear pulling up. A Porsche Carrera, naturally. Only the best for Jack. She wondered a little bitterly who he'd scammed it from. Another rich female, too in love with him to listen to her own common sense? "Why are you here?"

"Because I, apparently, know you better than your hosts do. Enough to know that your 'I want to be left alone' bullshit was just that. Bullshit." He grunted and shifted the bags a little. "Unlock the door, will you? These are heavy, even for a vampire. What did you pack, anyway? A metric ton of your native soil?"

"So amusing." Frowning, she inserted the key, turned it and swung the door open.

Jack stepped inside, setting the bags on the floor.

She walked in behind him and looked around the place. Had it been this way when her mother was here? Or had the decor changed? She imagined it had. Now it was nice, but modern. Prints by Mexican artists lined the walls, colorful and vibrant scenes of the ocean, of palm trees and sunsets. Brightly striped throw rugs and runners with tassels at the ends covered the hardwood floors. Horsehair vases with Navajo patterns, and Kokopelli dancing and playing the pipes, stood everywhere she looked. Jewel-toned walls surrounded her; bright green, burgundy, yellow.

Jack cleared his throat, probably because she wasn't paying him a lick of attention.

She glanced at him, then at the bags. "They're going to have to go upstairs sooner or later," she said.

"I realize that. I just assumed you hadn't picked out a room yet. Have you?"

"No."

"Well, once you do, I'll take the bags the rest of the way." He turned to head outside for the ones he'd left at the curb.

"You won't be here that long," she muttered.

He didn't give any indication as to

whether he heard her. He just marched on, grabbed the remaining bags and brought them inside. Then he stacked them by the door, closed it and stood there staring at her. "Well?"

"You're not staying here."

He shrugged. "I have a place."

The way he said it, with a "you're not the boss of me" tone, convinced her that he had absolutely nowhere else to go, even though his words claimed otherwise.

"That's bull. You didn't have time to make other arrangements."

"How do you know what I had time to do?"

"Because I only just arrived myself."

"Yeah, but you took longer getting here."

"I had to go home first. Pack some things." She tried not to sound too defensive.

"I flew in immediately. I've been in town two nights already. And I've had time to do plenty."

She hated it when he contradicted her and managed to be right about it. "Why did you follow me?"

"Technically, I didn't. I got here first. Besides, I didn't have to follow you. I knew where you were going. You told me, remember?"

She lifted her brows, clearly surprised.

"Not so you could follow me."

"Oh sure. Tell me there wasn't some part of you secretly hoping I'd show up, and sweep you into my arms and kiss you until you gave it up to me. Come on, Topaz, you know it crossed your mind." He put his hands on her shoulders and stared intently at her mouth, then jerked her just a little bit closer as he lowered his head.

She could almost taste him and, God, right then she wanted to, more than she wanted to wake up again at sundown. But she had her pride. She ducked his kiss and turned away from him, so he wouldn't see the naked hunger in her eyes. "If it did cross my mind, Jack, it was always preceded by the image of you handing me the rest of my money and telling me how sorry you were for taking it, and for using me and for hurting me." She shrugged. "One ain't gonna happen without the other, bud."

He lowered his head. She felt the motion rather than saw it.

"So have you got my money?" She felt a little stronger now. Strong enough to turn and face him again.

Without lifting it, he shook his head.

"I didn't think so. So I guess that means goodbye."

"No problem. I told you, I've got a place."

"And you still haven't told me why you're here."

Sighing, he reached into his long coat, which he didn't need, as the night was warm and vampires didn't feel the cold the way mortals did, anyway. They noticed it, but it wasn't uncomfortable for them. Jack's coat, long and dark, was more fashion accessory than necessity. And he looked hot in it, damn him. He pulled a manila envelope from somewhere within that sexy coat and tossed it onto a marble stand just inside the door. "I know why *you're* here, Topaz."

She jerked her head up, her gaze darting from that envelope to his eyes. "How?"

"Hell, woman, get it through your head that I know you better than anyone ever has. You look enough like her that I'm surprised it's not obvious to everyone. Or maybe I'm the only man who can see the real you. Tanya."

His words hurt. Probably because they were lies — beautiful lies, lies she'd wished some man would make true one day. But none ever had, nor ever would. Particularly not him. "Don't ever call me that."

"It's who you are, deep down."

"It's not. It hasn't been for a long time now."

He sighed. "Look, it doesn't matter how I

know. I know, that's all. So I made a call to an . . . acquaintance of mine who's connected. I got some inside info for you. And I don't like what it implies."

"I don't care what you like," she lied. She was burning with curiosity. She wanted to open that envelope and pore over its contents right this second. She wanted to thank him. She wanted to kiss him.

"Digging into your mother's murder could be dangerous."

She frowned hard, but before she could decide which of the dozens of questions to fire at him first, he was out the door. "Lock up tight, baby," he called. "It'll be dawn soon."

She watched him go, having no idea where the hell he was going — which should be the least of her worries, she knew. He walked to the road and got into his hot-looking black car, started the engine. Then he turned on the headlights and roared away.

Only then did she manage to close the door. She turned the locks not because he had told her to, but because it made sense. Then, her hands trembling, she took the envelope, opened the clasp and pulled out the paper-clipped sheets it contained.

The cover page read: *PROFILES OF PER-*

*SONS OF INTEREST IN THE MURDER OF
MIRABELLA DUFRANE.*

"What the hell? They had suspects? I
never knew of any suspects." Topaz moved
through the giant, sprawling foyer through a
wide archway into the living room, which
had a fireplace and soft sand-colored fur-
nishings, white carpet, and wide, wide
windows that were bare and uncovered and
looked out at the vista beyond. Rolling
dunes and the mighty Pacific. The scene was
so breathtaking that she paused for just a
moment to take it in.

Then practicality intervened, and she
glanced upward. Bamboo blinds, and window shades beneath them. Thank God, she
thought. Those windows would let in way
too much sunlight by day.

Okay. She sank onto the soft sofa — into
it, to be more accurate — and laid the sheets
out on the glass-topped bamboo coffee
table. And then she began to read.

Jack parked the Carrera in front of a meter
on a suburban street about a mile from
where he planned to spend the night. He
locked up the car, hoping no one would
bother it, and put the maximum amount of
change into the meter. It would get him
through most of the day. And if he got a

ticket toward sundown, so be it. It wasn't like he would ever pay the thing.

He took his bedroll from the passenger seat and, slinging it over his shoulder, began the walk to his temporary abode. It wasn't much, a family crypt in a cemetery beyond the suburbs, surrounded by rolling fields and with no one around to observe anything amiss. The crypt belonged to the family Carlisle, and it was roomy and spacious, and any corpses inside had long since turned to dust. They didn't keep it locked. Hell, who did these days?

There was utterly no reason why a vampire should sleep in a crypt. He liked the poetic cliché of it, though. It spoke to his whimsical nature. Besides, no one would bother him there — and if they did, he could scare the bejesus out of them without much effort, which would be good for a laugh, if nothing else. The crypt was completely impervious to sunlight, the main necessity.

Besides, it was the closest safe place to where Topaz would be sleeping today. And he didn't want to get far from her. Nor did he want to sit around analyzing just why that was, thank you very much. Suffice it to say, he was pretty sure she was about to tread on some dangerous ground, maybe ruffle a few feathers, stir up some long dormant evil and put herself at risk. That should be reason enough to want to stay close.

It wasn't. But it should be.

Of course, he had his other reason. She would be checking in with Reaper periodically, which he couldn't very well do himself. Not without raising suspicion, at least. He was too new to the white-hats, not really one of them yet. Any concern he showed would be suspect.

She could do it, though. And he could keep tabs on the big guy through her. That, too, should be reason enough to stay close to her.

And it, too, wasn't.

He sighed, set his backpack on the big stone bier and closed the heavy slab of rock that passed for a door, plunging himself into utter darkness. That didn't bother him. He could see just fine in the dark. Still, a little touch here and there to make the place homey wouldn't hurt.

Jack liked his creature comforts. And he'd done some shopping along the way to be sure he would have all he needed.

He hadn't spent a nickel of Topaz's money, though. He told himself he needed it, in case he had to return it to her. He paid no attention to the unfamiliar guilt that made him feel slightly ill whenever he thought of spending it.

He unzipped the backpack and took out a battery-powered lamp made to look like a gas-powered one. It was clever. He'd taken a liking to it right away. It provided the rustic ambiance of camping without the fuss. Then he took out his portable DVD player and flipped it open. He'd rigged it with a timer, and the lamp had its own. Both would shut off within a few minutes of sunrise.

No point wasting the juice while he was dead to the world.

He undid his bedroll, yanked on the cord and watched his air mattress inflate itself atop the bier. Quickly he made his bed with blankets and a pillow. All the comforts of home. Everything but a teddy bear.

He pulled out a pint of O-negative, sealed in a plastic bag. He would have preferred it warm, but this would do as a bedtime snack.

Finally he lay down in his bed and turned on a movie. *Dracula: Dead and Loving It.* Leslie Nielsen really bore no resemblance to Vlad. Jack had met the infamous vampire once, face-to-face. Moody bastard, and none too friendly. And while Nielsen looked nothing like him, neither did most of the actors who'd portrayed Dracula over the years. Bottom line? Nielsen made him laugh, so Jack was perfectly willing to overlook such minor issues.

3

Topaz pored over the dossiers on the three men who the police had considered "persons of interest" in her mother's murder. None of them had ever been charged, so she knew going in that she wouldn't find much evidence. But she also thought she would just *know.* If she saw the face, or read the details of the life of the man who had murdered her mother, she was sure she would know who he was.

And yet, the photos she saw — the politician, the actor and the businessman who'd raised her — said nothing to her. None of them whispered "guilty."

She couldn't even get an inkling for which one of them might have fathered her.

She ran out of time long before she'd had her fill of reading up on the men and their connections to her mother. Dawn was coming, and she was forced to turn in, to save the rest of her reading for nightfall.

She gathered up the pages into a folder and carried them with her up the stairs, where she checked out each bedroom before choosing one that faced west to the ocean and the sunset. It was perfectly dark in there, with the sun getting ready to rise on the opposite side of the house. There were perfect vertical blinds in the windows, and thick drapes as well. She drew them all nice and tight. Then, relishing her vampiric strength, she shoved the bed easily into a corner of the room where there was no chance of any light that might filter through, touching her.

She tucked the files underneath her pillow, then made a final round downstairs to be sure the entire villa was locked up tight, before finally curling up beneath the covers. She felt the sun rise. As it lifted, her eyelids sank.

Dead to the world, she thought. It's more than just an expression.

Briar sat on the carpeted floor of the vacant, unfinished home in Virginia. She and Reaper had headed north from Savannah, driving all night, until they came to this place. She didn't know who owned it. She didn't know if Reaper knew them and had permission to be there, or whether it had just seemed a likely place to rest for the day. She didn't know if they would be discovered and murdered while they slept, and she didn't particularly care.

"You've barely said a word all night," Reaper said as he tossed her a bag of blood, taken from a cooler in the car he'd rented. She didn't know where he'd gotten the blood or how long he'd had it or how much remained. She didn't care about those things, either.

"I have nothing to say."

"I could think of a pile of things." He chugged his own liquid meal, tossed the plastic bag and sank down onto the floor beside her. "You could thank me for saving you from Gregor. You could tell me I was right about him all along. You could explain how he managed to break your spirit in such a short period of time."

"I don't need to thank you for saving me, since I would have saved myself, sooner or later. I never had any doubt as to what Gregor was. I only thought he would show more loyalty to me, being that I'm just like him."

"You're nothing like him."

"You don't know me."

He drew a breath, seeming to consider those words, then finally nodded, conceding the point.

"And as for the condition of my *spirit* — assuming vampires even have such a thing — that's my business."

"I suppose that's true. I just thought it would take more than a day or two of torture to turn you into . . . this." He waved a hand her way.

"Into *what?*"

He shrugged. "A docile, quiet, brooding woman. A victim. Yes, that's it — you're acting like a victim."

"I *am* brooding," she admitted. "But you're wrong about the rest."

"Am I?"

She nodded, leaning back against the wall and closing her eyes. "There are things I need to work through in my own mind. I prefer to do it in silence, and in private. Just because I'm not clawing your eyes out at the moment, Reaper, don't assume I'm docile. It could be a dangerous mistake."

He sighed, and she felt his eyes on her for a long moment. She'd never raised her voice, nor infused it with any particular inflection. She'd spoken to him matter-of-factly, in the same monotone that she'd been using for days now, when she spoke at all.

She heard him sigh as he settled down

beside her to rest. And then, just before she fell asleep, he whispered, "I'd give a lot to have you trying to claw my eyes out. Better than this damn zombie you've become."

"Fuck you, Reaper."

"That would be even better." She heard him flip open his cell phone, heard the tones as he dialed a number. Then she heard the recorded voice of Topaz's voice-mail message.

Reaper muttered, "She must not be near her phone," and sighed. "Topaz, it's Reaper. Just checking in. Briar and I have headed north. We're just past Virginia Beach at the moment. I think we lost whoever was on our tails in Savannah. You can reach me at this number. I'll keep it turned on and monitor the voice mail. I hope you're all right. Call if you need me."

Briar breathed slowly, deeply, her body growing heavy with the lethargy brought on by the approaching dawn. "Pretty fond of the princess, aren't you?"

"Jealous?" he asked.

She made a choking sound, then rolled away from him and went to sleep.

When Jack arrived just after sundown, as she could have predicted he would, Topaz was sitting on the plush sofa with the file folders spread out around her, the DVD of her mother's life flashing across the television screen in front of her, and her own notebook open beside her.

He didn't bother knocking. Nor did he need to; she'd felt his approach long before he picked the locks with his mind and walked in as if he owned the place.

"Miss me?" he asked.

"Like a toothache." She didn't bother looking up to speak to him. "You know, you're very good at that, Jack."

He crossed the room toward her. "You're going to have to be more specific, hon. I'm good at so many things."

"Unlocking doors without a key."

He shrugged. "Psychokinesis. Any vampire can move things by mental manipulation."

"Yes, but I've seen very few who could open a lock in less than two seconds. It normally takes a bit more concentration."

He plunked himself onto the far end of the sofa, carelessly enough to appear casual but managing not to disturb a single sheet of her research in the process. "That should show you that I have a very strong will and am a very powerful vampire."

"What it shows me is that you're a crook through and through. That your strongest skill is breaking and entering really says it all, doesn't it?"

"Oh, Topaz, that is *far* from my strongest skill. As you well remember."

She just barely bit her lip in time to keep from smiling. And even then, she couldn't keep the delicious tingle of awareness from slithering up her spine. She remembered very well. Too well.

"So have you learned anything new?"

She sighed, raising her head to look him in the eye. Big mistake. When their eyes met, it was *always* a mistake. How a man could be so phony, so unable to feel true emotions, and yet look at her like that — well, it defied explanation. "I really don't want your help with this, Jack."

"Yes, you do. And I'm not leaving. This is the perfect way to kill time until Reaper's ready to reconstitute the gang and make another try at Gregor. At which time I'll get all your money back to you — if you let me stick around now."

"Oh, now there are conditions? I thought you promised to give me back my money either way, Jack. What happened to that?"

"You're right. How about if I add interest?"

"Twenty-five percent of the total, every month until you give it back."

"Are you a vampire or a loan shark?"

58

This time she let herself smile.

Jack sighed. "Ten percent of the half I still owe you, for every month until I give it back."

"Twenty."

He reached out a hand, stroked her hair where it had fallen forward over one cheek, tucking it back behind her ear, and whispered, "Fifteen," as if he were whispering words of love. Sensation sizzled through her, and she knew he knew it, even as she pulled back from his touch.

"I'll take the ten if you'll promise to keep your hands off me for the duration."

"I'll give you the twenty-five if you won't make me promise that."

They stared at each other for a long electric moment.

"I'll compromise," he said at last. "Fifteen percent and I won't touch you until you ask me to."

"Like that's gonna hap—"

"I'm not finished."

She clamped her lips and waited.

"I won't touch you until you ask me to. But you have to feel free to touch me any time you want. In any way you want to. Fully secure in the knowledge that I won't touch you back unless you want me to."

She frowned as she let the images of what

he was suggesting burn through her mind. Then she said, "You don't have the will-power."

"Try me."

She thought about leaning closer, maybe trailing her lips over his neck, just to prove her point. Because she had no doubt that he would wrap his arms around her, flip her onto her back on the sofa and mount her within about five seconds.

Or maybe it wasn't *his* reactions she didn't trust. Maybe it was her own.

"Chicken," he whispered. "Ten percent, then. Take it or leave it."

"And if I leave it?"

"I'll stay and help you anyway, return your money with no interest at all — as soon as I can lay my hands on it, that is — and touch you whenever the urge strikes me — knowing damn well you want it as much as I do."

She drew a breath and sighed. "Fifteen percent, your conditions." She held out a hand for a shake. "Deal?"

"Deal." He held his hand out, too, but he didn't take hers. He just waited. She finally closed her hand around his to seal the bargain, and when she took her hand away, she skimmed her fingertips over his palm and thought she felt him shiver.

Sighing, Jack managed to keep his control. But he was wondering, even before the touch of her hand on his had faded, what he'd gone and promised. The impossible, probably. Was he testing her — or himself?

Time for a new subject. "So you've read up on the men in your mother's life?"

"Yeah." She gathered her papers, shuffling through to the photos, and laid them out one by one. "The police seem to have focused on the men she was rumored to have been sleeping with in the year prior to her death."

"Including your father?" he asked.

She lowered her eyes, shielding them. "I don't know which of them is my father. There were a couple whose blood types made it possible, but there was no DNA testing back then, so the courts awarded me to the one they felt was most likely to provide a stable home." She picked out a five-by-seven black-and-white photo of the man who'd raised her, taken back in his younger days. "Thomas Martin, businessman."

"What kind of business?"

"Mostly government contracts. He owns

several manufacturing plants. They make weapons."

Jack looked up quickly. "He's an arms dealer?"

"Yeah. And according to the cops, there were rumors he wasn't too fussy about who bought his products. But no one could ever find proof he sold weapons to unapproved nations."

"Unless maybe your mom stumbled onto some."

"Yeah. That would give him a motive."

"He raised you?"

She nodded. "He and his series of wives. He got older. When his women did, too, he just traded them in for newer models. And I do mean models."

"Was he good to you?"

She glanced at him briefly, and he saw a flash of something — pain? — in her eyes, but she averted them so quickly that he couldn't be sure. He guessed the answer was no. Which made him wonder just how "not good" the man's treatment of her had been. Had he just been cold and uncaring, or something more? The notion sent a darkness through him.

She laid out the next photo. "Frederick Ramirez, state senator."

"Corrupt?" Jack asked.

"He accepted exorbitant campaign contributions from a reputed mob boss — Tony Bonacelli." She pulled another photo from a folder. "Interestingly enough, he was also sleeping with my mother. Or at least that was the gossip."

"Was the mob boss a suspect, too?" Jack asked.

"He was cleared early on. Airtight alibi."

"He could have had someone else do it for him."

"There was no evidence of it, though. If he did, he covered his tracks very well. Or maybe he had the cops on his payroll. Who knows?"

Jack whistled softly under his breath, then glanced at the one remaining photo in her hand. "And our final contestant?"

"Wayne Clark Duncan." She laid the photo down. The man was stunningly attractive, the shot unmistakably professional, even without the autograph scrawled in the corner. "Actor," she said.

"I could have guessed." He frowned. "But not one I've heard of."

"No, neither have I. And while he was questioned, there's nothing in the police reports about a possible motive. He's probably the least likely to have killed her."

"Those are the ones to watch out for,"

Jack said, and sighed. "So what's your plan? You want to talk to each of these guys, see what they have to say?"

"Yeah, later. First, though, I want to talk to Rebecca Murphy. She was my mother's agent and lawyer. I think she might know more than anyone — if she's even still alive."

He nodded. "Good place to start. You have any idea where we can find her?"

"As luck would have it, she's in the book. Or at least, someone with the same name is. I was just about to call when you arrived." She reached for her cell phone, flipped it open and frowned. "Damn. I had it on vibrate. Got a voice mail, just a sec." She hit a button. "It's from Reaper."

"Put it on speaker," Jack said. "I want to know how things are going, too."

With a nod, she hit another button, and Reaper's message played.

Topaz saved the message. "I'm glad they're okay. And especially glad they lost whoever was following them. That was creepy."

"Anything having to do with the CIA is likely to be creepy," he said with a smile. "At least, it seems that way to me."

Jack nodded at the phone. "Why don't you call this Rebecca person now?"

She nodded and placed the call.

■ ■ ■ ■

Rebecca Murphy agreed to see them that evening and gave them directions to her home, a small brick structure in an upscale suburb of Beverly Hills. It was a half-hour drive, and a surprisingly pleasant one. The Porsche was fabulous, and Jack drove it the same way he did everything else. Perfectly.

Rebecca answered her door wearing a kaftan with huge pink flowers all over it, a pair of fur-trimmed high-heeled slippers, and diamonds dripping from her wrist, throat and earlobes. Her snowy hair was cut close to her head on the sides and in the back, while the top was longer, giving her the look of some exotic bird. Topaz suspected she weighed in at about ninety pounds, if that. The kaftan was too big, so she thought maybe the weight loss was recent. The woman had an aura of physical frailty, perhaps even illness, about her, but it was nearly overpowered by the sense of mental power and emotional stability that exuded from her like perfume.

"Thank you for seeing us, Ms. Murphy. I realize it's after hours."

The woman waved a hand, glancing at

Topaz, then, her attention arrested, staring at her.

"This is my friend Jack. I'm —"

"Tanya," the woman whispered. "My God, you're Tanya, aren't you?"

"I'm sorry?"

"Everyone thinks you're dead . . . or worse."

Topaz lifted her eyebrows. "What's worse than dead?"

"Oh, child, there are plenty of things." Rebecca took Topaz by the arm, leading her into her house, a one-story brick ranch with brown shutters and trim to offset its stark look. "I can't believe you're here. After all this time."

"I'm sorry, Ms. Murphy, but —"

"Rebecca. And don't even try to tell me you're not her. I'd recognize you anywhere. You look exactly as you did before you vanished, ten years ago. God, you look so much like your mother." She shook her head as if to snap herself out of her reverie, and led them through her small, neat home, all the way to the rear. Topaz glimpsed a huge brown overstuffed sofa and chair, thick green carpeting, an aquarium and a ton of plants, and then they were being hustled through sliding glass doors onto a redwood deck in the back.

"Sit. Can I get you a cold drink? A snack?"

"No, thank you, we're fine," Topaz told her.

At Topaz's "we," Rebecca looked at Jack as if she had forgotten he was even there. Then she shook her head again. "I'm sorry, young man. I've already forgotten your name."

"Jack," he said, not adding a last name. She narrowed her eyes a little, but didn't ask. And then Jack pulled out a chair for her, and she forgot her suspicions as she smiled and took it, apparently pleased by the show of good manners.

He could charm the spots off a leopard, Topaz thought. Especially if the leopard was female.

"It's good to see you, Tanya. I kept tabs on you as much as I could until you disappeared — hard to believe it was ten years ago. No one knew what happened to you, but most of the speculation was that you died."

Topaz licked her lips. Admitting who she was had not been a part of her plan. But clearly this woman wasn't going to be talked out of believing it now.

Rebecca studied her, then tilted her head to one side. "You want to keep it that way, don't you?"

Topaz met her eyes. "For reasons I can't go into, yes. I would prefer to stay dead as far as the rest of the world is concerned."

"Well, I still have my law license. Give me a dollar."

"Excuse me?"

"Give me a dollar."

Frowning, Topaz set her tiny Coach handbag onto the glass-topped patio table and fished out a dollar bill. She handed it to the older woman.

"There," Rebecca said, folding it, and tucking it down the front of the kaftan. "You've just retained me. Anything we discuss now is privileged and completely confidential."

Smiling, Topaz said, "I get it now."

"So tell me why it is you've come to see me."

"You can probably guess," Topaz said. "I want to know who killed my mother."

The other woman sat back, blinking in stunned surprise. Then, her jaw firming, she nodded. "Well, I suppose that makes sense." She sat in her chair, arms crossed over her chest, and studied Topaz. "Why now? Why after all these years?"

Topaz lowered her head, darting a glance Jack's way as she did. He was sitting in silence, just observing, listening. Probably looking for any weakness he could use later to con her, she thought with a rush of anger.

"I just need to know, that's all. I've never . . . I've never understood who she was, or how she felt about me. I want to know everything about her. But especially who took her life."

The older woman nodded slowly, her gaze turning inward. "Your mother was the most beautiful woman I have ever known," she said softly. "She wasn't a great actress. But she had this energy, this spirit, that just emanated from her and drew people to her. Everyone who met her fell in love with her. Everyone."

"Well, maybe not *quite* everyone," Topaz said softly. "Someone killed her, after all."

Rebecca didn't let the comment sidetrack her. "She was a free spirit. Couldn't be tied to one man. She fell in love at the drop of a hat. I think it was the excitement of new love that thrilled her most. Once it got old — well, men pretty much fell into a predictable pattern with Mirabella. Once they had her, they wanted to own her. I mean, you couldn't blame them. Anyone could see how attractive she was, how many men wanted her. So whichever one she was with tended to feel threatened by that, and inevitably, he'd start trying to control her, manage her, you know? She couldn't tolerate that."

Topaz nodded. "Having a baby must have been the last thing she wanted. I mean, nothing is more controlling than —"

"Having a baby was the best thing that ever happened to her."

Topaz looked up slowly, trying hard to read the other woman's face, and then her thoughts, in search of a lie.

"She finally had someone in her life who loved her, without giving two hoots what she looked like or how well her career was going."

"Or how much money she had," Topaz murmured.

"She adored you, Tanya. She so wanted to make everything perfect for you. And she tried, she did. But her life was snuffed out before she had the chance." Rebecca dabbed at her eyes. "I really loved Mirabella, you know. She was my friend."

Topaz believed the woman. There was nothing in her mind to contradict what she was saying aloud. But there was something.

"Do you know who killed her?"

"No."

"But . . . ?" Topaz prompted, fully aware that there was something else, something Rebecca wasn't saying.

"There . . . was a lot going on in your

mother's life before she died. Let me dig into my files, so I can get my facts straight. My memory isn't what it used to be. I'll phone you in a day or two, and we can meet again. If you're going to be in town that long?"

"I am," Topaz said.

"Good." Rebecca nodded. "Good."

It was, Topaz sensed, the end of the conversation. She would get no more information from Rebecca tonight. She got to her feet, and Jack rose with her. "Thank you," she said simply.

"It was a pleasure meeting you," Jack added. He reached out to take Topaz's arm, then stopped himself, she noted, just before making contact. He really was trying to live up to his end of their bargain. It was slightly amazing to her. He was actually trying to keep his word.

They walked around the house, through the backyard and out to the front, where Jack had parked the Porsche. Topaz didn't say a thing until they got in. And then she said disbelievingly, "I can't believe she knew who I was just by looking at me."

He started the engine but didn't put the car in gear. Instead, he turned in his seat to look at her. "Well, her eyesight clearly hasn't gone the way of her memory."

71

"But I don't look anything like Mirabella."

He laughed. Just a soft sound, very short and more surprised than amused.

"What?"

"You look a lot like her, Topaz. You have the same bone structure, the same high cheekbones and delicate, angular jaw. The same little nose, the same full, sexy lips. Same milk-chocolate-brown eyes and thick lashes. Her skin tone was a little darker, her hair, too, but beyond that . . ."

"That's ridiculous. My mother was called the most beautiful woman alive."

"Yeah," Jack said with a firm nod, then put the car into gear and began to drive. "Exactly."

She shot him a look, but his face was unreadable. He focused on the road, not looking at her, intent on his driving, as if it were some challenging task that took every bit of his concentration.

"What are you trying to pull, Jack?" she asked softly.

He frowned, sending her a quick glance. "What do you mean?"

"Do you think flattering me is going to get you back into my good graces? Or my wallet?"

"I'd settle for back into your bed, but —"

"You never said shit like that when we

72

were dating."

He shrugged. "I didn't want you to get a swollen head. And maybe I was thinking like those men of your mother's. If you knew how beautiful you were, why wouldn't you go out and find someone a hell of a lot better than me? I sure didn't want to encourage that."

"No. At least not until you got what you were after."

He sighed, his head falling forward briefly. If she hadn't known better, she might have thought she'd hurt him, just a little.

But that was impossible, of course.

You couldn't hurt someone unless they cared, and she knew all too well that Jack didn't. He never had.

That thought hurt a little too much, so she distracted herself by picking up her phone, glancing at the time and dialing Reaper's cell.

He picked up on the first ring. "Topaz?"

"Yeah, it's me," she said. "How is it going? Are you still in Virginia Beach?"

"No, we're already moving on. Still heading north. I'll let you know where we decide to hole up next when we get there. How are things with you?"

"Fine. Everything's fine. The others?"

"Roxy and Ilyana are at Roxy's place."

"Really? Interesting. You think Ilyana will open up to her at all?"

"If anyone can get her talking, it'll be Roxy."

"She has secrets, that one," Topaz said. "How about Seth and Vixen?"

"They haven't checked in yet," Reaper told her. "Have you, um . . . Have you heard from Jack?"

She hesitated and glanced Jack's way. She got the immediate impression that he was listening closely to her conversation. He wouldn't have any trouble hearing Reaper's end, given all vampires' heightened senses. "Actually, he's here with me."

"Tell him I said hi," Jack said.

She didn't. Reaper could hear the greeting for himself. He sighed, and said, "Be careful, Topaz."

"Believe me, I am."

4

"Oh, hell."

Jack rejoined Topaz at the checkout counter of the 7-Eleven, having ditched her just long enough to place a call of his own. She was handing the cashier a wad of bills to pay for her shampoo, conditioner and the dozen other beauty supplies she'd insisted she couldn't get along without for one more night, things she hadn't packed because it was "so much easier to just buy them here."

At Jack's muttered curse, Topaz shot him a quick look over her shoulder. "Anything wrong?" she asked.

He didn't speak out loud, because he didn't think the checker had made the connection just yet and he certainly didn't want to encourage her to. *Take a look at the tabloid in the rack — upper left slot,* he told Topaz mentally.

Frowning, she glanced at the rack of

magazines and newspapers standing beside the cashier. Jack had no doubt that the banner headline and side-by-side photos of Topaz, back in her mortal days, and her mother, caught her eye just as quickly as they had caught his. When her eyes widened, he knew for sure.

DAUGHTER OF LEGENDARY ACTRESS RETURNS FROM THE GRAVE TO AVENGE HER MOTHER'S MURDER

She blinked in shock and quickly grabbed the issue, folded it over the sensationalistic front-page headline and dropped it onto the counter. "This, too," she said. He thought her voice seemed to quiver. Not so much that a mortal would detect it. Maybe not even another vampire. But he was more attuned to her than most — than anyone alive, he imagined. And that realization bore some further thought, but not right then.

The cashier nodded and snapped her chewing gum. Looking bored, she continued ringing up purchases and stuffing them into a bag.

Topaz gripped the plastic bag by its handles and hurried out of the store. Following, Jack hit the key ring button to unlock the car before she got to it, and by the time he slid behind the wheel she was in the passenger seat with the newspaper unfolded on her lap.

"Listen to this," she told him as he started the car. " 'Tanya DuFrane, daughter of the legendary actress Mirabella DuFrane, vanished a decade ago. It was rumored at the time that she had been very ill, and most of Hollywood assumed she simply wanted to die in privacy. However, a reliable source claims that Ms. DuFrane is alive and well, and has returned to L.A. determined to learn the truth about her mother's death.' " She looked up at Jack. "It goes on, sensationalistic blatherings about how Mirabella was shot and —" She lowered her gaze to the paper, scanning it again. "A half-dozen crackpot theories as to who did it and what became of her body. The fact that an eyewitness has seen me, and that I appear to be in 'the pink of health.' The *pink* of health. Do I look *pink* to you?" As she asked the question, she ran her fingertip over the pale skin of her forearm.

"Does it say where you're staying?"

"No, but it's implied." She ran a finger down the column of text. "Here. 'The younger Ms. DuFrane appears to be retracing her mother's steps on the final night of her life.' " She clenched her jaw and muttered "Idiots" through her teeth.

"Do you think Rebecca Murphy . . . ?"

"There hasn't been time," Topaz said. "We only left her ten minutes ago." She shook her head. "No, it couldn't have been her."

"So who else have you spoken with while you've been here? Who else even knew you were coming?"

She shrugged. "You knew."

"Oh, come on, Topaz, be realistic."

"These rags pay a lot for this kind of garbage. And it wouldn't be the first time you betrayed me for money."

"It wasn't me." He was wounded, actually, that she could even entertain the thought. He wished he could look her in the eyes or delve into her mind to determine whether she believed him. He tried, but she was blocking — not deliberately, he thought. It was anger and mistrust keeping his mind from probing the depths of hers. Digging any deeper would take more concentration than he could muster up while simultaneously driving and trying to think of convincing arguments.

"I gave you information to help you. Why would I do that if I were going to turn around and throw roadblocks in your way?"

"Oh, come on. You convince me you're on my side to find out more facts to sell, then stab me in the back."

"Topaz, I knew where you were staying,

and I knew why you had come out here before I ever arrived on that villa's doorstep. I could have sold that information to the tabloids without ever setting foot in California."

She lowered her head. "Maybe that's not all you're after."

He sighed, frustrated as hell.

"If you want to convince me, Jack, just tell me why you're really here."

He was quiet for a long moment, so long that he could feel her speculation, practically hear those wheels turning in her mind. She thought he was taking his time so he could make up a good lie, he realized. Say something, you idiot, he told himself.

"I have never felt remorse before. Not in all my years of conning women. Never once. But I felt it with you. I thought it would go away, but it's been getting worse instead of better. And there's more. I — I've *missed* you."

She was staring at him, probing. He wished he could let down his guard, let her dig around inside his thoughts and see that he meant what he said — but there were too many things she couldn't know.

"And besides all that, I kept getting the feeling that this mission of yours could be dangerous."

"So you want me to believe you're self-less?"

"Hell, no! I thought by coming out here, helping you do this thing that means so much to you, I might somehow atone for my sins and these feelings of regret would go away." He thumped a palm on the steering wheel. "I don't like feeling this way, Topaz. It's affecting my work."

"Your *work?*"

"Yes, my work. How am I supposed to move on to the next mark if I have to worry that I've somehow developed a conscience?"

She drew a breath, then blew it out slowly. "I suppose that's at least . . . plausible."

"Just assume it's the truth for now, and let's move on, okay? Who — besides me — knew you were coming here?"

She pursed her lips. "Besides you? The only people I've spoken with are the owners of the villa I rented. But I didn't tell them who I was."

"Could they have recognized you, like Rebecca did?"

"I haven't seen them face-to-face."

"All right. It's a simple thing to find out, really."

"Is it?"

He shot her a smirk. "Hello! We're *vampires.*"

"So?"

"So who wrote the story? Is there a byline?"

She looked at the piece again, then nodded. "Les Marlboro."

"Sounds like an anti-smoking ad. All right, so we find out where this Marlboro man lives, and we pay him a little visit. He'll tell us who his source is."

She shot him a look — a worried look. "I don't think we need to go that far."

"You're kidding me. You're okay with letting someone spy on you and report your activities to the press?"

"I just think there might be a less . . . violent way of finding out."

"I wasn't suggesting we torture him," he said. "Much."

"We can find another way."

He shrugged and turned into the driveway of the villa. "All right, if you insist." He glanced at the entry door, which stood slightly open. "You've had company."

She followed his gaze. "Son of a . . ."

Topaz got out of the car, slammed the door and strode up the walk. She shoved the front door wide and stepped inside, then stood there, sensing for a presence with her mind even while her eyes took in the mess around her.

Jack was beside her a heartbeat later. *Careful now. They might still be here.*

"No one's here," she replied aloud and waved an arm. "Look at this mess. Whoever it was, they went through everything."

"Was there anything for them to find?"

"The file you gave me. My own notes. The DVD." As she spoke, she moved through the place, checking the drawer where those things had been stored. "Odd."

"What?"

"They left the DVD."

He shrugged. "If they have an interest in your mother — or you, for that matter — they probably already have a copy."

"I'm going to check upstairs."

"I'll take a look around outside, though I don't feel anyone close."

She agreed, and headed up the stairs to the bedroom she'd been using. Her things had been tossed, every drawer opened, including the one in the bedside stand that had held the one thing she *never* wanted anyone else to see. Her journal and the little pen she kept with it were still there. That journal held her innermost thoughts. Her secrets. Her vulnerabilities. Every emotion she'd experienced about Jack. The intruder hadn't taken it, but he might have looked at it. And she knew Jack hadn't done it, because he'd been with her.

She felt violated. Red-hot fury came on the heels of that emotion, and she liked that a lot better.

"Topaz? Anything missing up here?"

She closed the drawer slowly and turned to face him. "I've changed my mind. Let's pay this Les Marlboro a visit tonight."

It wasn't difficult to locate the man. He wasn't listed in the phone book, but the paper's offices were in L.A., which was only a half-hour drive away, and breaking and entering came easily to vampires. Especially, Topaz knew, to Jack. Within ten minutes of entering the building, they had located Les Marlboro's cubicle and, after rifling the desk, his home address.

Which brought them to his door. He lived south of L.A., so it was on the way back to Santa Luna. His house was a pepperbox in the 'burbs, but the name on the mailbox was Adams, not Marlboro. She imagined writers with the scruples of this one probably had to use pseudonyms for their own protection. God, she thought, I hope he doesn't have kids.

All the lights were off. Either everyone was asleep or no one was home. Jack reached for the doorknob.

Topaz put a hand on his arm. "Wait."

He tensed. His bicep bulged underneath her palm, and she experienced a brief but powerful rush of desire. She'd always loved biceps. They were the sexiest part of a man, in her opinion. And his were sexier than most. Touching them had always turned her on.

She shook off the heat of wanting him and nodded at the little metallic tag affixed to the siding near the door: These Premises Protected by Sentinel Alarms.

"Yeah. Look how old that sign is," he whispered. "When people first get these systems, they use them religiously. Then they get complacent and stop setting them. Even people who do use them tend to set them when they're on vacation and leave them unarmed while they're home. Trust me, no alarm is going to sound."

"And what if you're wrong?"

"I'm never wrong." He said it with a look and a smile that did as much for her insides as his flexing bicep had. "But if I am, we can be out of here in short order. No harm done."

She nodded, knowing he was right. With their preternatural speed, they could move so fast that they would appear only as a blur to mortal eyes. In the darkness of night, even that much might not be visible. "All right, go ahead."

He put his hand on the doorknob, focused his attention on it. An instant later, she heard the lock free itself. Then he ran his palm up the surface of the door, past the dead bolt, and shook his head. "He didn't even throw the bolt."

Topaz made a "tsk tsk" sound, then stiffened in anticipation as Jack turned the knob and opened the door.

No alarm sounded. She glanced at the panel that was mounted to the wall just inside the door, and it read, The Adamses' System Is Secure. A green light glowed from its face.

"Not as secure as if you'd armed the darn thing, but still, secure," Jack whispered.

She frowned and studied him. "You're *enjoying* this."

"It's what I do. I'm *good* at it."

He sounded as if he were proud of the fact. Rolling her eyes, she continued through the house, which was small enough that it didn't take long. Les Marlboro/Adams apparently lived alone, so that was a plus. No children to traumatize, no mate to contend with.

They stepped into the lone bedroom and stood there, looking at the sleeping man.

He wasn't bad-looking, Topaz thought. Not attractive, but not repulsive, either. Must be his personality that kept him living alone.

Or maybe he's just a confirmed bachelor. Jack spoke to her silently, as the man lay sleeping.

There's no such thing.

Excuse me, but you're looking at one.

She shook her head. *When you fall in love, Jack, you're not even going to know what hit you, much less be content with living alone any longer.*

Ha!

She shrugged and gazed again at the man in the bed. Mid-thirties, brown hair, starting to show a little gray and some thinning in the center. He had a bit of a belly, too, expanding the blankets that covered him. Mortality sucked. She glanced at Jack. *So what's the plan?*

He grinned at her, then walked over to the bed and crouched low. Bending close to the man's ear, he said, "Wake up, pal. We've got some talking to do."

The man's eyes flew open wide, and he immediately sat up in the bed.

Jack slammed a palm into his chest, pushing him flat again. "You aren't to speak until I ask you to. I could kill you very easily, and way faster than you could get to the tele-phone."

"Wh-what do you want? You want money? Jesus, take it, just don't —"

Jack gazed hard at the man, and Topaz knew he was exerting the power of his mind. The man's jaw clamped shut and his eyes went wider. Jack was preventing him from speaking as effectively as if he'd clapped a hand over his mouth.

"I *said* not to speak until I ask you to." Then Jack smiled. "Oh, yes. That's right. We're not your garden-variety burglars. We're not even human. Now, there are two ways this can go. You can tell us what we want to know, and we'll leave here and you'll never see us again. Or you can be stubborn and make us torture it out of you. Either way, we'll get what we came for. Is that understood?"

Les strained to move his mouth.

Jack smiled. "Oh. Sorry. Go ahead, you can answer now."

Les opened his mouth experimentally, then rubbed his jaw with one hand.

"Do you understand your options?" Jack asked.

"Yeah. I got it."

"Good. This lovely lady has a few ques-tions for you. You will answer them. And you will tell no one of this visit. Unless you want it repeated in a far less pleasant manner."

Frowning, Les looked at Topaz. Then he looked again, his eyes straining.

"Who was your source for the Tanya DuFrane story that ran today?"

His eyes widened. "Holy shit. You — you're her, aren't you?"

"That is not the answer to my question, Mr. . . . Adams, is it?"

"You haven't aged," he muttered. "That photo I ran of you was ten years old. I couldn't find any more recent ones —"

"There *aren't* any more recent ones."

"But you haven't changed . . . except —"

"I'm paler, I know. I am *not,* Mr. Adams, *pink.* Now, will you tell me what I need to know?"

He shook his head. "No. I . . . I can't."

Sighing, she looked at Jack. "Make him tell me, Jack."

Nodding, Jack said, "I was getting hungry anyway." Then he bared his fangs and jerked the man out of bed by the collar of his pajamas. Jack held him a foot above the floor.

The man's scream was pathetic and loud.

Jack gripped Les's chin and tipped his head back, moving closer to his throat.

"Don't! Don't. I'll tell you! It was Argent."

Topaz blinked in shock. "Kimber Argent? The woman who owns Avalon?"

"No. Her husband, Albert. He recognized you as soon as he saw you."

"We never met face-to-face," she said.

"He's right next door in the apartment. Besides, he has cameras all over that place. He feeds me stories all the time. Makes more money for me than any other source. Hell, that villa of his is bugged till hell won't have it. There's video surveillance, too, but Argent says it's malfunctioning or something. Celebrities stay there all the time, and I get a ton of gossip on them from him."

Topaz muttered, "I should have guessed. So who broke in there tonight? Was it you, looking for more dirt?"

"Someone broke in?" he asked, wide-eyed.

"Yes, someone broke in. Was it you?" she repeated, growing impatient.

"No!" He swung his gaze from her to Jack and back again, afraid, she thought, that they didn't believe him. "I wouldn't *need* to break in, Argent would let me in if I asked him. But I haven't asked. And I won't." He was clearly terrified. "Look, I'm sorry. I didn't know you were — whatever the hell you are. I'll fix it. I'll print a retraction, say it was all a mistake."

"I'm afraid the damage has been done, Mr. Adams," Jack said. He dropped the man back onto the bed. "You'll sleep now. You'll remember this as a bad dream, nothing more. And you won't run any more stories about Tanya DuFrane, no matter how tempting those stories might be."

"I won't. I promise. I —"

"Sleep." Jack said the word firmly, with a piercing gaze, and the man sank back onto his pillows. His eyes fell closed. "It was a bad dream," Jack whispered, leaning closer. "It was nothing but a nightmare. We were never here."

Topaz touched his arm. "You could have used that same technique to get him to talk in the first place, you know."

"Of course I know. But scaring the hell out of him was much more fun. Besides, he had it coming. Bottom-feeding slug."

She didn't entirely disagree with him, she thought as they walked out of the man's house.

"Where are you taking me?" she asked as Jack drove through the rapidly fading night. "This isn't the way back to Avalon Mansion."

"It's almost dawn. Surely you don't want to spend the day there."

"That was the plan."

He sent her a look of disbelief. "We're completely defenseless when we sleep. You have no idea who broke in there, and they could come back."

"What for? They already searched the place and took what they wanted."

Jack drew a breath. "Unless what they wanted was you."

"Don't be melodramatic."

"I'm not. Topaz, consider what you're doing here. You're trying to unmask a killer, a person who has spent the past thirty-six years believing he got away with murder. You don't think that tabloid story made him nervous? You don't think he's still capable of killing to protect himself?"

She didn't answer, only lowered her head.

"You know I'm right," Jack insisted.

"Maybe." She sighed. "So where are you taking me, then?"

"My place. It's not much, but it'll have to do. We'll have time tomorrow night to make alternate arrangements. Right after I have a *conversation* with Mr. Argent."

"All right."

She didn't think he required her consent at this point, but she gave it. It was odd how it felt almost as if he were trying to protect her. It would be easy to believe that — too easy. So she refused. There had to be something in this for Jack. In the end, there always was.

At least she knew for sure now that he hadn't been the one selling information on her to the tabloids.

Jack pulled the car into an empty parking area off the side of the road. They got out, and he locked it up, pocketed the keys and said, "This way."

"Oh, Lord. We're not sleeping in the woods, are we? You didn't find a cave or a hollow tree or something equally putrid, did you?"

He looked at her briefly and kept on walking, up a hill, across a tree-dotted field, into the woods and then out of them again. The sky was beginning to fade to a lighter shade of gray. Sunrise wasn't far off.

Then she saw the cemetery and stopped in her tracks. He kept right on walking through, right up to the biggest crypt in the entire place. It was huge, ornate, made of gray stone, and came complete with a gargoyle guarding its roof.

"You have *got* to be kidding me."

"Do I?" He opened the heavy door and looked back at her. "It's quite cozy inside. Come on now, you don't have time to be fussy."

"I'm *not* being fussy, but for God's sake, Jack, could you have come up with anything more clichéd?"

"Nope. I tried, but this was the best I could do. Come on. We don't have all day. Or all night."

Shaking her head in disgust, she walked inside. He closed the door behind her, but it didn't matter; she could see perfectly well in the darkness. There were blankets and pillows spread over a bier, a lantern on the floor, and his backpack leaning in one corner alongside a cooler with the Red Cross's logo on the front.

"Sustenance?" she asked, nodding at it.

"Help yourself. Unless . . . well, if you want you could, um . . ." He tipped his head back a bit and ran his forefinger over his jugular. "Eat me."

"In your dreams, Jack."

"Sometimes, yes."

She punched him in the shoulder and moved toward the cooler to take what she needed from inside. "Any bodies in here?" she asked.

"Nothing recent. I think the newest has been here fifty years."

"That's a relief, at least. No decomposing corpses to sleep with." She finished the blood and returned the empty plastic bag to the cooler, to be disposed of later. Then she stretched her arms over her head as the lethargy began to creep in. She reached for a blanket, tugged it from the bier.

Jack gripped the corner and pulled it from her hands. "It's safe to sleep with me, Topaz. We'll both be dead to the world in a few minutes. There's no time for me to seduce you, even if I was planning to break our deal — which I'm not, by the way."

"So sue me for not trusting you."

"You're not fooling either of us. It's yourself you don't trust."

"Oh, please, you're not all that hard to resist." She let go of the blanket, and then, to prove her point, she peeled off her clothes, stripping down to her bra and matching panties, and climbed into the makeshift bed. It was surprisingly soft, and she realized he'd equipped it with an air mattress. "Nice touch."

Smiling to himself, Jack peeled off his clothes, as well, and got in beside her, wearing only his boxer-briefs. He pulled the covers over them both, but he was careful not to touch her. There was a mere inch of space between them, and he rolled onto his side, facing her, so close she could feel his breath on her cheek.

"You can kiss me good-night if you want

to," he said.

"Why on earth would I want to?"

He shrugged. "To thank me for my help. To show some gratitude that I'm trying to keep you safe. To —"

"To shut you up?" She rolled onto her side, facing him, and pressed her lips to his. It was a peck. It was brief, and firm, but when she pulled back, she could still feel those lips under hers. He had the softest lips. He always had. Her heart softened a little, and she leaned in again. This time she pressed her mouth gently against his, pulling back when he parted his lips and began moving them in that way he had that always drove her wild.

She could still taste him.

"Sleep well, Topaz," he whispered.

"No choice about that." Thank God, she thought. Because if there were, she knew she wouldn't sleep at all. Not with him this close. Not with every night they'd ever spent wrapped around each other replaying in her mind.

She felt the sun's energy rising, and with a rush of gratitude, she let her eyes fall closed.

5

When her eyes fluttered open at sunset, Topaz stretched and rolled onto her side. Someone was there — a familiar someone — and, still half-asleep, she nuzzled his lips with her own. His hands buried themselves in her hair, and his mouth captured hers. A mouth she knew, one she relished, one she loved kissing. And so she did. Her lips parted, her arms wound around him, and the kiss heated and grew until they were trying to devour each other.

And then, suddenly, she pulled free and lay there gasping, panting, hungering — and wide awake.

"Don't stop," Jack murmured. "Baby, don't stop. Not now." He reached for her.

She held up a hand, palm facing his chest. "You promised you wouldn't touch me, Jack."

"And I haven't."

"What do you call trying to swallow my

tongue just now, then?"

"You started it."

"I did not."

"You kissed me first, Topaz." He got off the bier and pushed both hands through his hair, heaving a sigh. "Hell, woman, I'm only human."

"No, you're not."

"You know what I meant."

Reluctantly, she nodded, unable to meet his eyes, knowing he would see the naked hunger glowing from her own.

"Topaz, come on. We both want to. You know it's the truth."

"Forget it."

"You can't deny what just happened. It's freaking explosive, what's between us."

"So's dynamite. Doesn't mean I'm going to put a stick down my pants and light the fuse." She shook her head hard, trying to drive her insistence into her own mind as much as his. "You broke my heart, Jack. I'd be stupid to give you a chance to do it again."

"So keep your heart out of it. You hate my guts now. It shouldn't be too hard. Let's just have sex."

She shot him a look, then got up. Without another word, she located her clothes and put them on.

"Fine," he said. "Deny it. Delay it. But it's gonna happen. Sooner or later, it's bound to happen, Topaz, and I think you know that every bit as well as I do and want it just as badly as I do. It's inevitable."

"Not if you leave."

"I'm not leaving."

She finished dressing, then snatched his clothes up and handed them to him. "Get dressed, will you?"

"Can't resist me without my clothes on, right?"

"I want to get back to the mansion. Take a shower, get some fresh clothes, do my hair and makeup."

"And what do you have planned for *after* midnight?"

"Very funny. I want to start talking to the men who were in that file. The ones the police thought looked good for my mother's murder."

"And your landlord?"

"I haven't decided what to do about him yet. If we tip him off that we know about the bugs in the house, he's liable to throw us out, or, worse, let us stay and find some other method of eavesdropping."

"I hadn't thought of that."

"Let's just find the bugs and watch what we say until we do."

Jack nodded. "Actually, I have a few errands to run while you're primping. I'll see if I can find us a sweeping device, so we don't miss any."

Topaz frowned at him. "Where would you find something like that in the middle of the night?"

He averted his eyes to begin dressing. Or maybe that was just the excuse he wanted to use. "I have no idea."

She had a feeling it was a lie.

What he wanted from her, Jack decided, was forgiveness. Okay, sex would be good, too, but forgiveness was tops. He'd been racking his brain to figure out what had drawn him here to her, made him feel as compelled to help her find her mother's murderer as he would have been to protect one of the Chosen. It wasn't love, certainly. He didn't believe in love. Love was a con man's most powerful tool, but it wasn't real. His reason for being here wasn't physical attraction, either — or at least it wasn't *only* that. It was something more, and it had been bugging him that he didn't know what.

Now, as he stood in a nearly empty parking garage, waiting for his contact to show up, he thought he'd figured it out. What he was feeling was guilt, plain and simple. And no wonder it had taken him so long to identify it. It wasn't something he'd ever felt before. But he felt it over her. If he'd known that all her life she'd been plagued by people who claimed to love her while coveting her money, he would never have chosen her as a mark.

How to convince her of that was the big question. He was going to give her back the money. He had intended to all along, deep down, and he realized that now. It was why he'd been unable to spend a nickel of it, why he'd carried it with him in cash ever since he'd been with her. So that he could return it intact. But he couldn't just hand her back the money — not yet, or she would realize he'd had it all along, and that wasn't likely to earn him the absolution he needed from her. Besides, if she got the money back now, she might send him packing, and he didn't want that to happen, either. Not while she could be in danger.

His feelings about Topaz were enough to drive him insane. Trying to figure them out and understand them was even worse.

Headlights cut into his thoughts, and he ducked back into the shadows and waited. The Lincoln stopped, and CIA Special Agent Frank Magnarelli got out, leaving his door open. His patent leather shoes tapped

100

on the concrete floor, then stopped. It was Jack's first face-to-face contact with the agent in charge of tracking down and capturing Reaper — former agent Raphael Rivera, that was. Up to now, they'd only talked by phone. Magnarelli had a face like rough pavement, a graying brush cut and a scar on his chin. He lit a cigarette, took three consecutive puffs, then dropped it and crushed it under his heel.

Nodding at the agreed-upon signal, Jack stepped out into the light.

"What have you got for me?" Magnarelli asked.

Jack looked him up and down. He was a tall, well-built man with ice-cold eyes and an attitude to match. "Depends. What have you got for me?"

"I gave you everything we had on the Du-Frane case already."

"Don't even think I'm naive enough to believe that. I know you have more. And I'll get to all of it eventually. But for right now, I want to know who fathered DuFrane's little girl. Tanya, wasn't it?"

Those cold gray eyes darkened with suspicion. "Why are you so into this shit, Heart?"

Jack only shrugged, but Magnarelli lifted his brows. "You're helping her, aren't you? That tabloid bit about her being back from the dead to seek vengeance is the truth. Is Tanya DuFrane a . . . one of *you?*"

"That's not the information we agreed to trade. And it's none of your business. Find out who fathered her, and I'll tell you what I have for you."

"Well, shit, it's not like I know off the top of my head. I'll find out, assuming it's even possible."

"You're the CIA. Anything's possible. But I'll settle for your promise to look into it, and a small parting gift."

Magnarelli shifted his feet, looking frustrated. "I'll look into it."

"And the gift?" Jack asked.

"Quit playing games, Heart, and just tell me what kind of *gift* you have in mind."

Jack grinned. Magnarelli was afraid he was going to demand a little sip from his veins. He didn't know that by reading the agent's mind — this particular CIA operative was a master at blocking his thoughts. Jack had discovered that in the time he'd been talking with the man. That was probably why they sent him when it came to dealing with the undead. But it didn't take mind reading to know what the fellow was thinking. Jack just loved messing with the guy.

"I need a sweeping device," he said at length.

Magnarelli's brows, steel-gray like his hair and eyes, arched, forming deep creases in his forehead. "Why?"

"Again, none of your business. You have one on you?"

Magnarelli sighed and lowered his head briefly. Then he turned, aimed his key ring at the Lincoln and started toward it. The trunk opened, and he leaned in and rummaged around. A moment later he came back with the device, handed it to Jack and quickly explained how to use it.

"Perfect," Jack said. "Thank you."

"Thank me by giving me something in return. Something I can *use* this time, Jack. That first bit, about Rivera heading north from Savannah was almost useless. By the time we got to the location you gave us, he'd been gone a day and a half already."

Jack shrugged. "I'm doing the best I can. Maybe this one will pan out for you." He tried to inject sincerity into his tone but wasn't sure he was successful. He dipped into his jeans pocket and extracted a slip of paper. "I know for a fact he was here."

Magnarelli glanced at the note. "Virginia Beach, huh? And you say he *was* there. How long ago?" He was still squinting at the paper in the dim glow of the parking garage, as if it might have more to tell him if he just

103

looked closely enough.

"As recently as twenty-four hours," Jack said. "It's the best I can do."

"The best you could do, Heart, would have been to give it to me twenty-four hours ago. When *you* got it."

"I *didn't* get it until tonight," Jack lied. "And I couldn't get away sooner without arousing suspicion." He tried again to look sincere. "Look, I'm doing the best I can here. And you're getting information you wouldn't have had otherwise, so I don't see why you should be complaining." He shook his head, turning away in manufactured frustration and taking long strides toward his car. "Fuck this. I'm working my ass off here, but it's never good enough for you assholes. I'm outta here. Find yourself another —"

"Hold on, hold on now." Magnarelli's shoes came tapping after him. Everything about him had changed: his tone, his walk. Even the granite face seemed to have softened. All phony as hell, Jack knew, but so was every word that passed between the two of them. "This intel is fine," the agent said, like he was talking to a ten-year-old who'd just failed a spelling test. "I just wish it was fresher, but it's good. You keep it up, okay?"

Jack stopped walking, his lips curving into

a slow smile, which he doused before he turned. "I really am doing my best here, Frank."

"I know you are. In fact, here." The agent tugged an envelope from his inside coat pocket. "A little bonus. You call me when you have anything else — the *minute* you have anything else, if it's humanly, er, if it's possible."

"You have my word on it," Jack said. And he didn't even cross his fingers behind his back.

Conning the CIA was the biggest game he'd ever run. And probably the most risky, because they were the best con men on the planet themselves. Then again, he'd always loved a challenge.

"Well, that didn't take long," Topaz said when Jack returned to the house. She wished it had taken just a bit longer. She was still in a satin bathrobe, with a towel on her head.

"I told you it wouldn't." He tugged the sweeping device from his pocket and held it up, carefully cupping it in his hand to block it from any video cameras, since they were undoubtedly working just fine. The thing was, a vampire's image wouldn't show up on tape, but the device might, unless he kept all its bits in direct contact with himself. "And I got what we needed."

"You know how to use it?"

"It came with a free demonstration. Why don't you finish getting ready and I'll, uh . . . sweep up."

She nodded, turned to head for the stairs, then paused and faced him again. "Are you going to tell me what your mysterious *errands* entailed?"

"No."

The bluntness of his answer made her blink in surprise. And then it made her wonder. "Are you seducing some wealthy, needy woman out of her life's savings, Jack?"

He frowned and leaned slightly forward, as if trying to see her more closely. "Is that a hint of jealousy I detect, Topaz?"

"In your dreams. I just can't bear the thought of some other woman going through what I did."

He moved closer, lifting his hands as if to stroke them down her outer arms, but then he paused, obviously remembering their deal. Instead of touching her, he looked directly into her eyes and said, "It's not another woman."

She hated the relief that surged through her with so much force that it left her knees weak. Hated it. But couldn't deny it.

"You're not going to tell me what it is, are you?"

"No."

"Is it legal?"

"Utterly."

When he said that, the dimple in his chin appeared, along with the twinkle in his eye that had melted her heart so many times. She wanted to throw herself into his arms with everything in her, as he held her gaze steadily and his smile slowly died. Some unseen force crackled between them. She felt herself leaning toward him, being pulled, and it startled her so much that she turned and bolted up the stairs, down the hall and into the master suite. She surged through it into the bathroom and closed the door hard, as if shutting out Lucifer himself.

And then she leaned over the sink, hands braced, and stared into the mirror, wishing she could search her own eyes in its reflection. But she couldn't. "What's the matter with me? Why am I still so drawn to him, when I know he's the worst possible choice for me? Why, when he's the biggest mistake I ever made? Am I stupid?"

The answer to that, she decided, was a resounding no. She wasn't stupid. She was broken. She'd never known any kind of love in her life, except the false, using kind. And so, naturally, that was what she attracted and was attracted to. The same kind of bullshit she'd always known. Even as a vampire, she was repeating the same cycles that had been ingrained in her since childhood.

She needed to break those cycles.

And she'd better hurry the hell up, she thought.

When she returned downstairs, looking drop-dead gorgeous in her own not-so-humble opinion, Jack was waiting at the foot of the staircase, holding a handful of tiny electronic thingies in his palm.

Topaz blinked down at them. "Are they . . . ?"

"Completely disabled. I decided we were better off just pulling them. Figured I can always tell our landlord to forget he ever planted them. I got them all, checked three times just to make sure. The only room left to go through is your bathroom. I thought I'd better wait until you came out to do that."

"Being that the alternative would have been pretty painful for you, Jack, I think that was a wise decision."

"Sure." He took the first two steps up, then glanced over his shoulder at her. "You look incredible, by the way. Do we have plans that I don't know about?"

"No."

"No? So that's all just for me, huh?"

"You wish." She smoothed a hand over the skirt of her black halter dress and wished his compliment didn't make her feel warm all over.

He shrugged and continued up the stairs. He was back minutes later, declaring her bathroom "clean."

Then they got into the car to head to the home of former State Senator Frederick Ramirez.

"I don't believe he's expecting you." The man who answered the door was more bodyguard than butler, but Jack wasn't concerned.

"No, that's true, he's not," Topaz said. "Would you please tell him that Mirabella's daughter is here and wants to speak to him?"

The man frowned, but gave a nod. "Wait here." And he left them standing outside, on the wide concrete steps of the impressive home.

"Friendly fellow, isn't he?" Jack glanced down at Topaz, noting the tension in her jaw. And the way her hair was as smooth as mink, hanging loose and sexy around her shoulders. "Relax. It'll be fine."

"Who said I wasn't relaxed?"

"I did." Then he glanced at the closed door. "He's coming back. The senator will see us."

"I just hope he's as easy to read as his man Friday."

The door opened, and the butler/ bodyguard stepped aside. "He'll see you. Follow me."

The place was shamelessly opulent and colder than ice. They moved through a foyer, then turned to traverse a long hall, every footstep echoing. At the end, a pair of double doors stood open, leading into a book-lined office that smelled of leather and aging volumes. Their escort stopped outside the doors and waved them in.

Jack could feel Topaz's tension build as they walked through those doors. The senator stood near a large fireplace, his eyes on Topaz as she entered. Then he plastered a warm and mostly-sincere smile on his face, and came toward them, reaching out his hands.

He clasped hers in both of his. "Tanya. My God, I thought you were dead."

"Everyone did."

He held on to her hand as his eyes roamed

her face. "You look so much like your mother."

"Thank you."

"It must be cold outside. Your hands are freezing." He was still clinging to her hands, and Jack was getting a bit hot under the collar about it. Not that he had any reason to be. The guy could be her father, after all. But if he wasn't, then he'd damn well better let go, and soon.

As if on cue, Ramirez did, turning toward a sofa and several chairs that formed a half circle around the fireplace. "Sit, please. Be comfortable. Can I have Rodney get you anything? Wine, tea, coffee?"

"No, thank you," Topaz said.

"We never drink . . . wine," Jack quipped. Topaz elbowed him in the rib cage, but discreetly, as they both sat down on the brown leather sofa.

The senator glanced at the door. "That's all for now, Rodney."

Nodding, the man-at-arms pulled the doors closed and left them alone. The senator glanced at Jack. "I'm sorry, I seem to have forgotten my manners. I'm Frederick Ramirez."

"Jack Heart," Jack said, extending a hand to shake his.

"Tell me, what brings you here?" the sena-

111

tor asked, turning his attention back to Topaz.

"Well, two things really. I'm curious as to who my birth father truly is. And I'm even more curious to learn who murdered my mother."

Ramirez was silent for a moment, thoughtful. Then he said, "And I imagine you consider me a suspect on both counts."

"I just wanted to talk to you about it," Topaz said. "I'm not accusing you of anything."

He sighed and nodded.

"You must have thought you could have fathered me. You tried to gain custody after my mother's death."

"I did. Because I cared for her." The older man drew a deep breath and met her eyes. "The truth is, Tanya, I knew I couldn't have been your birth father, because I was, am, sterile. I wanted to raise you anyway, out of love for your mother. And I hoped the courts would never know about my deception. But they found out."

"Really?" Jack asked. "Because I didn't see any note of that in any of the court documents."

"I'm a powerful man, Mr. Heart. With powerful connections."

"That much is obvious," Jack said, with a

pointed glance around the room. "Clearly all this wasn't acquired on a state senator's salary."

The senator chose to ignore that remark. "Suffice it to say I had enough influence to ensure that my sterility was never recorded in the public documents, but the judge was aware of it." He returned his full attention to Topaz. "I wish you had been mine. I honestly do. And if it will put your mind at ease and help you in your quest for the truth, I'll gladly cooperate with DNA testing. Hell, I'll even pay for it."

Jack knew it wasn't necessary. The man wasn't too tough to read, and he knew Topaz was picking up on the same things he was. Ramirez was telling the truth. Jack saw the disappointment in her eyes and felt a rush of emotion that was totally unlike him.

He cleared his throat, forced his gaze back to the senator. "What do you know about the murder, Mr. Ramirez?"

Ramirez dropped his gaze. "It's been a long time, but it's etched in my memory. I loved her, you know. I wanted to marry her, but she wouldn't be tied to any one man. She was such a free spirit. I always suspected that one of the men she was seeing killed her in a jealous rage. But the police investigated thoroughly and, while I hate to say it, Tanya, if they failed to find the guilty party, I don't hold out much hope that you'll be able to."

"Maybe not," she said. "But I have to try."

He nodded. "I *will* tell you this. I had no reason to wish her harm. None. I wouldn't have hurt her for the world. I even put up a substantial reward for information at the time."

Topaz glanced at Jack, met his eyes. *He's not lying.*

I know.

"Do you have any theories about what might have happened to her body?"

"That was a desecration. I don't know. Some crazed fan. Some obsessed lover. I just don't know, Tanya."

The telephone shrilled once, then stopped. A moment later, the butler was back, poking his head in. "It's the governor, sir."

Ramirez nodded, held up a hand for patience and addressed Topaz. "Is there anything else you want to ask me?"

"I have something," Jack said, when she shook her head. "Right after Tanya arrived here and the tabloids blasted their gossip about her mission, the house where she's staying was broken into. Possibly by someone very nervous about what we might have

114

learned. Do you know anything about that?"

Ramirez's brows drew together. "I know it's not a good sign. Tanya, it could be that the killer is still nearby, living locally, close enough to be a threat to you." Then he shot his attention Jack's way. "I can get you some Secret Service people. Talk to the police and see to it you have —"

"That won't be necessary," Jack said. "Believe me, I can protect her."

Topaz shot him a quick glare. Jack grinned. He really did know her well, he thought. "Let me amend that. She can protect herself. I'm just the backup."

Topaz rose from the sofa, so Jack and the senator got up as well. "Go ahead and take your call, Senator. We have what we came for," she said. "Thank you for taking the time."

"If there's anything else you need, don't hesitate to call. I'll instruct my staff that any calls from you are to be put straight through to me."

"That's kind of you."

"It was wonderful meeting you, Tanya. I hope I'll see you again." Then he glanced at the butler. "Rodney, show our guests out."

"You're disappointed," Jack said, as he drove them back toward the mansion.

115

"Yeah, kind of. He seemed like a decent person."

" 'Seemed' being the operative word. There *is* that bit about him accepting contributions from mob bosses."

She nodded. But her face was shaded with sadness, and he found he couldn't stand to see it there. Odd. Empathy had never been a strong point of his. Still, he was compelled to distract her from her sadness.

"You never told me your story, Topaz."

"Which story would that be?"

"The story of your transformation. Who made you and when, and how it came about."

She slanted him a sideways glance. "You really want to know?"

Oddly enough, he did, and he told her so.

She shrugged and shifted in her seat a little, leaning back as if getting comfortable. "There's not a lot to tell, but I suppose it's one of the more unusual makeovers you'll hear about."

"Makeover, huh? That's a cute way of putting it."

"Yeah, I'm a cute person." She shrugged. "When I turned twenty-five, I got control of my own money for the first time. And there was a lot of it. By then I was well aware that my father — the man who'd raised me —

was more interested in my fortune than in me. I'd been living with that knowledge for years. In fact, it seemed to me then that everyone in my life who was supposed to love me only cared about my money."

Regret burned through his veins and straight into his heart. He'd been one more in a long line of those who had used her.

"I was sick by then. The belladonna antigen's effects were kicking my ass. I was depressed, tired all the time, lethargic, weak, dizzy. The doctors knew what caused it, said it was par for the course. But they said there was no known treatment, much less a cure. I was basically told I wouldn't live far past thirty."

"And you knew nothing about what else that antigen meant — that you could live forever?"

"No, I didn't know there even *were* vampires, back then."

"Well, few people do." He was watching her face, glancing at it often while driving. He'd meant to distract her from her sadness, but it seemed to him that this conversation was only making her sadder than ever. Maybe he should change the subject, but she was into her story and he didn't know how.

"I decided to take off," she said. "I decided

117

to take every bit of money I had and just blow it all. I was going to party until I dropped."

"I suppose you needed to rebel."

"I hated that money. Because of it, I thought I would never find anyone who could love me for just me. I went to Mexico. A resort on the Gulf Coast. I spent six months there, most of them so drunk I could barely walk. And it took its toll on my body. I think I shortened my life expectancy to almost nothing — to absolutely nothing, in the end. I got weaker and weaker. I barely ate, I just drank and partied and had sex with anyone who wanted me."

"That would have included anyone who saw you."

She sent him a quick look, and he thought her lips tightened slightly at the corners, as if a smile were lurking just beneath the surface. A sad one. But it pleased him that he'd elicited it with his compliment. He had never given her enough of those, he realized.

"One night I staggered out of a *cantina* and into the street, and just collapsed there. I could feel myself dying, I think. I thought so at the time, anyway. I thought it was all over. And my only regret was that I hadn't managed to put much of a dent in my inheritance, so some undeserving asshole would probably end up with all of it."

"You were suicidal," he said. "Only instead of a gun, you were using a bottle."

"Many bottles," she corrected.

"So what happened?"

"It's a blur. I only remember it in small bits, like a puzzle with most of its pieces missing. I remember a woman gathering me up from the dust and into her arms. It seemed odd, how easily she lifted me. I didn't weigh much at that point, but she wasn't much bigger than I was. I remember her breath on my throat. Her hands were so soft, and so cold. And her voice was just a whisper, but one that got through to me and gave me comfort, somehow. When I woke, I was in my bed in the room I had rented. The windows had all been completely covered. I felt so different. Not sick or weak, but strong and powerful, strong like I'd never felt, even before I got sick."

"It's a rush in the beginning, isn't it?" Jack asked.

She nodded.

"And the woman who brought you over?" Jack asked.

"Gone," she whispered. "All she left me was a note."

He was turning the car into the driveway of Avalon by then. And even as he shut it off and killed the headlights, Topaz was digging in her handbag. She pulled out an old-fashioned silver cigarette case, with the initials MD engraved on its face.

"Was that your mother's?" he asked.

"Yeah. I've had it forever. I never smoked, so I use it to keep special things in." She opened it, and though she kept it turned toward her, he glimpsed the little cards that had been attached to the flowers he'd sent her on occasion when they were dating. She'd kept them. God, he really had meant something to her once.

"Here it is." She took out a folded sheet of paper and snapped the case closed, returning it to her purse. "You want to read it?"

He nodded, and she handed it to him. He unfolded it there in the dark, intimate interior of the car. He didn't need lights to see. He glanced at the resort stationery, and then at the elegant scrawl of the handwriting.

Dear Fledgling,

I'm very sorry that I have to leave you to learn of your new nature on your own, but I had no choice. So I'm leaving you this note to tell you the most important things, the ones you need to know in order to survive. When I found you last night, you were near death. You would not have seen another day, and though I could not manage to get your consent, I did what I sensed you would want, had you been given the choice. I made you into what I am — a vampire.

You are stronger now than any human, and that strength will only increase with age. Your senses are enhanced. You can read thoughts, and send them, and control the minds of others, given time and practice. And you must drink blood to survive. It needn't come from humans, or even living beings. Blood banks and animals will suffice. But food and ordinary beverages are no longer an option. Your body cannot and will not tolerate them.

You must never expose yourself to direct sunlight. You will sleep during the day, whether you want to or not. You are highly flammable, so be very careful around fire. And you can bleed out with ease. Those are the ways you can die.

Any injuries you sustain will heal with the day sleep. So if you can stanch the blood flow of a potentially mortal wound just until the sun rises, you will survive.

Pain is magnified. But so is pleasure.

Only humans with the belladonna antigen can become vampires. We all had it. As vampires now, we sense those humans who possess it, and we are compelled to watch over and protect them.

Those are the things you need to know. I wish you a long, powerful and happy life-eternal.

Jack refolded the paper and handed it back to her. "She didn't even sign it."

"No. And she abandoned me. But I was used to abandonment by then. And at least she didn't take my wallet with her when she left."

He winced at the barb. "I probably deserved that."

She only shrugged, making no move to get out of the car.

"You know, our stories aren't all that different," he said.

She said nothing, just sat still, waiting, so he went on. "My father died when I was a kid. I don't even remember him. My mother was a drunk, pretty much worthless. I raised myself, for the most part. When I was eight, she dropped me off at her brother's for an afternoon and never came back."

Her head lifted slowly, her gaze turning to

focus on his. "You were abandoned, too?"

"Yeah. And Uncle Frank was none too happy about it — not at first, anyway. But I was a smart kid. See, Uncle Frank was a confidence man, old school. I picked up on that, and one day, when we were in the park, I made sure he was watching and then went up to some kind-looking woman with a broken waffle cone I'd found on the ground. I cried about how I'd used my last fifty cents to buy an ice cream, only to have it fall apart and melt on the ground. She handed me a dollar, patted me on the head and told me to go get another."

She was gaping now, lips slightly parted, eyes wide.

"Proudest moment in my life was when I walked up to Uncle Frank and handed him that crisp dollar bill. I remember how it smelled, and how he smiled as he took it. Then he took me by the hand — first time he'd ever done that. And he said, 'Boy, I think this just might work out after all, you and me.' "

"And you've been conning people ever since," she said softly.

"Women. I've been conning women ever since. Mostly."

She shook her head slowly, reached for the car door, pushed it open.

123

"If I'd known then what I know now, Topaz, about you and your past, I never would have conned you."

"That's not the question, though, is it?" she replied. She got out of the car, closed the door and walked toward the house.

He followed quickly and caught up. "If that's not the question, then what is?"

She stopped walking and looked up at him. "You don't know?"

"No. Tell me." The wind was moving her hair gently, and the stars seemed to reflect in her eyes.

"The question is," she said, her voice softer than before, "without the con, would you even have given me the time of day? Would you have bothered with me at all?"

He blinked and decided honesty might be the best course here. "I was looking for a mark, Topaz. Not a romance."

She turned away, moving toward the house again.

Again he caught up, then opened the door before she could and let her go inside ahead of him.

"But if I *were* looking for . . . that . . . you'd be the one."

"Not anymore I wouldn't."

Her cell phone rang before either of them could speak again. Jack had a lump in his throat and a knot in his chest, and he was damned if he knew why. He'd been honest. He wasn't looking for love, hadn't been looking for it in the past when he'd met her, and he sure as hell wasn't looking for it now. It would be pointless to look for something that didn't exist.

She yanked out her phone, glanced at the screen, then flipped it open. "Reaper?"

And then she listened, and as she did, her eyes met Jack's again. But it wasn't hurt that shone from their depths this time, and it wasn't the sparkle of nighttime stars. It was suspicion.

6

"We're being followed again," Reaper said.

"Are you sure?" Topaz wasn't as much surprised as she was worried. "I thought you said you'd lost them."

"We had. That's the point. Someone must have tipped them off to our location. And the only people I told were our people. You, Seth and Vixen, Roxy and Ilyana."

She lifted her eyes to spear Jack with a steady gaze, having no doubt he could hear every word of the conversation. Could he have been the one? "How sure are you about Ilyana?" she asked.

"We barely know her. But I do think she hates Gregor as much as the rest of us do, having been his captive. Don't you?"

"Yes. But we know she has other motives. Secrets she's keeping. Who knows what they might cause her to do."

"Hang on, Topaz. Got to check something out." And then he switched from speaking aloud, to speaking mentally. She knew he was allowing his thoughts to be heard only by her, and she quickly blocked her own mind to keep Jack from listening in.

We have to at least consider the possibility that it could have been Jack.

She thinned her lips. *All right. What do you suggest we do about it?*

Tell him I'm heading to Pennsylvania. Say . . . Philly. I'm not, I'm actually going to the western end of the state to meet with some vampires who might be able to help us with this situation. But you tell him Philly. I'll have someone watching. If the CIA end up in Philly, we'll know.

Did you tell anyone else about this plan?

No one. And then he returned to speaking aloud again. "Sorry. It was nothing. Here's the address where we'll be spending the next day or two."

She nodded slowly, committing it to memory as he recited the phony address. "Philly, huh? Ring the Liberty Bell for me, will you?"

"Thanks, Topaz." *I hope to God I'm wrong.*

I do, too. "Goodbye, Reaper." She disconnected, a thumbnail to a button, then slid the phone back into the holster that rode on her slender hip.

Jack was studying her closely. "He okay?"

127

"You must have heard. The CIA spooks nearly caught up to them again. He can't figure out how they knew where he was."

"They're the CIA, that's how."

She nodded. "Yeah. Well, they're heading to Philadelphia. We've got this safe house out there. Vampire-owned, usually vacant, safety features built in —"

"The one on Mariposa. I know it."

"I figured you did. I just hope those assholes don't find them again."

"Me, too. Or if they do, that they're still a few steps behind."

She narrowed her eyes on him.

"So who's the next daddy candidate on your list, hmm? The actor or the mobster?"

"Wayne Clark Duncan's last known address was all the way down in Laguna Beach, so he'll have to wait for tomorrow night. The mob guy, though . . ."

"What?"

"Well, it's a Saturday night. According to the police reports, he's a silent partner at a nightclub not far from here — or he was, then, anyway."

"I think a night out is exactly what you need," Jack said with a smile. "Besides, I'm starved."

"I don't have anything stored up. Maybe we could go find a blood bank or a hospital on the way?"

As he thought, the dimples in his cheeks deepened, making her gut tighten and clench. She found it extremely difficult to believe he would betray Reaper for money. And then she wondered why, when he'd done it to her. And why it was she had some idiotic desire to trust him again.

"What would you say to a good old-fashioned vampire hunt?"

"Human prey?" She widened her eyes at him.

"We don't have to *kill* them. Come on, it would be fun. And this nightclub, if it still exists, should provide a ton of potential victims."

She smiled slowly. It was her nature to relish the hunt. It couldn't be helped. "We erase their memories afterward?"

"If you insist."

"I'm in." Then she glanced down at her attire. "But if we're going to do this, we really need to, uh, dress for dinner."

His smile was quick and bright and devastating. And everything in her reacted to it, just as it always had. She ran upstairs to change into an elegant, full-length dress, scarlet, with a slit up one side that would make Jack's eyes pop. She lowered her head, shaking it slowly. What was wrong with her?

She shouldn't want to make any part of Jack pop.

But she did. And in spite of their history, in spite of the fact that he'd already proven himself untrustworthy, she still didn't believe he was informing on Reaper. She couldn't.

The club was called The Underground, and it didn't look like a mob hangout. Music thrummed from inside, strobe lights flashed blindingly through the windows, and the last thing Topaz wanted was to go inside. So instead they struck up a conversation with the doorman to try to find out what they needed to know.

As they'd approached him, Topaz had flashed a smile and a good bit of thigh as she said hello.

He looked her up and down, unimpressed, then picked up a clipboard. "Names?"

"You won't find them on the list," she said.

"You aren't on the list, you don't get in. Move along."

She pursed her lips. "I didn't want to go in, anyway. I just wondered, didn't this place used to be owned by Tony Bonacelli?"

His head came up slowly, and he met her eyes. "Who's asking?"

Topaz held his gaze and exerted the full

strength of her will. "*I'm* asking. And you're going to answer me. You *want* to answer me. You want to tell me anything I need to know. You know you do."

He blinked, looking dazed. "Tony Bonacelli's been dead for five years. His son Vic owns the place now. Took over the . . . family business."

"And is Vic here tonight?"

"Yeah. He's here with his girl. Tiffany Skye."

Tiffany Skye. The name rang a bell. "Should I know her?"

"She's done a few movies. Recording a CD now."

"Right," Topaz said. Another of the young blond celebrities who appeared to have gained fame for no apparent reason. "I really would like to talk to them. Are you sure you won't let us in?"

"Yeah, if you want, but they're leaving. I just called for the limo. It'll pick 'em up around back."

"Why, thank you, Bruno. You've been very helpful."

"Name's Dave," he muttered.

"I don't particularly care." She placed her palm on his cheek. "You're not going to remember any of this conversation, Dave. Not even that it happened."

He didn't answer as she turned and walked away, Jack falling into step beside her. Once they were out of sight, she released the bouncer's mind from her control. From around the side of the building they watched as he frowned, blinked and looked around, clearly aware that something had just happened, but at a loss as to what.

The vampires stalked the night, moving silently through the shadows near the rear of the nightclub. Or at least, they were silent when Topaz could suppress her occasional laughter — and it was odd that she could laugh at all, but Jack was right. She was having fun. Stalking, hunting, using her vampiric powers to elicit the information she needed — it gave her a rush. Vampires, for the most part, had become far too civilized. Most rarely embraced their nature these days.

"It's a shame Bonacelli's dead and gone," Jack said.

"There's still hope. He might have let something about my mother slip to his son. And if this Vic knows anything, he'll tell me."

"Oh, I believe it. You had Bruno eating out of your hand." Jack shrugged. "Then again, he *is* male."

He sent her a wink, and she averted her

eyes. She loved flirting with Jack. Always had.

He nudged her with an elbow. "There's a limo skulking toward us," he said. "No headlights."

"That's a good sign. She's a celeb, so they probably want to be discreet."

Near the rear door, which had Dumpsters flanking it, they waited as the limo pulled to a stop.

Eventually the club's back door opened, and a young starlet staggered out, a hot-looking Italian on her arm. He was, Topaz guessed, twenty years older than she was, but he didn't look it. Both of them were wasted, though, and she was pretty sure Tiffany was underage.

Topaz met Jack's eyes, and he nodded. This had to be Tiffany Skye and Vic Bonacelli.

They stepped out of hiding, blocking the couple's path. The drunken pair came to an unsteady halt, looking at them, false smiles beginning to falter. Vic's hand instantly moved toward his side. Topaz felt the rush of Jack's power as he stopped the motion with nothing more than mental force.

"You want to invite us to ride with you in the limo," Topaz said softly. "You're compelled to."

"She's right," Jack said. "You need some-one you can trust to be sure you both get home all right. And you know the driver's probably on some tabloid payroll. But you trust us."

"You trust us more than anyone," Topaz added.

The couple's smiles had died completely by now, and their eyes seemed vacant.

Jack slid his arm through Tiffany's, which was about as big around as a pretzel. Topaz did the same with Vic, pleased to feel some decent biceps lurking beneath his shirtsleeve. Smiling and chatting as if they were old friends, they walked toward the limo.

The driver emerged to open a rear door, glanced at Vic and asked, "Mr. Bonacelli?"

"These are friends of ours, Ralph." He spoke in a monotone, his voice without any hint of inflection. "They're going to . . ."

"See you home," Topaz told him.

"Yeah. They're going to see us home."

"Yes, and put the divider window up, Ralph," Topaz said, sending him a killer smile. "We have private things to discuss."

"Very well."

He held the door as the four of them climbed in. They settled in seats facing one another. Jack sat beside Tiffany, Topaz beside Vic. The driver got in and put the car into motion. A second later, the divider window, darkly tinted, rose with a soft hum.

Topaz turned to the man. "So you're Vic?"

"Yeah," he said, staring into her eyes, mesmerized.

"You're Tony's son?"

"Yeah."

She patted his hand. "And you're dating an actress. Like father like son, I guess."

"I guess."

"I think your father knew my mother. She was an actress, too. Mirabella DuFrane. Have you heard of her?"

He nodded, his gaze still stuck to hers like glue. "Everyone's heard of her."

"Well, yes, but I meant — did your father ever speak of her? There's a rumor they were lovers."

Again, he nodded.

Impatience jabbed at her, but she fought it down, took her time. "What did your father say about her, Vic? I'd really like to know, and I know you want to tell me."

He nodded slowly. "He put a hit out on the guy who killed her. Called a sit-down with the other bosses. Put up a million bucks to the guy who could take out Mirabella's murderer."

Topaz felt her brows rise as he spoke those

words. Tony Bonacelli would hardly have done that if he'd been behind her mother's murder. Dammit.

"Did anyone ever collect on it?" she asked.

"No. The offer stands to this day. He made me promise to see it through."

She swallowed and glanced at Jack, who was gently moving Tiffany's platinum curls behind one ear, exposing her slender neck.

Don't take too much. She's bird-sized.

Yeah, I noticed that.

She focused again on Vic. "Did your father ever tell you that you might have a sister out there, Vic?"

"You mean Mirabella's baby?"

"Yes. That's who I mean."

"He told me once that he wished she was his. But the timing was way off. He didn't say more than that."

"I see."

Jack was looking at her again. *Let's get on with this and get out of here, Topaz. We got what we came for.*

She nodded. "Vic, you know what a rush you get from drugs? Like ecstasy?"

"Yeah."

"I'm gonna give you an even bigger rush." Topaz leaned in to brush her lips over the guy's neck. She found it corded and firm. Nice. "You want this. You know you do. Just relax," she whispered. "Close your eyes, and let your head fall back and rest against the seat. Oh, it'll be so good for you."

"Yeah," he said, obeying her every word.

She glanced at Jack and found his gaze on her, his eyes ablaze with the bloodlust, just as hers must be. She smiled at him, and he smiled back. And then they bent to feast at the throats of the two lovers.

It was good, Topaz thought. The guy's blood was strong and vital and rich, and packed just enough toxins to give her a slight buzz above and beyond the normal rush of feeding.

She drank, relishing it, lifting her eyes every few sips to glance toward Jack, always to find his gaze fixed on her.

When she'd taken all she could without doing harm, she lifted her head and dabbed at her lips with the back of one hand. Vic was unconscious — not from blood loss, but because she had mentally commanded him to be.

She saw that Jack had done likewise with his party-girl waif.

"Mmm," he said. "That was good, what little I dared take, at least."

"It was. I'm glad you suggested it."

"I'm glad you're open to my suggestions."

She glanced at the sleeping beauties.

"Now, what sort of memory shall we give them? That this was all just a dream, or maybe a bad reaction to too many drugs and too much booze?"

"The latter," Jack said. "Might actually do them some good."

The limo came to a halt. "Better hurry, so we can wake them. Ride's over." She took a tissue from a built-in dispenser and dabbed the droplets from their victims' necks, then stopped in mid-motion when the driver's door suddenly opened, and Ralph dove from it and ran like his pants were on fire.

"What the —"

Then a voice from outside shouted, "Get out of the car, hands in the air. You're completely surrounded."

She met Jack's eyes, her brows raised. "You have *got* to be kidding me."

Jack was peering out the tinted window. "I don't think *they're* kidding, babe. I think we'd better cooperate. Stay behind me, okay?"

"It's not like they're going to *shoot* us."

He was still studying them, and she looked, as well. Armed men with shotguns pointed their way stood on all sides of the car. She frowned. "Jack, those don't look like cops."

"I don't think they are."

138

"Shit. Leave it to me to pick a victim with his own private army."

"Driver must have known something was off," Jack said. "I should have seen it coming." He hit a button and lowered the window slightly. "We're coming out. We're unarmed. And we've done nothing wrong."

He pushed the door open and slowly, with his hands over his head, got out of the limo. He moved about three steps forward, then waited for Topaz to emerge.

"Vic! Tiffany!" the guy who'd spoken earlier yelled. "Are you all right in there?"

Topaz closed her eyes. "Shit. We really should have woken them up."

"Looks like they're down," one of the armed men said. "You two," he commanded Topaz and Jack, "take five steps forward and then lie facedown on the ground, hands behind your heads."

They took a step, then another. *On step four, run for it, full speed.* Jack sent the words mentally. *I'll be right behind you.*

Okay.

Three. Every shotgun muzzle was aimed directly at them.

Four. Topaz hesitated.

Go! Jack ordered.

She flew into motion, and shots rang out. Jack launched himself with a burst of speed a heartbeat after she did, and they vanished like blurs of color in the night. They didn't stop until they were miles from the scene, at the edge of the desert, a sprint that took them only minutes.

Topaz sank into a dune and waited. "Jack," she called, verbally as well as mentally. "Where are you?"

He came into sight then, walking slowly, exhausted — more so than he should have been from the brief burst of speed. She smelled blood.

"Jack!" Surging to her feet, Topaz ran to him.

Blood soaked his shirt. He'd lost the elegant black dinner jacket he'd been wearing somewhere along the way. "God, you're hit."

"Yeah, slightly."

"Slightly, hell, you're bleeding out." She eased him down into the sand, then reached for the high end of the slit in her sexy red dress and tore it all the way around. Using her teeth, she tore the fabric into sections, then wadded up several pieces as she dropped to her knees beside him.

She was glad the feelings roiling in her belly hadn't paralyzed her. The sight of Jack bleeding and the fear of losing him permanently were raging in her mind and in her heart. But instead of slowing her down, they only seemed to spur her into quick action.

She tore open his shirt. The wound was low, just above his hip bone on the right side. And it was pulsing blood at an alarming rate.

"Hold on, Jack," she told him, and willed it with everything in her. She pressed the wad of fabric into the wound, using all her strength to exert pressure. Then she took his hand and laid it over the makeshift dressing. "Press hard."

"Pressing." The word was more of a grunt. His eyes were on her face, but she couldn't look into them. She would lose track of what needed doing if she looked into those eyes. They did things to her.

She took a larger piece of fabric and wrapped it around him to hold the dressing in place, knotting it as tightly as she dared.

He grunted in pain. "Jesus, woman, you can't tourniquet a waist."

"I can damn well try." When she finished, he let his body fall backward in the sand, his eyes heavy. She sensed his pain, and as magnified as it was in their kind, she knew it was crippling him.

"Jack, you can't rest here. Not here."

"Just for a minute."

"We need to get you to shelter." His eyes closed, his head falling to one side. She shook his shoulder gently. "Jack, we're in the desert. And the sunrise is . . ." She looked at the sky. The stars were fading, and in the distance, a thin ribbon of gray, paler than the midnight-blue above, had appeared. "We've got less than an hour. Come on."

She hooked her arms beneath his and tugged him upright. "Come on, Jack."

He tried, bending a knee and pressing his foot into the sand in a weak effort to rise. But he only toppled again. "Can't. I'm too weak."

"Dammit, Jack!"

He hooked his hand around her neck, cupping the nape, tugging her face close to his. "I have something to say."

"There's no time —"

"I'm sorry I hurt you, Topaz. I really am."

She stared into his eyes, shocked into stillness by those words. She had never expected an apology. And that it came now, when he was hurt and maybe bleeding out — she believed it. She believed he meant it. And, unable to do otherwise, she kissed him. Something possessed her, something beyond reason. His fingers threaded in her hair, and his tongue danced over hers, and he kissed her like he'd never kissed her before.

She was aching, hungry, when their lips parted, but he was still kissing, his mouth trailing over her cheek, her jaw, her neck.

She tipped her head back. "Do it, Jack. Drink."

As his mouth moved against the sensitive skin of her throat, he spoke. "No. Not from you. The bond —"

"I know it forms a bond. The truth is, Jack, we already have one, as much as I hate to admit it. Now drink, dammit, before we both roast in the sun."

His lips trembled as they parted. She felt the graze of his teeth on her skin and shivered from sheer pleasure. And then he bit down, and his fangs sank through her flesh, popped through the vein. His lips closed, and he sucked from her.

Pleasure — no, *ecstasy* — washed through her like a warm elixir. Her entire body writhed and heated, and her head fell back. She closed her eyes and moaned in pleasure even as she clutched the back of his head to hold him to her, to offer him more and still more.

He pulled away at last and enfolded her in his arms as he lay back. She relaxed atop him, lying across his chest as the sensations slowly ebbed. She knew he was feeling the rush of power now. It would surge through him with the influx of powerful vampiric blood.

Eventually he sighed. "Thank you."

"Thank *you*." She said it jokingly, but she meant it. God, that had been so good. Only sex could have come close. "Think you can walk now?"

"Yeah. Let's get out of here."

She got up off his chest, regretting the loss of that intimate contact with everything in her. He sat up, got to his feet, reached a hand down to help her. She swayed just a little.

"I didn't take too much, did I?" he asked, concern etched on his face as he searched her eyes.

"No. I'm fine." She wasn't, though. She was drunk with passion, with need. And he was the only man who could fulfill it. The only man who ever had.

"You suppose there's time to get the car?" she asked.

"No, and we can't make it back to the mansion, either. There's barely time to get to the crypt," he said with a brief glance at the night sky.

"We'll make it," she promised, and, clutching his hand in hers, not even wondering why, she got moving.

Jack's pain was excruciating, but at least it was less than it had been before Topaz had replenished him with her blood. Damn, even with the physical agony, his body had come alive when he'd been feeding from her tender throat. Smelling her, tasting her, touching her. He'd felt as if he'd been about to burst into flames.

He wanted her more than ever now; there was no question about that. And he knew that the bond between them, whatever it had been before, had been magnified by the sharing of their blood. It was inevitable. It was also why he'd never partaken of her when they'd had sex in the past, no matter how sorely he'd been tempted. He hadn't wanted to make her any more attached to him than she already had been, knowing he would leave her in the end.

But now they'd done it. Topaz would never get him out of her system now. That thought made him smile just a little, until its echo whispered through his psyche. *And you'll never get her out of yours. Then again, you never really have, have you?*

His smile died.

Jack was lying on the air-mattress-enhanced bier inside the crypt, while Topaz secured the door, changed her clothes and unfolded a blanket. He watched her every movement, though she never revealed enough to sate him. He didn't think all of her would be enough for that. As hard as he tried, he'd never been able to forget her, to stop wanting her, thinking about her.

She climbed into the makeshift bed beside him and tugged the covers up around them both. Then she rolled onto her side, facing him. He was on his back. "Twenty more minutes, give or take. How's the wound?"

"It's bleeding again, but only a little. I'll last."

"You sure?"

He turned his head toward her. "You'd care, wouldn't you? If you woke up to find me dead tonight, you'd really care."

She lowered her eyelids, hiding her emotions behind them. He could have probed her mind for them, but he was too weak and tired to make the effort, and she was probably blocking, anyway.

"When you have sex with someone, especially if it's only them and for an extended period of time, it creates a bond. It doesn't matter if you want it or not, it just does. That person becomes important to you. It can't be helped. So yeah, I may hate your guts most of the time, but I care."

He nodded. "Is that what it is, you think? A physical bond created by all the sex we had?"

She nodded. "And it'll be stronger now, with the blood sharing. But you know that."

He hadn't thought it could get much stronger. But he liked her theory. He was this drawn to her and this obsessed by her because they'd shared intimacy over a long period of time. It made sense that sex could create a bond as surely as the sharing of blood could. It wasn't any sappy emotional thing, like love, for example. It was physical. Simple. Cut and dried.

"We didn't really get anywhere tonight, did we?" she said. "With the Bonacelli connection, I mean."

"Yes we did, Topaz. We learned a lot. Enough to rule him out."

"As my mother's killer, yes," she said softly. "He wouldn't have put out that reward just to make himself look innocent. A man like him wouldn't worry about looking innocent to his peers. He was too powerful for that. And he certainly didn't broadcast the reward to the authorities to avert suspicion."

"No, that would have gotten him arrested."

"But we still don't know if he was my

father," she said.

Jack sighed. "If he told his son the timing was off —"

"I know, but he could have been lying. It's just not as compelling to me as the reward and the hit and all that."

"We'll find out the truth, Topaz. We're getting closer all the time."

She sighed softly. "It's just that we're running out of options. One more interview to conduct. And I don't know where we go from there."

"Mmm, the actor. Retired by now, no doubt."

"It's a long shot," Topaz said, and he could hear the disappointment in her voice. "He didn't even try for custody."

"Don't assume anything." He reached out to brush a stray lock of hair from her face, breaking their deal by doing so, but grateful when she didn't object. "Thank you, Topaz. You probably saved my life tonight."

"You're welcome," she said. He held her eyes for one long moment, and he thought she might just be willing to let him kiss her. But then she lowered her lashes, rolled onto her back and took a long deep breath. "Good night, Jack."

"Good day, Topaz."

■ ■ ■ ■

Jack had another one of his "errands" to run shortly after sundown. He dropped Topaz at the mansion and left, only to return an hour later with a thick file folder.

Topaz wasn't in the house. Frowning, he opened his senses and felt her outside, on the beach. So he went, file folder in hand, and found her there. She was sitting in the sand, legs stretched out in front of her, staring out over the nighttime sea as the waves rolled lazily, not quite reaching her bare feet. The way the wind moved her hair mesmerized him, and for a moment he just stood there, a few feet from her, watching.

"It's beautiful, isn't it?" she asked. "I love the ocean."

"Well, it's wet." He kicked off his shoes and moved closer, setting the folder across her thighs.

"What's this?"

"Dossier on the actor. Thought we might as well go in prepared."

She nodded, but she wasn't looking at the folder. She stared at his face instead. "Where are you getting all this stuff?"

"I know people. Can't tell you more than that."

"Are you blackmailing someone? Conning them?"

"Does it matter?"

She studied him intensely. "I've been thinking about you, you know."

His smile was slow and deliberately suggestive. "Oh, believe me, I've been thinking about you, too."

"I mean about your childhood. Your mother abandoning you. I got to wondering if that's why you treat women the way you do. If maybe, every time you take a female for a bundle of cash and then walk out, you're kind of getting payback. Punishing your mother symbolically."

He pursed his lips, saying nothing.

"Do you think that's why you do what you do?" she pressed.

"I do what I do because I'm good at it, and because it's lucrative. And if I want a shrink, I'll make an appointment with one, okay?" He got to his feet and stomped back to the villa.

"I hit a nerve, didn't I?" she called after him.

"Don't try to analyze me, Topaz. This isn't some kind of mind-meld we've got going on here. We want to fuck each other's brains out. And we will, before this is over, I guarantee it. But that's all it will be. The sooner you figure that out, the easier it'll be for you when it's over."

She would have winced at the words, but she didn't, because he hadn't blocked, and so she felt what he was feeling in that moment. He was afraid, she realized, stunned to the marrow. Jack Heart was scared to death — of *her.*

7

She should have realized it sooner, Topaz thought as she rose to her feet and took her time about brushing the sand from her clothes. She'd been so wrapped up in her own pain that she hadn't taken time, until now, to wonder what made Jack the way he was.

He'd experienced the same kinds of loss and betrayal in his life that she had. He had the same bitterness eating away at his soul, and it stemmed from the all-consuming pain of abandonment. He was still that wounded little boy whose mother had dumped him and never looked back.

She knew that child. She'd *been* that child.

And now she knew that he was hurt and he was scared, whether he would admit it or not. Knowing that made *her* feel frightened, too. It was far easier to think of him as a heartless con man out for a buck and some sex on the side — providing the sex was good and hassle free. Now, though, she was seeing him as so much more. That was a dangerous path for her to walk, one that was treacherously steep, booby-trapped with potholes and loose stones, and skirting a bottomless pit. She could fall all too easily, treading this particular path. If she did, she would fall hard, and the landing was going to make the pain she'd felt so far seem like a hangnail.

"So be careful," she told herself. "Just don't fall."

Squaring her shoulders and carrying the folder with her, she trudged through the sand back to the villa. Jack had hit the shower. By the time she'd settled herself on the sofa with the file open on the coffee table in front of her, he returned, and he seemed to have forgiven her for the dime-store analysis. He trotted down the stairs wearing jeans but no shirt. His feet were bare, his hair still wet, though he was rubbing it vigorously with a towel. He wore his usual expression: a smirk that said nothing.

"So, anything interesting so far on our friend the actor?" he asked, nodding toward the file.

"Plenty," she said. She moved over a bit on the sofa, and he took her cue, sitting close beside her. Really close. She didn't move away, either. She liked him close. She cleared her throat and refocused her attention. "Wayne Duncan was married, but as an up-and-coming actor with aspirations of becoming a leading man, he and his handlers opted to keep his marriage secret."

"Not all that unusual, I suppose," Jack said. "Gay actors pretended to be straight, married actors pretended to be single. Some still do."

"It's all about the image," Topaz agreed. "According to the file, his affair with my mother was a long one. Probably could have been great for his career, if it could have been public. But he had to keep it from his poor wife, and he had to keep his poor wife from the public at large." She gave her head a shake. "Can you imagine trying to juggle so many secrets?"

"It would be enough to make some men snap," Jack said softly.

Topaz nodded. "I wonder if my mother knew he had a wife."

"I wonder if his need to keep his secrets was why he didn't fight for custody of you. It would have meant admitting the affair, possibly ruining his marriage."

"Couldn't have been much of a marriage anyway," Topaz said. "The reports here suggest he was very much in love with my mother."

"He'd have been a fool not to be."

Jack was staring at her as he said it, reminding her without a word of his insistence that she resembled her mother, and she felt herself warm in reaction in spite of herself.

"Topaz," Jack said.

She glanced up at him, saw in his eyes that he was about to veer off topic and take this moment into a dangerous direction. Dangerous to her heart, at least. She shook her head slightly, just barely, and then focused again on the file. "No one seems to have known anything about Wayne Duncan's wife," she said. "But there is one photo. Let's see, I just saw it a minute ago." She shuffled papers. "Ah, here it is. Her name's Lucia Duncan. Looks like she's been through the mill, huh?"

She handed Jack the grainy three-by-five black-and-white photo. He took it, stared at it, said nothing.

"It surprises me that he married her. I mean, she's probably his age, but she looks a lot older in that photo, doesn't she?"

"Yes, she does," Jack said softly. "A lot older than the last time I saw her."

Topaz frowned. "Jack? You *know* her?"

"I don't think I ever knew her." He surged

to his feet, and the file folder flew from the table, papers scattering everywhere. The photo landed faceup on the floor. He stared at it for one frozen moment, then spun and paced away.

"Jack . . . ?"

"Where is he?" As he strode toward the door, Jack snatched his key ring from the rack on the wall with so much force that the entire thing came down. "Where the hell is this actor?"

"Um, the address is in the —" As she spoke she scrambled to gather up the fallen sheets, searching for the actor's last known address. "Jack, what the hell is going on?"

She found the sheet she was looking for and knelt there on the floor, looking up at him.

"That woman," he said, pointing an accusing finger at the photo that lay on the floor, as if he could send a blast of power from his fingertip to annihilate it. "That woman . . . is my mother."

"You need to try to calm down," Topaz said softly. She was driving. She'd insisted on it, because Jack was in no condition to. His jaw was tight and clenched, his entire body trembling with barely contained emotion. He clutched the photo in one hand, crumpling its corner with the force of his grip.

And all Topaz wanted to do was comfort him. God, she knew what he was feeling. She knew it so well. No one could hurt you like your own mother could. No one.

He didn't answer.

"We'll talk to him. Duncan. The actor. We'll just talk to him, right? You can't go in there looking for blood, Jack. Remember, he isn't guilty of anything here."

"Except taking a mother from her only child."

"You don't know that. He may not even have known she had a child. He may have met her after she'd left you." She looked up, increasingly nervous as the actor's house came into view. It was a modest Cape Cod in a quiet suburban neighborhood. There were palm trees lining the edge of the lawn. She reached out a hand to cover one of his. "I'm with you on this, okay? I'm here."

He glanced at her from the corners of his eyes. There was emotion roiling there, but she glimpsed a hint of surprise beyond the unbearable hurt that photograph had dredged up from the depths of him. There might have been a touch of gratitude there, too. She couldn't be sure.

As soon as Topaz stopped the car, Jack got out. She had to hurry to keep up with him as he strode toward the house, knocked on the front door.

"Are you sure you're ready for this? We could have phoned first, given you both time to prepare."

"I just want to look her in the eye and ask her why. It's been a long time coming, Topaz."

She nodded. "I understand." Lowering her head, she whispered, "To be honest, Jack, if I had the chance, I'd want to do the same thing. Look my mother in the eye and ask her how she could leave me. And I suppose it makes even less sense for me to feel that way. She didn't leave on her own. She was taken from me. And yet, it feels the same. It feels like she walked out on me."

She glanced at the door then, but there were no sounds from beyond it. Impatient, Jack stepped closer and pounded on the wood, ignoring the doorbell.

"Coming, coming," a male voice called from somewhere within.

Soft footsteps came closer. Finally the door opened, and Wayne Duncan stood there, a dim echo of the publicity photos in the file. His hair was no longer striking black, but silver. His brows were salt-and-pepper. His face still bore the bone structure that had given him leading-man potential, though he'd never achieved movie-star status. He was thin, but held himself erect and proud, and he was an impressive figure, even in a flannel robe and slippers.

Jack looked him up and down, and then looked past him, scanning the rooms beyond. "Where is she?" he asked.

Clasping Jack's shoulder to try to instill calm, Topaz intervened, taking the confused looking man's attention away from Jack. "Mr. Duncan, I'm sorry to bother you, but —"

"My God," Duncan whispered. His eyes were riveted to her face, and then his hand rose to lightly touch her cheek. "Tanya."

She licked her lips, lowered her eyes.

"You *are* Tanya. Aren't you?"

"Yes. Yes, I am." She lifted her eyes again and held his gaze. "And this is my friend, Jack Heart."

He ignored the introduction. "I read you were in town, but I couldn't believe it. There were no photos. No proof. Oh, Tanya, I'm so happy to see you."

She nodded and tried to smile. "That's lovely to hear, Mr. Dunc—"

"Wayne, please."

"Wayne," she corrected. "But Jack and I really need to talk to you. Can we come inside?"

He lowered his head, his expression guilty. "Of course. And I know what you want to talk about. You know about the break-in, don't you?"

Jack snapped to attention, his gaze shooting back to the actor. "Yes, we know," he lied. "We know it was you."

He nodded. "I'm sorry. I'm so sorry. I just . . . I read that tabloid report, and I needed to know what you'd found. What you suspected."

"Why?" Topaz asked.

He sighed, shaking his head slowly. "Come inside. Sit down, and I'll try to explain." He stood aside to let them enter, and they did, side by side.

Save the questions about my mother until he tells us what he knows about yours, Jack's mind whispered to Topaz's. *She doesn't seem to be here at the moment, anyway.*

Topaz nodded, noting the framed photos of the couple together. One hung from a wall, and two others stood in facing frames on an end table. He led them to a cozy nook, set between curving windows that looked out onto the stars. Four chairs stood there, velour and comfortable, and they surrounded a small wicker table.

"I'll get right to the point, Mr. Duncan," Topaz said softly. "I'd like to know who murdered my mother. Was it you?"

He held her gaze, and she probed his mind. "I loved her. I could no more have hurt her than I could fly to the moon. She was the love of my life, Tanya. But I couldn't be with her. Not fully. I was married, and I couldn't leave my wife."

She nodded, then asked the next question without hesitation. "Are you my father?"

He dropped his gaze. "It's very likely. I never claimed you, never tried to gain custody."

"Because of your wife," she said.

He nodded.

"If you didn't kill my mother, then why the break-in?" Topaz asked. She was amazed at Jack's restraint, and yet he kept silent, just watching, and no doubt probing.

Duncan faced her. "Because I know who did kill her. At least, I think I do. I have no proof, you understand. And yet, I had to know whether you had found any. I thought you might have uncovered —"

"You think your wife did it," Jack said slowly. His patience had run out, and he saw the same things in the aging actor's mind that Topaz did. The difference was, he said them out loud. "You think Lucia found out about your affair and murdered Mirabella DuFrane."

Duncan met Jack's eyes. "Yes. I think it. I've always feared it. It's eaten away at my soul, not knowing. Wondering. Believing it to be true."

"My God." Topaz was stunned to the core. "How could you stay with a woman like that? Why would you choose someone capable of —"

"Lucia was sick, Tanya. Pancreatic cancer. She needed me."

Topaz sucked in a breath, her eyes flying to Jack's. He sat there looking as if he'd been hit between the eyes with a mallet.

"Where is she now, Duncan?" she asked, her voice shaking as she reached her hand out to clasp Jack's as firmly as she could.

And then the final blow fell.

"She died twenty years ago," Duncan said. "She never told me whether or not she'd killed Mirabella. But I believe in my heart that she did."

Jack shot unsteadily to his feet and stumbled from the room. Topaz got up to follow, but he held up a hand behind him, telling her to stay. Then he staggered out the door into the night like a punch-drunk boxer heading for his safe corner.

"Is he all right?" Duncan asked.

"I seriously doubt it," Topaz told him. "Mr. Duncan, Lucia was Jack's mother."

162

"What?"

"You didn't know, did you?"

"Lucia had a *son?*" It was his turn to look blown away. He pressed a hand to his forehead, his eyes wide and inwardly focused. "It can't be. She wouldn't have kept something like that from me. No."

Topaz nodded. "Yes. Her maiden name was Heart. Spelled like the organ, not in the more typical manner." When he shot her a look, she knew he'd known that much. He had to believe her now. "She abandoned Jack to her brother when he was only eight. He never heard from her again, never knew what happened to her."

Wayne Duncan lowered his head, abject agony painted on his face. And he wasn't acting, Topaz was certain. "I never knew her. I never knew her at all, did I?"

"I'm very sorry for your loss, Mr. Duncan, and for bringing you this sort of news. I —" She looked toward the door Jack had left hanging wide open. He was sitting in the car, but at an angle that put his face beyond her sight. "I have to go after him."

"Of course," Duncan said. "Please, Tanya, contact me again before you leave town. I'd like . . . a chance to get to know you."

She gazed at him, felt her heart clench a little tighter in her chest. "You *had* the chance to get to know me, Mr. Duncan. But you abandoned me, instead, denied me, kept me a shameful little secret. You abandoned me just the same way Lucia abandoned Jack," she said.

"But . . . you had a good life. The courts saw to it that —"

"Is that how you sleep at night? By telling yourself I had a good life? My childhood was hell, Mr. Duncan. My mother was taken from me by your wife, because of *your* lies. I was awarded to a man who knew he wasn't my father, who wanted to use the money I inherited to build his own fortune, and never gave a damn about me at all. You left me to that, even though you knew I was probably yours. And you tell me now that you want to get to know me?"

He swallowed hard, his Adam's apple swelling in his throat. "I'm sorry, Tanya."

"I'm sure you are. But it's too little, too late. You weren't around when I needed you. And now . . . well, now I don't."

He turned away, but before he did, she thought she saw a tear in his eye. But she had no time for his tears. God knew she'd shed enough of her own to know that they would pass sooner or later.

She had to go to Jack.

■ ■ ■ ■

Jack rode back to the mansion in utter silence. Aside from asking if he was all right once or twice, Topaz respected his need for stillness. He couldn't talk about it, not yet. He couldn't speak or he might explode.

His mother was dead.

Well, that should come as no surprise. He'd always assumed she'd managed to drink herself to death long before now. But having it confirmed . . . and knowing she'd left him and gone on to find this Hollywood life for herself, married an actor, lived in a nice home . . . Why hadn't she sent for him?

He didn't know whether to cry or scream with rage. His mother had murdered Topaz's mother. Good God, that didn't even compute in his mind. He couldn't even grasp it.

When they arrived at Avalon, Topaz parked under the shelter of the portico, looked at him for a long moment, ran her hand briefly over his, and then got out of the car and started toward the house. He didn't follow. He exited the Porsche, then simply stood by the car, hands pressed to the hood, head hanging between them. He was torn between opposing urges to pound something to bits, or to sink to the ground and curl into the fetal position.

And then her hand was on his shoulder, tugging, and against his will, he turned to face her. He didn't want her reading the emotions on his face, didn't want her seeing his weakness or, worse, pitying him.

He didn't get any of those things. Instead, her arms slid around his waist, and she pressed her body tightly to his. One hand slid upward until she threaded her fingers in his hair, moving them there, and it was soothing.

"She's gone," he said, and he said it in a voice that was so carefully controlled that it came out shivering and tight. "I got all worked up to confront her, and she's just gone. She even robbed me of that."

"I know," she whispered, and he knew she truly did. If anyone knew, it was Topaz.

He shook his head beneath her hand. "How can you comfort me? Jesus, Topaz, it looks as if my mother murdered yours."

"Looks that way. That's not you, though."

"I've done just as bad to you."

"Yeah, and you'll probably do it again, given the chance. And yet . . ." She tipped her head up to his, staring into his eyes, and her own were wide and wanting.

His body responded to that look exactly the way it always had. Before he could think better of it, he was lowering his head, taking her mouth. Her arms twined around his neck, and she stood on tiptoe to reach him better. He hugged her waist close to him, held her so there wasn't room for air to pass between. And the kiss heated and deepened, grew more urgent, until their bodies were straining and they were feeding from each other's mouths.

His hands fumbled with her jeans, and hers with his, until they struggled free of them. He slid his hands down her thighs and lifted them, and she used them to hug his hips. He turned her, settling her backside on the still-warm hood of the car, holding her there, and then he drove into her, and everything in him caught fire.

She clutched his shoulders, let her head fall back. Eyes closed tightly, she moaned his name. "God, Jack. Yes, Jack. More, Jack. Harder. It's been so long, Jack. I've wanted you for so damn long."

And he gave her what she wanted, what she needed, and he knew exactly what she was feeling, because in those moments it wasn't just her body that opened to him. Her mind opened, as well. And his melded with it, until he could feel everything she felt, every sensation, every tingle. And so he knew when the sensations began to build beyond endurance. He knew when her body tightened, clenched and strained for release. He knew exactly how to move, how to touch her to push her over the brink. And he knew how to let her hover there, whimpering and begging and yearning. When he let her come, it was an explosion, and her sensations raged through him and became his own, driving him over the edge alongside her. He sank into her deeply, gathered her into his arms, and held her to him as he emptied himself into her.

Her arms were around him. Her legs enclosed him. Her body milked him. Her essence filled him.

And in those moments, as they clung to each other and slowly came back down from the stratosphere, in those moments when she was vulnerable and open to him and needing him as much as she needed blood to survive, he felt her thoughts, her doubts, the almost paralyzing fear that whispered through her brain as her physical senses and the ecstasy they'd just shared slowly released their hold on her.

Don't you do it, Topaz, her mind warned her. *Don't love him again. He'll hurt you, you know he will. Just like he did before. You can't trust him. Not with your heart, never with your heart. God, Topaz, don't. For your own fuck-*

ing sake, don't love him again. It would kill you this time. It almost did the last time. And if you let yourself believe it would be any different, then you're lying to yourself.

8

She didn't trust him. She didn't trust him as far as she could throw him, Jack thought, as he tried to keep his hands from shaking and managed to get back into his clothes. He'd heard her thoughts, felt her emotions. And they were big ones. She was damn near swamped in emotions surrounding him. But they were too confused to fully identify. For some reason, that bugged the hell out of him.

But why should it, when he was just as confused about his feelings for her?

No, no, he wasn't. He knew what he felt for her. It was simple. He wanted her. He liked her. And yeah, he felt guilty for hurting her. That was it. Simple.

You're sticking with that bull, even after what just happened between you?

He ignored the voice of reason in his head, or maybe that was the voice of insanity in his heart, and continued his cool analysis.

Topaz's feelings for him must be pretty similar to his for her. She wanted him; she liked him, in spite of her better judgment; and she was still stinging from the hurt he'd dealt. She'd loved him once, but she didn't anymore. That much was clear in her own inner determination never to love him again.

But she didn't trust him.

Damn, why did that bother him so much? She *shouldn't* trust him. He was a confidence man. She would be *stupid* to trust him.

Except she wouldn't be, because he wouldn't betray her again. Not come hell or high water. And he wanted, right then, to give her back the rest of her money to prove it to her. But if he did that, she would know he'd had it all along, that he'd lied to her. Again. And that certainly wasn't going to do much to make her trust him. He would have to figure out a way.

In the meantime . . .

"Just so you know, that didn't mean anything, Jack. We're not getting back together." She was righting her clothes, buttoning her blouse, running a hand through her long, mink-soft hair the way he'd been doing a few moments before.

"I know."

"I just want to be clear on it. What happened between us doesn't change things."

She started for the house.

"It changes things. Don't kid yourself." He caught up to her, went ahead to open the door.

She preceded him inside before turning to face him, her hair sailing over one shoulder with the motion. "Like what?"

"Like . . . now I know you still want me. As much as I want you."

She rolled her eyes. "You already knew that."

"I wasn't as sure of it as I pretended to be." He closed the door, flipped the lock. "And I know that you care. You pretend to hate me, but you don't. You can't. There's our bond."

"The blood bond. I know, but I couldn't just let you die."

"Because you care. But that's not the bond I was talking about. It's the other one. The one we share because of our mothers and our childhoods and everything that's led us to become who we are. Our stories are so similar, Topaz."

"And yet we turned out so differently."

"You'd like to think so. But you know better. We're alike, you and I. Two peas in a pod."

"That's bull." She started toward the stairs but stopped when he went on.

"There's one more thing that's changed."

"What's that?" she asked without turning.

He walked up behind her, slowly. She didn't move away. He brushed the hair away from the back of her neck and leaned down to trail his lips over her nape. He felt her shiver.

"It changes our bargain. I said I wouldn't touch you until you wanted it. And now I know you do."

"I should have known you'd never keep your word," she whispered.

Even though he knew she was lashing out in self-defense, it stung. He drew back from her.

"I suppose it's safe to stay here while we rest," she said, changing the subject completely. "Wayne Duncan doesn't have any reason to come back and bother us now."

"I suppose that's true."

"I'm not sure there's any reason to keep digging into this," she said. "I don't think we're ever going to find any proof one way or the other. The only person who really knows who killed my mother is dead."

"So what's next?"

"We pack up and leave. Go our separate ways."

Jack closed his eyes and felt a blade sink deep into his heart. God, why? Why did the thought of never seeing her again cause him this much pain?

The good thing about being a vampire, Topaz thought, was that you could never lie in bed awake, tossing and turning and worrying, when you were supposed to be sleeping. The day sleep didn't give you a choice.

She put on a lime-green satin nightgown, thin and light, with spaghetti straps, cut to midthigh length, with lace around the hem and neckline, and slid in between the cool, clean sheets. Moments later, Jack slid into the bed beside her, wearing boxers and nothing else. She didn't argue. And she didn't argue when he pulled her against his chest, wrapped his arms around her and held her close.

It was the last time they would ever be in bed together, after all. And she didn't have the strength to deny herself the pleasure of drifting to sleep in his arms. Or of waking there again, come sundown.

She didn't *want* to deny herself those things. Even though they made her heart ache like it hadn't ached since he'd left. Why the hell did she still have this weakness for him, when she knew he was no good for her?

When the sun went down and she stirred

awake, his arms were still around her, but his eyes were already open, scanning her face. And they were deep and welling with something she knew damn well was false.

"Don't look at me like that."

"Like what?" he asked with all the innocence of a six-year-old.

"You know like what. Don't try to make me think you feel anything for me, Jack, when we both know you don't."

"That's not true. I care about you."

"You destroyed me," she told him. And she realized that it was high time she told him all the things she'd never said. Things that had been eating at her, things she'd buried. They all came tumbling out in a rush of release and emotion she hadn't seen coming, a rush so powerful it seemed to launch her from the bed to the floor without thought.

"How could you hurt someone the way you hurt me if you cared about them? I *loved* you, Jack. I adored you. And you walked away, left me like I didn't matter. Do you know what that did to me? *Do you?*"

"I know," he whispered.

"No, you don't," she said, pacing the floor. "You couldn't possibly know. I felt worthless. I felt like the worst fear I'd ever had — that no one could ever truly love me — had just been verified once and for all. I felt unattractive, unwanted, rejected, humiliated, beaten. I cried — no, sobbed — violently every waking moment for almost a month, Jack. And then, for the second month, I only woke up crying every evening and cried myself to sleep again every morning, but managed to keep the tears in check during the night. Unless I thought of you, or saw something that reminded me of you, or heard your name. The third month I managed to get to where there were a few days every week when I didn't cry at all. By the end of the fourth month, those days even outnumbered the ones when I did.

"But even then, I dreamed you would come back, and I was so stupid that I prayed for it. I would have taken you back, even after what you did to me. That's how bad it was. I barely fed. I got weak and sick and went half-insane."

"I'm sorry. I know it's not enough, but —"

"I actually thought about ending it, you know that? There were several days, not just one, but four or five of them, when the pain was so bad, I thought about just walking into the sunrise and letting it all go. It didn't seem like there was any other way to stop the hurting. I planned it all out. What I would wear, whether I'd leave a note, whether anyone would really give a damn that I was gone. I was close, and that's not me. That is *so* not me. I'm a strong, powerful woman, Jack, but you reduced me to nothing. Less than nothing. A pain-wracked, desperate, broken shell of a woman with nothing left of herself or her soul. That's what you did to me."

Tears had somehow managed to flood her eyes, and they were streaming down her face now. He stared at her, shaking his head, regret in his eyes, though God only knew if it was real or just another mask. He was too good an actor for her to tell.

"And now, Jack, now at long last, I thought I was over it," she whispered, brushing her cheeks with a hand. "But I guess it's just been lingering inside me all this time. And I'm not sure I'll ever get rid of the hurt you caused me. Not entirely. But I did get past letting it cripple me. I found a way to pick myself up, dust myself off and go on living. I got my strength back. I got my power back. I convinced myself that you had lost something incredible when you let me go, and that I hadn't really lost much at all. Only a man who never loved me, a man who used me, took all I had to offer, and gave nothing in return. A man cruel enough to take the love I gave him and toss it on the floor, and then step on it as he walked away. I didn't lose much."

She stomped right up to the edge of the bed. He'd sat up now, feet on the floor, watching her as she ranted, with something like shock in his eyes.

"But *you* did, Jack," she said, her voice hoarse, tears flowing even harder. "You lost so much. Because I am the most incredible woman you are ever going to find, if you live ten thousand years. I'm beautiful, and I'm smart, and I'm funny. I'm generous and kind, and successful, and let's not forget wealthy, and when I love, I love with everything in me. You'll never find someone to love you the way I did, because it was beyond physical or even emotional. It was soul-deep, what I felt for you. And you're never going to have sex like you had with me, either. It'll never be that good again. Sex like that doesn't just happen with anyone. That's what you threw away, Jack. And I've been waiting a long time to tell you so."

He nodded slowly, taking a breath, waiting as if to be sure she was done. Then he said, "I deserve every bit of that. And I can't even argue with you."

"I am the best thing that ever happened

to you, Jack Heart."

He lowered his eyes. "Don't think I don't know it."

"All I wanted was your love." A sob choked her. She spoke around it, her voice tight and hoarse, as her heart asked the question she'd never been able to answer. "Why couldn't you just love me?"

He was quiet for so long that she didn't think he was going to answer. She turned and started to walk away from him, but then he said, "I never thought love was real. But I guess it must be, if you felt it that strongly. I guess it's just not real for me. I don't think I'm capable of it."

She nodded her head. "Everyone's capable of it. You're just too damn selfish to offer it. Loving someone is a risk, and as I've learned the hard way, you're not going to risk yourself for anything or anyone. It's not that you can't, it's that you won't. You weren't even willing to try. Not even for the only person in your entire life who would have gladly died for you." She shook her head slowly. "It's your loss, Jack. I don't think you'll ever know just how much you threw away. Way more than what you took me for, though. Immeasurably more."

She left him then, heading into the bathroom to shower away her tears.

■ ■ ■ ■

She'd been right about one thing, he thought. He'd had no idea how she'd felt. A whole month before she could even stop crying? And he didn't doubt her. She wouldn't lie, not about that. What she'd said to him had been fed by raw emotion, contained too long. It had erupted without forethought, like a volcano when the pressure gets too intense. He *couldn't* doubt her, because she had been utterly open — as open as the gates of hell — as she'd let those pent-up feelings come rushing out at him. He'd *felt* the pain he'd caused her, and it didn't feel good.

His remorse was multiplied. And he knew she was right. He *had* thrown away the best woman he would ever find. The problem was, he didn't *want* a woman. All right, he wanted one — this one — but not as a partner, not in some kind of *relationship,* not in love. Hell, maybe he *was* selfish. Or maybe he just didn't know how to fall in love, but . . .

It didn't matter. What mattered was that he had hurt her far more deeply than he had ever realized, and she wasn't going to let him get close enough to do it again. She would never trust him again, no matter what he did to try to show her that she could. And he still didn't know why the hell it mattered to him.

He only knew that it did.

While she showered, he drove to the crypt and gathered up his things. Then he headed back to the house, feeling oddly empty and almost lethargic.

She was waiting in the living room, hair damp, wearing a bright sundress, her eyes still red.

"Topaz, I —"

"I'm sorry," she said.

"*You're* sorry?"

She nodded. "I guess all that stuff needed to come out. And you probably deserved it, but not now. I mean, it's over now. It's in the past. If I was going to dump on you, it should have been then. I know you regret hurting me, and that you've been trying to make up for it by helping me now. I also know there's nothing you can do that will ever make it right for me. So all that venting was pretty useless."

He licked his lips, shook his head. "I had it coming. I didn't know most of what you told me, and I probably needed to know it. And if it got some of the hurt out of your system, then it did some good."

Nothing will ever get the hurt out of my system.

The thought was like a slip of the tongue, Jack realized, because she slammed her mind closed on it almost instantly.

"You were right about one thing," she told him. "I don't hate you. I never will."

He nodded, relieved to hear that. "Topaz, I regret hurting you like I've never regretted anything in my life. And I will spend eternity regretting it. I hope you believe that."

"I think I do."

"Friends, then?" he asked.

She held his eyes but didn't answer. And then there was a knock on the door that prevented her from saying she would never be his friend, which was what he was pretty sure he'd seen in her eyes.

Jack went to answer the knock when Topaz made no move to do so. He sensed no malice coming from the person on the other side, so he opened the door. A man in a familiar uniform stood there, a twenty-four-hour delivery service truck in the driveway at his back. "Yes?"

"I have a delivery for Ms. Tanya Du-Frane."

"She's here. I'll see that she gets it."

Nodding, the man handed Jack an electronic box with a stylus attached. "Just sign on the screen, there by the X."

Jack scrawled something illegible and handed it back. The delivery man handed him an eleven-by-thirteen cardboard envelope. "Have a nice night."

"You, too." He watched the guy leave, keeping track until the truck was down the road and out of sight. Then he closed the door and looked at the envelope. "It's from Rebecca Murphy."

"My mother's lawyer," she muttered, and she met him halfway, taking the envelope from him with a sigh. "I don't suppose it matters at this point, but . . ." With a tired shrug, she tore it open and fished the documents from inside. There was a single sheet of paper on the attorney's letterhead, along with a small, business-sized envelope, plain, white and sealed, with nothing written on its face.

Frowning, Topaz walked to the sofa and sat down.

"Dear Tanya," she read aloud. "Your mother asked me to deliver this letter to you when you turned thirty years old, but by then you had dropped out of sight. I kept it, always hoping. And I offer it to you now, to give you the closure you obviously need. Having read this myself, right after your mother's death, it's my opinion that she wasn't murdered at all, but that she arranged her own death. Suicide by hit man. I swore to myself that I would never reveal that theory to anyone other than you, unless they arrested someone for the crime — someone innocent. If they got the actual killer — the one I believe she hired herself — I would gladly have watched him fry.

"I couldn't bring myself to tell you any of this when we met the other evening, not without the letter from your mother, so you could read it for yourself and draw your own conclusions. I had to retrieve it from the safe-deposit box where I've kept it all these years before I could proceed.

"If there's anything else I can do for you, please don't hesitate to call. I loved your mother more than any client I've ever had. We were more than business associates. I thought of her as I would have, I think, had she been my own daughter. And that affection extends to you.

"With sincere concern and sympathy,
"Rebecca."

Topaz lifted her head, met Jack's eyes. Hers were damp. Damn, he hated seeing her cry, and twice in one day was almost too much. More than that, he knew exactly what she was going through right now. He knew the feelings, the turmoil, the shock.

With trembling hands, she lifted the small envelope and held it out to him. "I can't."

He took it, caressing her hands with his as he did. They were cold and shaking. "You want me to read it?"

She nodded, the motion jerky, and Jack sat on the sofa beside her and opened the envelope. The single sheet of stationery still held a faint trace of scent — lavender. A mortal probably wouldn't have detected it after so much time, but to a vampire, it was still fragrant.

"My precious daughter," he read aloud.

"I've loved only once in my life, and that love was the love I felt for you. I hope you will never doubt it. I am more sorry for leaving you the way I'm about to do than I've ever been about anything before, but I have no other choice. I'll regret it more than you will ever know. I'll watch over you, always, and my love for you will never die.

"With all my heart, I wish you happiness.

"Your mother, Mirabella DuFrane."

When Jack stopped reading, Topaz snapped her head up. "That's it? That's all?"

"That's all," he said. "I'm sorry. I know how you must be —"

"That can't be all. There has to be more." She snatched the letter from Jack's hands and looked at it.

And then everything in her seemed to freeze. She stared at the letter, her eyes registering shock and disbelief.

"What?" Jack asked. "Topaz, what is it? What's wrong?"

Blinking, she laid the letter flat on the coffee table and got to her feet. Her gait was leaden as she moved across the living room, like an accident victim wandering in shock from her wrecked, flaming vehicle. She took her handbag from where she'd left it, on the stand just inside the front door, snapped it open as she made her way back, and then poured its contents onto the coffee table, burying the letter.

"Topaz, will you tell me what's wrong?"

"I'll show you," she whispered, her voice tight as she fumbled through the pile, tugging out the silver cigarette case. She opened it, took out the other letter, the one left for her by the vampiress who'd made her. The one she'd kept all this time in her mother's monogrammed cigarette case. Holding that letter in one hand, she pushed all the other items aside, to uncover the letter from her mother. And then she placed the vampiress's letter beside Mirabella's and stared at them, blinking back tears.

Jack was still watching her face, feeling sick with worry for her. She was taking this far harder than he would have expected her to.

"Don't you see it, Jack?" she asked, gaze still riveted to the letters. "Don't you *see it?*"

With an effort, he dragged his gaze from her face, and focused instead on the letters resting on the table. And then it was his turn to go still, his eyes widening. "The handwriting —"

"Is identical," Topaz whispered.

She lifted her head and turned to him, and he met those moist eyes and held them. "My mother isn't dead at all. She's undead. Like us."

Topaz was in shock. So deeply in shock that a half hour passed before she could bestir herself enough to do more than sit on that sofa, staring blankly into space as tears streamed down her face and a thousand thoughts battled for prominence in her mind. Mostly she just ignored them and lost herself in her pain.

For a while.

Then she felt other things. The warmth from the fireplace, which hadn't been burning the last time she'd looked. The surge of power from the blood Jack must have managed to coax down her. She didn't remember swallowing, didn't remember the taste, but she felt it inside her, coursing through her veins, clearing her mind, and she realized that she had indeed fed.

Even as she blinked past the fog in her mind, Jack was draping a fire-warmed blanket around her. Without noticing, she'd shifted on the sofa. She was reclining now, with her back against the arm. He slid onto the other end, pulled her feet into his lap and began massaging them.

Her voice like ice, she said, "You don't have to do that."

"I want to. Trust me, it'll help." His thumbs pressed the balls of her feet, fingers kneading the tops.

"She didn't have to leave me, Jack," Topaz whispered. "She didn't really die. The whole thing must have been staged to give her an out. That's why the body was taken. No one stole it. She just got up and walked away." Fresh tears welled. "She walked away."

"I know."

"Why didn't she take me with her?"

He started rubbing each toe in turn, tugging them gently. She felt some of her tension starting to melt away under his hands.

"Come on, Topaz, how is a vampire going to raise a child?"

"It's been done before," she reminded him.

"She had no way of knowing that." He moved up to her ankles, and his touch was magic. Muscles in her shoulders eased; her spine softened. She relaxed a little more deeply against the cushioned arm. "Besides," Jack said, "you were famous, too, as famous as she was simply because you were her child. How was she going to cover you both disappearing? She couldn't fake your death, as well, could she?"

"Of course she could have. She could have taken me with her," she said. "We could have just run away. Vanished. We could have hidden."

"Your mother's face would have been instantly recognized, no matter where she went. She was loved by the entire world, Topaz. It probably seemed impossible to her. On her own, maybe she could have flown under the radar, vanished into the protective world of the undead, but with a baby . . . ? It would have been impossible."

He was massaging her calves now. Topaz's neck muscles went warm and soft, and she let her head fall back on the sofa cushions and rest there.

"She said she had no choice."

"She was definitely shot that night," Jack said. "False reports might show up anywhere else, but not with the CIA. Their investigations showed gunshot wounds, blood everywhere. They found the casings, for heaven's sake. Those had to be real."

"Part of the cover. She had someone shoot her. Had someone else waiting there to transform her before she actually died."

Jack shook his head, kneading his way back down her legs to her ankles and feet again. "Too risky. Someone would have seen. She couldn't have counted on staying alive until she got to the hospital, where whatever vampire helped her could get to her to make the exchange. There's no way she could have been sure she would live that long, not with three gunshot wounds to the abdomen."

Topaz sighed, relaxing now into his ministrations, welcoming them. "It doesn't make any sense. If she planned this herself — and it's clear from her letter that she did — then she must have figured out how to stay alive long enough to be transformed. It makes no sense."

"Maybe we'll never know how she did it." He sighed. "Selfishly, I'm glad it wasn't my mother who killed yours. That takes a load of guilt from my shoulders."

"It was never your guilt to bear."

"Knowing that is easy enough. But I felt it anyway."

She closed her eyes. "That really is helping."

"Reflexology. Every point in the foot corresponds to a point in the body. You work them, the body responds."

"A hidden talent I never knew about."

"I have all kinds of talents you don't know about, lady."

She opened her eyes, met his. They were soft with sympathy and what looked like genuine caring. "I need you tonight, Jack."

His hands stilled on her feet. Then he rose and leaned over her, sliding his arms around her, beneath her shoulders, and gathered her to him, drawing her closer until she was sitting across his lap. She draped her arms around his shoulders and kissed him. She didn't hesitate at all. And he held her even closer, tightening his arms around her waist, bending over her, kissing her back and feeling as if his very soul was pouring itself into hers.

He wanted to take her hurt away. And he only knew one way to do that, so he gave it his all. He rose from the sofa, carrying her with him, and continued kissing her all the way up the stairs and into the bedroom. Soft kisses. Long, deep, lingering kisses that kept the fierceness of his desire controlled, doling it out in lingering bits. He lowered her to the bed, and there, in the darkness of the room, he undressed her, one piece of clothing at a time. The sundress. The bra. The lacy panties that matched it. And then he moved over her body, kissing a path from her breasts to her navel, then lower. As he pushed her thighs apart, he kissed her most intimate places, then used his tongue to give her the relief she so desperately needed tonight. And also to try to convey his feelings. He cared. He really did.

He held her, fondled her, licked and tasted her, until she was screaming with ecstasy and pushing his head away. And then he climbed up her body and sank himself inside her.

It was heaven to feel her surrounding him. So warm. So wet. So welcoming. And it felt right, this union. When they connected this way, he didn't see anything lacking in his life. It was perfection as he moved inside her, as she arched her hips to meet him every single time, whether he quickened the pace or slowed it, deepened his thrusts or held back. She always knew, always anticipated. It was as if they were one mind, one soul, when they made love.

Made love. It felt like that, he thought. He'd never thought of it that way before, he realized.

And then he was through thinking anything at all, because she was moaning his name, and her head was twisting back and forth on the pillows, and he knew it was time to push her to the brink again. So he slid his hands beneath her bottom and held her to him, as he thrust into her harder and deeper and faster than before.

She clutched his shoulders, her nails digging into his flesh. Her eyes flew open and met his, and he saw tears pooling in them as she came this time. Just as he reached the precipice himself, those tears of hers began rolling down her cheeks.

Spent, Jack relaxed onto his side and pulled her into his arms, cradling her, rocking her there. "Baby, please don't cry. Everything's going to be all right."

She sighed. "They're tears of relief, Jack. Thank you for that."

"In that case," he told her, "there's a hell of a lot more where that came from. Come here." And he pulled her on top of him.

At a quarter to dawn, Topaz lay sated, glowing with satisfaction in Jack's arms. Her heart and mind were still reeling, but he'd given her an outlet for all the emotion that had been overflowing in her. He'd taken it all from her, as if drinking away toxic blood. He'd taken it onto himself, bearing the brunt of her emotions, which she'd left lying open to him. As open as her body was to his.

All of that, he'd taken somehow. And it had to hurt, because he was feeling exactly what she felt. She knew that. She knew how it worked among their kind. And yet he didn't block it out. He made love to her, straight through her storm, pushing and pushing, until the physical pleasure became bigger than the emotional pain and finally drowned it out.

All in his arms.

If he never did another thing for her, Topaz thought, he'd done enough that night — more than enough — to make up for all his past wrongs. He'd ridden out the storm with her, helped her to get through it without losing her mind. Not an easy battle. In a vampire, emotional pain was as magnified as the physical variety. It could have driven her mad. Perhaps sent her into catatonia, or even killed her. She would never be sure.

Thank God, she thought.

Then . . . no, thank Jack.

"Thank you," she whispered. "Thank you, Jack."

"Don't thank me for spending the night in ecstasy. Trust me, it was no sacrifice."

"You took the pain, and we both know it."

"Penance."

She shook her head, thinking it had to be more than that.

"What are you going to do next, Topaz?"

She drew a breath, snuggled closer in his arms, and didn't give a damn that she was letting herself fall in love with him all over again. Then again, who was she kidding? She'd never really stopped.

"I'm going to find her," she whispered. "I have to."

His arms, muscles like whipcords, tightened around her in a way that felt so incredibly safe and reassuring that she could almost believe it was real. "Do you even know where to begin searching?"

She nodded against his chest. "The last place I know for sure she was. Mexico."

He nodded. "Makes sense." And *he* was tense then. It was in his jaw and in his voice. She felt it.

"I don't want to go there alone, Jack," she whispered, and it was like laying her heart on a guillotine and waiting for him to drop the blade. That was how vulnerable it felt to put herself out there for him again after his rejection, his betrayal.

"You're not going there alone, Topaz," he told her. "Not as long as I'm undead, you're not."

9

"Topaz needs you."

Reaper recognized the voice on the other end of the cell phone. It was the voice of a man he didn't trust. Topaz was in love with the jerk, though. Reaper knew the signs. Jack Heart was the biggest mistake Topaz had ever made in her life. He was no good for her, and what was worse, she knew it. And yet she loved him. Who could figure women out?

"Reaper? Are you there?" Jack asked.

"Yes. I'm here. What's going on? Is Topaz all right?" He had no doubt in his mind that Jack was somehow to blame for the CIA knowing his location. They'd been just two steps behind him, no matter where he'd gone in the past week.

"She's a mess," Jack said.

"I have no doubt, if you've been out there with her all this time. If she's a mess, Jack, just who do you think is responsible for that?"

Reaper felt the hesitation on the other end of the line but could read nothing more. Jack's mind was closed to him.

"Not that it's any of your business, Reaper, but I know I messed her up. A lot. More than I ever realized, but that's in the past. I've been trying to make up for it. But that's not what's bothering her right now. Or maybe it's part of it, I don't know."

"Yes, you do. It's a part of everything for her."

Jack's sigh was soft but audible. "Yeah. I guess I do."

Reaper nodded at the phone. At least the bastard could admit it.

"Despite that, there's more now," Jack told him. "Her mother — her mother was the actress, Mirabella DuFrane. Have you heard of her?"

"Not really."

"Why am I not surprised?"

"Just get to the point, Jack." Reaper wasn't entirely comfortable engaging in long telephone conversations, particularly with this guy. For all he knew, one of Jack's sleazy contacts could be tracing the signal.

"Her mother was murdered when Topaz was an infant," Jack said. "Her body was stolen from the morgue, never to be found.

It was a big Hollywood mystery, the stuff of legend. Only it turns out Mirabella Du-Frane never really died at all. We're pretty sure she was the vampiress who transformed Topaz ten years ago in Mexico. We're heading there now to try to track her down."

Reaper blinked. "Are you saying Topaz's mother faked her own death and walked out on her when she was an infant? Deliberately?"

"It looks that way."

No wonder Topaz was a mess, Reaper thought. He had a million questions racing through his mind, and he tried to sort them logically, ask them in order of importance. "Is she in any danger?" he asked.

"Depends on how badly her mother wants to avoid being found," Jack said. "My instinct is that she's only in danger of having her heart broken again. And I don't think she could handle it this time. She's got this notion that she's . . . unlovable. That no one's ever cared for her, only for her money."

"Gee, I wonder where she could have gotten that idea?" Reaper said, his tone as cruel as he could make it.

Jack paused before going on. "I probably deserved that, Reaper, but I'm not going to take a lot more from you, deserved or not.

So could you put a sock in it and focus on Topaz for a minute here?"

"She's all I'm focusing on."

"Me, too," Jack told him. "Whether you believe it or not. She's hurting right now, and I'm afraid it's going to get worse before it gets better. *If* it gets better. She used to believe that at least her mother, out of all the people in her life, had truly loved her. Now, though, knowing the woman has been more or less alive all this time and basically abandoned her . . . even that belief has been shattered."

Reaper understood that. "There had to be extenuating circumstances . . . The woman must have felt she had no choice."

"Yeah, sure, you and I know that, but all Topaz can feel right now is hurt and rejection. I've never seen her like this, Reaper. If it goes badly, I don't know what she might — I'm freaking terrified of what she might do."

Those words hit Reaper on a level far deeper than anything he'd felt in a long time. Many a vampire had given in to despair and ended it all by simply lying down for the day sleep in an open field or walking into the sunrise. He'd seen it happen too many times. He'd seen it happen when he hadn't believed it could. He'd seen it happen to someone he'd loved.

"She needs to be with people she trusts, people who care about her, if she's going to get through this," Jack went on.

"And that's not you, right, Jack?"

"What I feel for Topaz is between the two of us. But we both know she doesn't trust me."

"Do you blame her?"

"Look, enough already. Will you gather the others and join us in Mexico or not?"

Reaper searched his gut but found no guidance. This could very well be a trap, set up by Jack. The lifelong con man might simply be trying to trick him into walking into a well-baited snare, so he could collect a hefty payoff from the CIA. Or from Gregor — Reaper's sworn enemy and Jack's former partner.

"I need to talk to her," Reaper said at length.

"If she finds out I called you, she'll be madder than ever."

Reaper sighed. "If this is some kind of a game you're playing, Jack . . ."

"It's not a game. Or a con."

Narrowing his eyes, Reaper said, "The CIA's been on my ass all week, Jack. They always seem to know where to find me."

"Interesting that they never quite find you

soon enough to do you any harm, though, isn't it?"

Reaper frowned. "What are you saying?"

"Only that I've known where you were all week. If I wanted to tip them off, help them catch you, I would have done it by now, don't you think?"

It was a valid point. Unless Jack had been playing with him like a cat with a mouse. But that wasn't Jack's M.O. He was out for the payoff — always. He wouldn't waste time in collecting it or take a chance on it slipping away. And the agents *had* been lagging behind him. Always a day late and a dollar short, so to speak.

Maybe he'd misjudged the bastard. Hard to be objective, when he'd felt Topaz's heartache firsthand. Briefly, but he'd felt it. This guy had damn near destroyed her. And Reaper hated him for that. Because in spite of himself, he cared about Topaz. He cared about them all.

In the end, that was what made the decision for him. "I'll contact the others. We'll meet you there. Give me a location."

Jack seemed more attentive, Topaz thought, than he had ever been. His worry and concern for her were a little too convincing, a little too believable. She didn't want to fall into the deadly trap of trusting him again. She knew herself too well.

And yet, she was already halfway there. The ground beneath her feet was crumbling, and she sensed herself getting perilously close to a fall.

She was nearly done for, wasn't she? Her body still craved his touch, still responded to him in a way it never had to any other man. Her heart still cried out for him, still ached for his love, still wept with the knowledge that he was incapable of giving it. And now her mind was following the other parts of her. She was actually beginning to trust him again.

She must be a complete idiot.

They'd been on the road for hours, had taken turns driving. They'd spent the previous day in an abandoned barn, and Topaz had made sure they'd stopped close enough to dawn to avoid any opportunity for sex. Sheer, desperate self-preservation had been her motivation, painful self-denial the result. She wanted him more than she wanted to see another moonrise.

It was 3:00 a.m. They were following the coastline along the midnight sapphire waves of the Gulf, and she distracted herself by staring out the window at the passing waters. They were as dark and deep and every bit as fathomless as her own feelings, and just as unsettled.

"This is it, isn't it?" Jack asked, breaking into her thoughts. Then again, she thought, he was never very far away from her thoughts, was he?

She drew her attention away from the water, focused ahead and saw the entrance to the posh resort, Corona, where she'd booked them a private cottage — *one* private cottage for them to share, because she was a fool — on the beach. "Yes, that's it. Pull up by the front. I'll run in, sign the register and get our keys."

"I'll come al—"

"No, really. Just wait here."

He frowned, puzzled. But she'd been in such close proximity to him for so long now that she honestly needed a break. To sit there in that car beside him, remembering with every mile that passed the way it felt to touch him, to be touched by him. Longing to slide closer, to cover his hand with her own, to stroke his neck and lay her head on his shoulder.

Her throat tightened with emotion, and she quickly got out of the car.

The resort was a sprawling complex, the hotel an adobe mansion that hadn't changed a lot since she'd been here last. Ocean prints hung on the walls, and a vaulted ceiling towered high with a cactus-shaped chandelier in the center. The night clerk at the front desk greeted her warmly, her smile broadening when Topaz gave her name — Tanya DuFrane. She saw no need to hide her identity any longer. It was all over the press that she was alive and well and seeking to solve her mother's murder. She would have a hell of a time disappearing again when this was all over.

"*Señorita* DuFrane!" The desk clerk clapped her hands together. "It is an honor to have you with us. It has been years, no?"

The girl couldn't possibly remember her. She would have been a child the last time Topaz was here. But Topaz assumed someone had recognized her name when she'd phoned to book the reservation and had done a bit of homework.

"I am a huge fan of your mother's work," the clerk went on. "So tragic that the world lost her so soon. And for you, more so, yes?"

"Thank you. Is my bungalow ready?"

"*Si,* ready and waiting. It is *Numero Tres.* Follow the road that curves to the right. You'll see a row of cottages along the beach. It's the off-season, so very few are occupied. Just one other, in fact. You should have all the privacy you could desire."

"Thank you. I'll need two keys."

"Of course." The girl handed them to her. Not modern plastic key cards, but actual keys hanging from tags with numbers on them. "You'll find the number to call when you want to arrange housekeeping service, a schedule of events, a listing of restaurants and another of all our vendors waiting in your cottage. We have boat rentals, Jet Skis, surfing, snorkeling —"

"Yes, thank you. I'm just too tired right now to even think about all that."

The girl smiled and nodded. "Of course. *Buenas noches,* then, *señorita.*"

"Good night."

Taking the keys, Topaz went back to Jack's car and got in. He didn't take off right away, just looked at her. "Are you okay, Topaz?"

She glanced at him and nodded. Even knowing it was a lie. She'd never been less okay. She hadn't been okay since he'd walked out on her. And sometimes she wondered if she ever would be again.

Aloud though, she only said, "That way. Cabin Three."

He looked at her for a long moment, then finally nodded and put the car into motion again. It was only as they pulled up in front of the cabin that Topaz felt the presence of the others. Other vampires lingering nearby in the night. Several of them. She tensed and quickly opened her mind. She'd been trying so hard to block out her feelings for Jack that she'd failed to scan the area.

"It's okay," Jack said, reaching over to pat her hand as if she were a frightened child. "It's just the gang."

Frowning, Topaz opened her door, and even as she got out of the car, they came walking from the cabin right beside hers. Reaper, Roxy, Vixen and Seth. She couldn't move for a moment, she was so surprised to see them there. And then, as they closed in around her, and as Roxy wrapped her in a warm embrace, Topaz burst into tears, in spite of her best efforts to hold them back.

Jack felt a little bit unwanted, like an outsider, an interloper. The others were like a family as they embraced her and all talked at once. He was unreasonably relieved when he heard someone say that Ilyana and Briar were inside. They were outsiders, too. And in fact, of them all, he thought he would be happiest to see Briar again. So he headed into the cabin marked with the green 2 in search of her, and left the little group to catch up in their sappy way without him.

The cabins were made of adobe, forty by forty or so, with two stories each. They all looked pretty much the same; full front porch, big windows on either side of a red door, clay pottery overflowing with exotic-looking plants, and rattan lawn furniture on each porch.

Jack opened the red door and stepped into the large living-dining area, and looked around. He didn't see anyone, but he could feel them. Ilyana, the newcomer to the group, was mortal. One of the Chosen. Her energy was impatient, frustrated, a little bit afraid. She was nervous around vampires. She had every reason to be, having served as Gregor's bedtime snack for God only knew how long. She was presently in one of the rooms off to the right of this one. A kitchen, he thought.

Briar's energy, on the other hand, didn't even feel like her. It was dull, and had a sickly element to it. It was contained, reserved, quiet, withdrawn. None of it was Briar. At least, not the Briar he remembered.

He followed his sense of her energy all the same, up the stairs to the second floor and along a hall with four doors, stopping at the third. The door wasn't locked, and he didn't bother to knock. He had let her feel his approach, so she knew he was coming.

He opened the door and let his gaze sweep over the small bedroom. She sat on the bed, knees drawn to her chest, eyes on him. "What do *you* want?"

Jack lifted his brows and went inside, leaving the door open. "Nice to see you, too, Briar. I've been fine, thanks. How about you?"

She didn't react, aside from the slight flaring of her nostrils as she exhaled.

"I can see you haven't been fine at all," he said.

"What is there to be fine about?"

He shrugged, crossing the room. "I don't know. We're alive. Eternally strong and young and powerful."

She turned her head slightly toward the window, and he followed her gaze to the small group gathered on the lawn. "What good is it? This world isn't worth living in. There's nothing good about it."

"Never knew you were so into goodness."

She shot him a look. "What good is strength if you aren't allowed to prey on the weak? What good is eternal life, when it's only filled with people who'd just as happily kill you as look at you?"

He sighed. "You trusted the wrong guy, Briar." And it occurred to him that he could say the same words to Topaz, and they would be just as true. "He turned on you. But it was Gregor, for God's sake. What did you expect? He's evil."

"So am I. So are you."

"I'm not evil. Selfish, maybe, but not evil. And I don't think you are, either."

"No? What am I, then?"

He shrugged, opened his senses to hers, then lowered his head. "You're in pain. And it's intense. Excruciating. You need to let it go, Briar, or you're not going to last. No one can hold up under that kind of anguish."

"And how do you suggest I let go?"

"I don't know. Stop focusing on it. Find something else, something you can get a little pleasure out of, a little joy. Focus on that, and the pain will start to die. It can't live if you aren't feeding it. It'll starve without your attention."

"So you've turned from a heartless con man into some kind of philosopher now?"

"Not really. It's just the best suggestion I can come up with on short notice."

"Yeah, well, it's a lousy one."

"Why?"

"Because if there were anything in this world capable of giving me joy or pleasure, I would have at least caught a glimpse of it by now."

He sent a meaningful look toward the window. "I think maybe you have. You're just too busy wallowing in misery to let yourself see it."

"I should get off this bed and hit you."

"But you can't even work up the enthusiasm to do that, can you, Briar? And that should tell you something."

"What, pray tell? What gem of wisdom is my lack of enthusiasm supposed to impart?"

He met her eyes, saw the pain in them, felt it. "Only that what you've been doing up to now isn't working for you. So you might as well try something else. What have you got to lose?"

"Self-respect. Dignity. Pride. My mind . . . Should I go on?"

He shook his head. "Why are you still with Reaper? I'd have expected you to run away again by now. Particularly if you're so miserable."

She lowered her head, focused on her hands where they were clasped around her knees. "Sooner or later, he's going to get back on Gregor's trail," she said. "Reaper's good. I don't have any doubt that he'll find him. And when he does, I intend to be there."

Jack sensed the feelings she still had for that sadist and rolled his eyes. "I'm the last person who should be saying this, but how stupid would you have to be to go back to

211

that idiot after what he did to you?"

"You're right. You're the last person to be saying it. Your precious Topaz did the same thing, didn't she?"

"Not by a long shot. And all I did was take her money. Gregor tortured you, Briar."

"If you don't think what you did to Topaz was torture, you'd better think again," she said. "Women like her fall hard when they fall for a man. Thank God I never have and never will."

"Not even for Gregor?"

She snapped him with a look, like snapping someone with a rubber band. "It's not what you think. It was never . . . that way between Gregor and me."

"Not because he didn't want it to be."

She was quiet.

"And yet you want to get back with him," he said with a slow shake of his head as he lowered it.

"No. I want to get back *at* him. You're right, he tortured me. I owe him."

Jack snapped his head up, met her eyes, saw a dull glow of anger, of hatred, simmering in their almost black depths. He felt his lips lift at the corners. "Now that's the Briar I know and . . . know."

She held his gaze for a moment, then sighed and lowered her eyes.

"What about the others? Reaper and his pups?"

"What *about* them?" she asked.

"How do you feel about them?" he asked.

"I don't like them. I don't like *him*. I don't want to be friends, not with any of them. Not with you, either, for that matter. I never trusted anyone in my life, until Gregor. He taught me what a mistake that was. It's not one I'll ever make again."

He nodded slowly. "Not everyone is like him, you know."

"Yes," she said. "They are. And the ones who pretend otherwise are hypocrites."

Sighing, Jack got up from the bed.

"Why did you come in here, anyway?"

He shrugged. "Of all of them, we're the most alike. I just wanted to see how you were doing, that's all."

She frowned, as if puzzled. "What's happened to you, Jack? Have you gone soft?"

He shook his head, even as the question echoed in his mind and he found himself wondering about the answer. "Never happen."

"Are you working a con, then?"

"I was, but —" He broke off. "Doesn't matter. I'm not at the moment."

"Then what are you doing here? With them?"

He walked to the window and stared down at them, where they were still deep in conversation below. "I guess I'm trying to make up for some of the harm I've done in the past. Not sure it can be done. But I'm trying."

"You *have* gone soft. In the head, as well as everywhere else."

"Maybe I have."

As the group broke apart, Topaz saw Jack leave Cabin Two and head toward Three, with the key she'd given him in hand. Her eyes followed him, in spite of herself.

"We can split things up differently, you know," Seth said. "If you're not comfortable having him in your cabin."

She met his eyes. "No, it's fine."

Seth probed, and she guarded. That should have told him to mind his own business, but he never had been the sharpest tool in the box, she thought with an exasperated sigh when he spoke his question aloud.

"You're not falling for that jerk again, are you?"

"Of course not."

"Good, 'cuz I don't trust him as far as I can throw him, Tope. I never have, and I trust my gut on this."

Vixen put a hand on Seth's shoulder.

"He's not all bad," she said.

"Maybe not. But he's not all good, either," Seth said. "Better to err on the side of caution where he's concerned."

"Hey, you don't have to convince me," Topaz told him. "I know better than anybody."

Seth nodded. Then he reached out and hugged her, and she was so surprised that she stiffened at first, then sighed and hugged him back. "He gives you any crap, you let me know, okay? I'll knock him into next week."

"My hero," she told him, loading a heavy amount of sarcasm into the phrase.

He grinned, and then he and Vixen turned and headed for the beach, arm in arm. Roxy came over and gave her a hug, too. "If you want advice about men and relationships, sweetie, you come to me. Don't waste your time listening to that young pup, Seth. He only wound up with Vixen by the skin of his teeth, through dumb luck and my help."

Topaz nodded, and then Roxy left her and headed for her cabin. Leaving Topaz alone with Reaper.

He studied her face for a long moment, his expression pensive.

She was almost afraid to ask the question, but she forced herself. "Did the CIA show up in Philly?"

"Not yet."

Relief nearly melted her muscles. She closed her eyes and felt it washing through her like a balm.

"That doesn't mean they won't, nor does it mean he's innocent of feeding them information prior to this."

She gnawed her lip. "Why are you so sure it was him?"

"I'm not," Reaper admitted. "I don't have a shred of evidence, let's be clear on that. I just think . . . I think you should be very, very careful where he's concerned."

She lowered her head. "Thank you. I will be."

He nodded. No hugs, not from him. He wasn't comfortable with casual physical contact. She'd learned that about him early on in their time together. "Let me know if you need anything, all right?"

"Yeah." She looked at the sky. "Thanks for coming, Reaper. It means a lot to me."

"That was Jack's doing," he said. "He called, told me you needed people you could trust around you for this." Sighing heavily, he shook his head. "I hope to God I'm wrong about him, Topaz."

He turned and walked back into the cabin as she whispered, "So do I."

10

An hour before dawn, Jack's cell phone rang.

"Where are you?"

The voice belonged to Frank Magnarelli, the last person he'd wanted to hear from tonight. He glanced around, sensed the area. Topaz was outside with the others. "I've left the state. Game over."

"The game is over when we say it's over, Jack. And since we don't have Rivera yet, it's not over."

"You've got nothing left that I need."

"No?"

"No, and you didn't give me the information you had to begin with."

"We gave you —"

"Let's talk about what you *didn't* give me, shall we? You didn't tell me about my mother. You didn't tell me what you knew about Topaz's mother, either."

There was silence for a long moment.

Then, "So you know."

"I know. So does she."

"I'll contact you tomorrow night."

"Don't bother. This cell phone number will be out of commission by then."

"I wouldn't do that if I were you, Jack. We know where you are."

He blinked, stunned.

"Sorry, pal. It just doesn't take as long to triangulate a signal as it used to. Tomorrow night, Jack. I guarantee you, we'll have something you want *very badly* by then."

The line went dead, and Jack sat there, feeling, for the first time, afraid of what those bastards at the CIA might be up to. He'd used them, played them, fed them tidbits that would do them no real good, so he could get information on Topaz's mother. But they knew, they'd known all along, that Mirabella DuFrane wasn't really dead. Magnarelli hadn't exactly confirmed it on the phone, but Jack sensed it to his bones. Which meant they'd been playing *him*, using *him*, feeding *him* tidbits that would do him no real good.

They wanted Reaper. And they would do anything to get him. Reaper had been right about that.

And now Jack was between a rock and a hard place. He couldn't warn the others without admitting the game he'd been playing. Doing that would lose him any hope of regaining Topaz's trust for good. No, he had to play this out, see it through to the end.

No one would get hurt. He would make sure of that. He just had to out-con the biggest con artists in the business: the federal government.

By the time they'd unloaded their things and chosen bedrooms — separate bedrooms, at Topaz's insistence — the day sleep was already tugging her under. And she was glad of it. She didn't know how she felt about Jack anymore. Reaper's suspicions made sense, and yet she couldn't quite convince herself that Jack was the one feeding information to the CIA. She couldn't. And it was stupid of her, because she, of all people, knew how duplicitous he could be.

That alone told her that her heart was in dangerous waters. Again.

Maybe it always would be, where Jack was concerned. She ached for him, cried over him, missed him even when he was only in the next room, and yet she expected him to hurt her again if she gave him even half a chance. And, she realized, she was giving him way more than that. Everything she had once felt for him had come rushing back during this time with him, and it was stronger than ever.

She felt doomed.

When the sun set again and she came awake, Jack was already out of bed and taking up space in the bungalow's only bathroom, which irritated her. Feeling irritated with him was a relief, though. Far better than wanting him and aching for him and expecting him to break her heart all over again at any moment.

She pounded on the door when she heard the shower running. "Hey! Since when do you get first dibs on the shower? You know I need my time in the bathroom first thing in the evening."

He didn't answer, though she knew perfectly well he could hear her. The door was unlocked, so she went in. He was safely on the other side of the shower curtain, after all. "Jack, come on. I know you heard me. How much longer are you going to be, anyway?"

He opened the curtain and stood there in the spray, naked and gorgeous, water running in rivulets, clinging in droplets, making his skin gleam and her blood heat. She couldn't look away, no matter how hard she tried. God, she'd never seen a man more beautiful or a body more perfect. And she'd never wanted anyone the way she wanted him.

"You're welcome to join me."

Forcibly, and with no small effort, she lifted her gaze to his, though she hadn't had nearly enough of a lingering look at the rest of him. She shook her head.

He shrugged and yanked the curtain closed again. "Your loss. I have to go out for a little while, and I thought I'd get it over with early."

"Go out where?" Her suspicions were already aroused.

"Just going to do a little reconnaissance."

"Uh-huh. And you're taking one of the gang with you?"

"Wasn't planning on it."

"Why not?"

The water stopped abruptly, and he yanked the curtain aside again. She couldn't keep her eyes away, so she handed him a towel and didn't bother to try.

"Because they're not my gang," he said. "But I'm more than willing to take you along. You want to go with me?"

She thought about it. If he were offering to take her along, then he must not have anything to hide. Unless, of course, he was counting on her saying no. Jack was too smart not to have thought of that angle.

God, what kind of a relationship could she ever hope to have with a man she trusted so little?

That wasn't the problem, though, and she knew it. If he loved her, she could and would trust him to the moon and back. But he didn't. Never had. Wouldn't even say it. That was one lie even Jack couldn't bring himself to tell.

"I think I'll sit this one out," she said at last. And she had her reasons, even though she felt as guilty as hell for them.

"Okay. I'll fill you in if I learn anything. Shouldn't be more than an hour." He finished rubbing himself down, anchored the towel around his lean hips and headed for the door. "Shower's all yours."

"Thanks."

"Are you sure you don't want me to stay? Maybe, scrub your back or, uh . . . something."

"I think I'll manage without you, thanks."

He sent her a wink and left the room.

Topaz undressed and got into the shower as soon as he closed the door behind him, rushing through her morning rituals, because there was something she needed to do before he returned.

As soon as she was dressed, she checked the bungalow to make sure he was gone.

He wasn't around, and the others seemed to be leaving her to herself for the moment. So she went into Jack's room and began a methodical search through his belongings.

And what she found there was like a red-hot blade sliding cleanly into her heart.

The money — *her* money — was in the bottom of his duffel bag, wrapped in plastic. It was sorted into neatly banded bundles of crisp, cold cash. Her cash. She had no doubt of that. She even counted it, and it was exactly 250,000 dollars. The exact amount he'd taken from her, minus the half he'd returned. This was the other half, the half he'd claimed he didn't have and promised to get for her.

He'd been lying to her. Again. She wasn't even surprised.

But her heart broke all over again, just the same. She hadn't expected anything different from Jack. She would have been a fool if she had. But, God, how she'd let herself hope.

"Since when does it take three of you to talk to me?" Jack asked. Magnarelli was familiar to him, of course, but the other two were strangers. "Doesn't matter. I have nothing for you."

The three men, wearing nearly identical

gray suits and sunglasses, stood around him in what he imagined was supposed to be a menacing manner. And it might have been, had he been human. But he wasn't. He was stronger, faster and smarter. And he would sense an attack coming before they could go from making the decision to moving on it.

Even if he couldn't read their thoughts — the agency had apparently trained these special agents to block them — he would still sense danger. At least, he was fairly certain he would.

"Of course you do," Magnarelli said. "You're going to tell us where Rivera is."

"If I knew, I might. Providing you could come up with something for me in return. But since you can't, and since I have no clue where the Grim One is keeping himself these days, I'm afraid we're at an impasse."

"You *are* going to help us, Jack."

Jack met Magnarelli's steel-gray eyes, which he could see clearly behind the dark glasses. "Look, I've been keeping you informed as to his whereabouts for more than a week now. It's not my fault you let him slip away yet again."

"We think maybe it is. We think you've been doling out your information to us too late to do us any good. And we think it's been deliberate."

"Look, I can't help you anymore. He suspects me already. He tried to trick me into sending you to Philly just to confirm it. Fortunately, I saw through the ruse. Hell, if the whole CIA can't keep track of one vampire hit man, how the hell do you expect *me* to?"

"You know where he is," Magnarelli said, while his two colleagues stood silently, feet shoulder-width apart, hands clasped in front of their dicks. "And you're going to tell us. When you do, we'll tell you where to find Mirabella DuFrane for your girlfriend."

Jack tilted his head to one side. "Hell, even if I knew where he was, that wouldn't be enough. You guys have been holding out on me. To even *tempt* me to give you that kind of information, I'd need a hell of a lot more."

"Such as?"

Jack pretended to mull on it a bit. "I'd still need Mirabella's location, of course. And I'd also need the recipe you all used to create Gregor's goon squad. The drones, I believe he called them." What a mild word, he thought, for that army of killers.

"Not in a million —"

"And," Jack went on, not even waiting for the agent to finish his refusal, "the second of Rivera's trigger words. I already know the first one, the one that sends him into a mindless killing rage. For my own protection, I'd like to have the one that snaps him out of it."

"If you're going to turn him over to us, you won't need it."

"Tell you where he is, you mean. I'm not volunteering to gift wrap and deliver him for you. And to reiterate, I said I *might* tell you, *if* I knew. Which I don't."

Magnarelli shook his head slowly, then removed his sunglasses and met Jack's eyes. "For that kind of compensation, you'll have to deliver him into our hands. Drug him, bind him and deliver him. Right here. Tomorrow night."

"Right," Jack said with an exaggerated roll of his eyes. "You're asking for the impossible."

"Yes, but we're offering a bonus. Something better and more valuable to you than any of the stuff you've demanded. Something you didn't even think to ask for."

Jack frowned, and his senses went on alert. "What would that be, Magnarelli?"

"When we tell you where to find Mirabella DuFrane, she won't be dead."

Jack went stock-still and probed the agent's mind. But he found nothing there

226

but an impenetrable brick wall. "In other words, you're threatening to kill her unless I do as you ask."

"We're not asking you, Jack. We're telling you. Bring us Rivera, or the woman dies."

Jack studied the other two men. They weren't quite as adept at shielding their thoughts as Magnarelli was, but it didn't matter, because they didn't know anything.

Jack contemplated his reply for a long moment, and finally settled on what it would be. "I think you're bluffing."

"Do you?"

"Yeah, I do. If you had Mirabella Du-Frane, you'd have brought her here, shown her to me as proof. It would be a far better way to leverage me into doing what you want."

"You're very good, Jack. You're right, we don't have physical custody of the woman at the moment. But it doesn't matter if she's with us or not. We know where she is. We have her under surveillance, and we have an operation in place and ready to launch. We can grab her at any time."

"I don't think so," Jack said, pushing his slight advantage. "I think that if you knew where she was and had the ability to do so, you'd have grabbed her already."

"Is that what you think?"

Jack nodded. "That's what I think."

"Are you willing to bet her life on that, Jack?"

Jack wished he could read the man. But he couldn't. Still, he knew better than to show any sign of weakness or uncertainty. This bastard would pounce on it if he did.

"Tomorrow night, Jack," Magnarelli said. "Right here. Midnight. Bring Rivera, or your girlfriend's mother dies."

When he left the agents, Jack did so in a blinding blur of motion too fast for human eyes to detect. He couldn't risk being followed. And just to be sure he wouldn't be traced again, he tossed the cell phone into the fathomless waters of the Gulf on the way.

Hell, what was he going to do now?

He couldn't risk Mirabella's life. She was Topaz's mother, for God's sake. But if he told Topaz the truth, he would also have to admit what he'd been doing, and he doubted she would ever believe that he had never truly put Reaper at risk, much less that he'd been working for information that would help her in her quest, rather than for money.

He supposed there was really only one option. He had to find Mirabella before the agents did.

And come what may, he was going to have to talk to Reaper.

He intended to do that the minute he got back. But he felt a ripple of emotion that turned into a wave as soon as he got within range of the bungalow. Topaz. Something was wrong.

Jack surged inside, then up the stairs, following his sense of her all the way. It was coming from his room, not her own. He flung the door open, then stopped and just stared.

She was sitting on the bed, her eyes red and wet, her entire body shaking. His duffel bag was in front of her, the stacks of bills all around her. As he stared at her, searching for words, she lifted her head and met his eyes.

"I can't believe I was starting to trust you again."

"Topaz —"

"I don't understand, Jack. I don't understand. Why carry it around with you like this? Why didn't you spend it or put it into a bank or a safe or —"

"Because I was going to give it back."

She closed her eyes, and her head fell forward. Her pain was so intense, and he felt it so keenly that it made his stomach churn.

"Please don't lie to me anymore," she whispered.

"I've had it all along, Topaz." He came the rest of the way into the room, but he didn't touch her or get too close. "My original intention was to give you back half, convince you Gregor still had the other half, and keep it for myself. I admit that. I know it was a lousy plan, and I'm an asshole for ever having concocted it. But the fact is, Topaz, I couldn't go through with it."

"Why not?" She didn't look at him.

He couldn't believe she was actually listening to him. But she seemed to be. She wasn't yelling or arguing or accusing. Just listening.

"To tell you the truth, I've been going nuts trying to figure that out myself. I only knew I wanted you to trust me again. I wanted to make up for the pain I've caused you. And if I admitted I'd had the money the whole time, I was sure you would never trust me, and never give me the chance to make things right. I've been trying to figure out a way to give it back without admitting I'd had it all along. Maybe that's cowardly of me. But that's the truth, Topaz. That's why I haven't spent a nickel of it or put it away. Hell, I've never spent a cent of your money, ever since I took it from you. I think maybe, deep down, I knew all along I couldn't do that to you. I think I knew from the day I left you that I had to give it back."

Again her question was simple. "Why?"

He sat on the edge of the bed, reached out to touch her face, to tip it up so he could look into her eyes. "Because I love you."

She blinked. Tears flooded her eyes, and she closed them against the pain. The hope. "Don't say that unless you —"

"You know I wouldn't say it if I didn't mean it. I've never said it before. That was the one thing I could never bring myself to lie about, Topaz. But as it turns out, it wouldn't have been a lie. I've loved you all along. This isn't a con, and it's not a game, and it's not some kind of penance I'm trying to pay. I love you. I didn't realize it until I walked in here and saw you with that money, and thought I'd finally lost you for good."

She opened her eyes again. She was still crying.

"Do you believe me?"

"I want to," she whispered. "God, I want to."

"Then why don't you?"

"Because if I believe that and then you take it away from me again . . . I don't think

I'll survive. You're asking me to reach into a bear trap, to grab the bait and trust that it won't snap my hand off. No, it's worse. It's way worse than that. Do you know how long I've dreamed of hearing you say those words to me? Do you understand that there's nothing I've ever wanted more, not in my entire life?"

He just held her eyes. Her questions didn't require answers.

"It's too late, anyway," she said.

"Too late?" he asked.

"For me, I mean." She got up from the bed and moved closer to him. "If you're lying to me, Jack Heart, I'm done for."

And then, to Jack's utter astonishment, she flung her arms around his neck, and kissed him. Hungrily, desperately, passionately kissed him, and he could taste her tears on her lips. She shoved the duffel and the money off the bed, pushing him back and climbing on top of him, wrestling with his clothes and her own. Jack was overwhelmed with the power of her desire and of his. It was a thunderstorm of emotion and release, of yearning and denial, of pain and relief. Their lips never broke contact as their clothes tore and flew, and then they were flesh against flesh, straining and pressing to get closer, then closer still, kissing as if they were starving for the taste of each other, as if they would never stop.

She was straddling him when she took him inside her, and she tipped her head back, closed her eyes. "Say it again, Jack."

"I love you," he told her, driving into her and feeling almost too much pleasure to bear. "I love you, dammit. I love you."

Topaz lay in his arms, spent and sated and feeling as if she'd been lifted from the pits of hell to the heights of heaven, all on the wings of those three words.

And at the same time she felt the dizzying fear that she was going to fall further than ever before, and that it would surely be fatal this time. She loved him. She loved him with everything in her, but she didn't trust him. She wanted to believe he loved her, but the best she could manage was to believe he might think he did, for the moment, but that it wouldn't last. And it wasn't so much that she was willing to take the inevitable pain just for the bliss of having him back, even for a little while. It wasn't that she was willing at all. It was that she had no choice. She'd been trying to get over him for almost a year and hadn't managed to even come close.

So let it kill her this time. It would be better if it did.

"Much as I'd like to lie here, holding you until sunrise," he said, "we have things to do. We need to be looking for your mother."

She nodded, her cheek rubbing against his chest. "I know."

"Have you thought about what you'll say to her when we find her?"

"Endlessly. But I still don't know. I suppose I'll just look into her eyes and see what words come tumbling out of me." She bit her lower lip. "If she even wants to see me."

"She will."

Lifting her head, Topaz looked into his eyes. "How can you be so sure?"

"I just am. Trust me."

Those two words were like a blade twisting in her heart. She looked away quickly, then got out of the bed and began to dress. Jack got up, too, threw his clothes on, and then gathered up the bundles of money that were scattered across the floor like the bricks of a fallen building and put them into the plastic bag that had held them. He set the bag on the bed. "You should put this somewhere safe, until you can get it home."

She looked at the money. "I don't want it." And then she looked at him. "I didn't want the other half, either. I never did. All I ever wanted was your love, Jack. Money

234

doesn't mean shit to me. *You* do."

He smiled a little, came closer and ran a hand through her hair. "Well, now you've got both." Then he smacked her on the bottom. "Go on, go put it someplace for now, and we'll get moving."

"All right." She took the bag and left the room, tucked the money deep into her own bedroom closet and locked the bungalow when they stepped outside. The others were gathered on the back porch of their own cabin, which faced the ocean.

"It really is beautiful here," Topaz said softly.

"We were beginning to wonder about you two," Reaper said, rising from his chair.

"*I* wasn't." Roxy sent Topaz a knowing wink, followed by a puzzled frown. And no wonder, Topaz thought. If her expression matched what was going on inside her head, then she must look more frightened and resigned to a cruel fate than sated and well loved.

"Do you have any sort of a plan?" Reaper asked, and Topaz realized that Jack must have communicated mentally with the gang leader to enlist everyone's help in the search.

Jack nodded. "There are two places within a fifty-mile radius that vampires tend to frequent. I think we should split up into teams, check out both of them, and question every vampire we come across. Moreover, we elicit their help, if they seem trustworthy and willing. Have them ask all their contacts, too."

"Sounds like a good plan," Reaper said. "Briar, you can come with me. Seth and Vixen —"

"I'm not going," Briar said.

Reaper shot her a look — more disappointed than surprised. "Why the hell not?"

"It's not my problem. And I think all this is a waste of time. We should be looking for Gregor. That *is* what you're getting paid to do, isn't it, Reaper?"

"I'm not on anyone's time clock."

She nodded. "You might want to at least sniff the air for him while you're out hunting for Topaz's long-lost mommy. Maybe even ask around. If you find out anything, you can let me know."

"Are you really so eager to get back to the man who tortured you?" Reaper shook his head sadly, then just sighed as Briar stalked into the bungalow and let the screen door slam behind her.

"Reaper, I'd like you to ride with me tonight," Jack said.

Topaz was surprised, and judging by the look on his face, Reaper was suspicious.

"Fine by me," he said. "Topaz, you can team up with Seth and Vixen tonight."

"How about Ilyana and me?" Roxy asked. "As mortals, even though we're Chosen, we can't very well go poking around known vampire haunts asking nosy questions."

"No, that probably wouldn't go over too well," Jack said.

"I was thinking you could work online tonight," Reaper said. "Find any references to Mirabella sightings that have appeared in the tabloids in the past six months or so, cross-reference them with Mexico, and see what comes up."

"Hell, Reaper," Roxy said. "The only thing that could possibly give me more search results would be if I were looking for Elvis."

He smiled. "I know. It's a big job, but there just might a grain of truth in one of them, and it could help."

She nodded. "I brought my laptop. I'll go up to the main hotel and see what they have to offer by way of an Internet connection. God, please don't let it be dial-up."

Jack snagged a notepad from his pocket, jotted down an address and handed it to Topaz. "You guys can check out this one. Reaper and I will take the other. Call Reaper's cell if you find anything, and if not, we'll meet back here as soon as we've finished, all right?"

She nodded.

"All right. I'll see you in a few hours, then."

She waited for him to wrap his arms around her and kiss her goodbye, but he didn't make any move to do so. She could feel his uncertainty. God, was he regretting his impulsive words already? Was he already changing his mind?

He gave her a small, secret smile, then hurried to his car.

"Come on, Tope. The car's in the parking lot," Seth said.

"What are you driving?" she asked him.

He just met her eyes and smiled. "What do you think?"

11

Jack got into the passenger seat of his own Porsche, too distracted to drive. Reaper looked at him oddly for a moment, then, without a word, took the driver's seat. He didn't speak, and Jack was glad. He had to go through what had just happened between him and Topaz, and try to figure it out.

He'd told Topaz that he loved her.

Those were words he'd been certain he would never say to any woman, because he knew they would be a lie. He didn't believe in love, didn't think it existed. And women, they craved it, hungered for it like nothing else. Especially Topaz.

And he knew, dammit, he *knew* it was the one thing she wanted from him, the one thing that could get to her when all else failed, and he'd vowed never to use it against her like a sweet, seductive weapon. Or like a drug that would convince her to do whatever he needed her to do.

Those words were as effective on Topaz as Reaper's trigger words were on him. Just as overwhelming. Just as impossible to resist. Just as dangerous to her. Hell, to both of them.

Right now, for some insane reason, logical or not, Jack was compelled to make Topaz trust him. So for one brief, insane, desperate moment, he'd lost his mind and said the words he knew would win him that trust.

He'd told her that he loved her. He'd told her that he felt something he didn't even believe himself capable of feeling, much less living up to. And he hated himself for it. What's more, he couldn't undo it now that it was done. And when things went to hell between them, as they ultimately would, she would be even more crushed and broken than she had been the first time he'd stupidly betrayed her.

Damn. There was no solution to this. None.

He didn't know why the hell he'd said what he had. When he'd seen her with that money all around her, when he'd seen the tears on her face, he'd somehow been driven to say and do anything to take her pain away, to remove the distrust from her eyes. The words had come tumbling out of him before he'd given them any forethought, much less had the chance to bite them back.

And they had worked. They were magic words, those three monosyllabic bits. They were magic words. I love you.

And they were a lie. Which sooner or later she was going to figure out. And it would do her in this time. She'd said so, and he didn't doubt it for a minute.

He was guilty of a crime of the heart, and he was a bastard, and he deserved to burn in hell for it.

"You're unusually quiet," Reaper said.

Jack dragged his attention away from the cyclone going on in his gut and glanced sideways at the Grim One as he drove. "A lot on my mind."

"I can see that. Is it Topaz, or does it have to do with me?"

"You?" Jack frowned.

"I assumed you wanted to talk to me about something. Otherwise you'd be with her right now. Or am I guessing wrong?"

"Oh, that." Jack shifted his attention to the other matter weighing on his mind. It was a relief, actually, to think about something besides the unforgivable sin he had just committed against a woman he honestly cared about. "Yeah, actually, you're right. I did want to talk to you. Could you do me a favor, though, and agree not to wring my neck until I've finished what I have to say?"

"I haven't wrung it yet, Jack, even though I have a pretty good idea what you're gearing up to say. I suppose I can put it off until I've heard the rest."

Jack stared at him, blinking.

Reaper shrugged. "Well, *someone* has been keeping the CIA informed of my whereabouts. And there are precious few people who knew. I'm fairly certain it was you. What I'm waiting to hear is why, and whether you've told them I'm here in Mexico. And now that I think about it, whether this little date of ours tonight is going to end in you trying to hand me over to them."

Jack was stunned. "You *knew?*"

"I've suspected for a while. *Now* I know."

Jack sighed and lowered his head. "You probably won't believe any of this, but it's the truth. At first, yeah, I was considering informing on you for the money. God knows they were paying Gregor a lot to try to get hold of you. I made contact, made a deal with them."

"And then . . . Wait, let me guess. You fell in love with Topaz and found you couldn't go through with it. Either because you cared too much to hurt her that way, or because you knew that betraying her again would ensure that you lost her forever."

Jack shrugged. "Something like that. But we needed information on her mother. They offered to supply it if I would keep them informed as to where you were as you moved around the country."

Reaper looked sideways quickly, his expression registering surprise. "So you kept feeding them information to get help for her?"

Jack nodded. "Only I gave them vague locations and always a day late. I made sure you would be able to stay a step or two ahead of them."

Reaper opened his mouth to respond, then closed it again and frowned. "They *were* always a few steps behind."

"I know. I made sure they would be. And, Reaper, you probably won't believe this, either, but that was my plan all along. Even when I was in it for the money, I never intended to actually put you at risk. I thought I could outcon them, that's all."

Nodding, Reaper drove, deep in thought. Then, "So why did you decide to tell me this tonight?"

"Because I tried to tell them I was done, it was over, I had no more to give them and they had nothing else I wanted. But they tracked me down, used my cell phone somehow, probably called it while I was resting by day and traced the ping or something. They're here."

"Where's your cell now?"

"At the bottom of the Gulf somewhere."

"Good," Reaper said. "Do they know I'm here?"

"They guessed. I told them you weren't, and that I had no idea where you were, but they didn't believe me. So I tried a new tack, told them they had nothing I wanted. And they said to try them. So I suggested they tell me how to create the drones and give me your trigger words, and that I might consider helping them out again. And they said they had a better idea."

"And here it comes." Reaper shook his head slowly, almost as if he knew what was coming next.

Then again, Jack thought, he might have a notion. He'd worked for those bastards himself in life. He knew how they operated.

"They told me they have Mirabella. Topaz's mother. That they'll kill her unless I deliver you into their hands."

Reaper sucked in a breath. "When?"

"Midnight tomorrow."

His eyes turning dark, Reaper said, "Did you see her?"

"No," Jack said.

"Talk to her?"

"No. No mental contact, either. I've tried, but she must be very well blocked."

Reaper nodded. "They don't have her, then. They wouldn't give you that much time to deliver me if they had her. That's just asking for trouble. Giving you time to try something. Giving me time to get clear. Besides, they would have shown her to you — more leverage."

"I thought the same thing, even called them on it. They couldn't show her to me, so I knew I had guessed right. But they claim they know where she is and can pick her up at any time."

"They're lying," Reaper said. "If they knew where she was, they'd have had her already."

"My thoughts exactly. The thing is, we have to find her before they do."

Reaper nodded his agreement. "I assume you've told Topaz all this?"

"You assume wrong. I don't want her to know. Not yet. I'll lose her trust forever if I admit I was working with the CIA all this time. She'll assume it's the only reason I stayed with her, the only reason I'm with her now. That I'm using her to earn some big payoff from them at your expense and hers, and . . . God, now her mother's."

"Yeah. I imagine you're probably right, that's exactly what she would think. I'm wondering about it myself, to be honest."

"I don't blame you for wondering." Jack sighed and pointed to a road sign ahead. "Take a right up there."

"So you're trusting me not to tell her, and I'm trusting you not to get my ass drugged, hog-tied and taken in for what the Agency would call 'reprogramming.' "

"That's it in a nutshell," Jack said. "Just until the deadline. Just until I manage to make this right. And then I'll tell her the whole truth."

Reaper fixed him with a stare that penetrated to his soul. "If you double-cross me, Jack, I *will* kill you."

"I don't doubt it for a minute." Jack sighed. "If this goes badly, I won't even mind."

Reaper seemed to contemplate that for a moment, and then he nodded once, firmly. "All right, then. It's a deal."

Jack whispered, "Thank you," as Reaper turned into the parking area outside a small adobe house that was pitch-dark and boasted a solid, no doubt well-locked door. There were no signs of life from within or anywhere around the place. No obvious ones, at least.

To Jack and to Reaper, however, the signs were abundant. They could feel the energy of a dozen vampires and, interestingly, a handful of mortals. Not the Chosen, either, just ordinary mortals. Since when did mortals and vampires hang out together? What the hell was this place?

They felt that energy go tense and taut as they shut off the engine and opened the car doors. All senses within that building perked up and focused on them, wary, defensive, distrustful and ready for battle.

Seth, Vixen and Topaz walked side by side by side straight up to the giant arched door that led into the private club. Seth was between the two women, and Topaz thought they must look incredible. Seth, tall and lean and hot as hell. Vixen, with her coppery mane and pixie features, and a sexy aura that spoke of things untamed and untamable. And Topaz herself, brunette, beautiful and feeling better about herself than she had in months.

And yeah, she was well aware that letting her feelings go up and down based on someone else's actions — based on Jack's actions, on three simple words he'd spoken — was a dumb-ass thing to do. And yet she felt good. Because he had come back to her.

Because he had finally told her he loved her. Because he had made her feel like a woman again.

"You ever been here before?" Seth asked.

They'd stopped walking, but the wind still blew dust behind them and moved their hair. Topaz shook her head, enjoying the way it made her hair lift higher in the wind's embrace. "Never."

"How'd Jack hear about it?"

"Grapevine," he said. Topaz saw the suspicious look cross Seth's face but chose to ignore it. She knew he didn't trust Jack. Hell, she didn't, either, so she couldn't even be mad at him for it.

"They're gathered on the other side of the door," Vixen said, holding out a hand that trembled a little and taking an involuntary step backward. "They're not happy about our visit."

Topaz gazed at the door, while Seth reassured Vixen, taking hold of her hand.

Hey, in the house. We're friendly. There are three of us, Topaz, Seth and Vixen.

Vixen?

There came a murmuring of thoughts and emotions. Some of the fear and wariness seemed to change into curiosity. Then a male spoke mentally. *The shapeshifter?*

"How can they know?" Vixen asked, then

clapped a hand over her mouth as her eyes widened. She hadn't been blocking.

"News about someone as unique as you would travel fast," Topaz said. "Gregor's band has scattered. Briar and Jack are with us, but there were others. They've obviously been talking to those they meet."

Vixen blinked her huge brown eyes three times in rapid succession, then turned her gaze to the closed door. "Yes," she called, speaking aloud. "I am the shapeshifter. And these two who are with me rescued me from captivity by the rogue band that held and tortured me. Please, we only seek entry and conversation."

Tension eased still further beyond the door. And then, slowly, it opened with a low groaning creak that could have been a Hollywood sound effect in a classic horror flick.

A pair of vampires stood on the other side of the entrance, a male who was as tall as a flagpole and about as big around, with jet-black hair that hung to his shoulders and a gaunt, hungry look about him. His partner, a petite female with short brown hair that looked as it if had been combed with an eggbeater, stood staring at them.

Other vampires lingered in groups of three and four, around the room. A handful of young men who looked for all the world like a typical rock band. A few young females who hung in pairs. None of them more than a few years undead. Except, perhaps, for the couple who'd let them in.

"Vixen," the male said, making it a question as his eyes roamed her face, taking in her foxlike characteristics, Topaz thought. It was obvious once you knew. The slightly pointed ears, the hair like a lush fox tail, the slanted, deep brown eyes, the way she walked up on her toes, the tiny, delicate frame. As far-fetched as it had once seemed to her, Topaz thought now that it would be harder to believe Vixen was anything *but* part fox.

"Yes," Vixen said to the man. "This is Topaz, and this is Seth. They're friends. Good ones."

He glanced at each of them as they were introduced, but only briefly. "I'm Reynold. This is my mate, Crisa."

Crisa gripped Reynold's forearm and stared hard at Vixen. "Could you show us?"

Reynold shot her a quelling look, but before he could say anything, Seth spoke. "It's not a parlor trick, hon. Or a spectator sport."

"Yeah, and she's not some kind of circus bear waiting to dance for you," Topaz

250

snapped.

Crisa lowered her head quickly. "I'm sorry. I've made you mad. I've made them mad, Reynold, haven't I? I didn't mean to. I only wanted to see her change into a fox. I've never seen a vampire change into a fox before."

She continued muttering as she walked away, head bowed. Some of the others stepped out of her path as she moved amongst them.

Vixen frowned after her.

"She's . . . different," Reynold said softly. "She meant no offense, she just doesn't . . . understand some things."

Mentally, Topaz realized as she delved into the girl's essence a bit more deeply, Crisa was childlike. An innocent. "I'm sorry I snapped at her like that. I didn't realize," she told Reynold softly.

"She'll have forgotten all about it in a few minutes." Reynold turned, waving a hand at the large room before them. A small bar, perhaps six feet long and made of pounded copper, took up one corner. A handful of stools stood in front of it, and there were small overstuffed chairs and settees grouped around tiny coffee tables in various spots around the huge room. Behind the bar, built into the wall, there were refrigerators. It didn't take much imagination to figure out what they contained. The liquor bottles on the shelves were clearly just there for show, in case some mortal should venture too near. The layer of dust on them ought to give away the truth, but an ordinary human wouldn't notice.

The lights were electric, but muted by amber shades that gave them a softer glow. The place was painted in red and yellow, lined with clay pottery, some of which held cacti and desert flowers. The walls were decorated with figures of skeletons playing various musical instruments and dancing, and, here and there, crosses made of tiny *papiermâché* skulls. Topaz smiled, recognizing the symbols of *Dia del Muerte,* the Day of the Dead. Brightly colored handwoven rugs lined the floors, and Mexican music played softly from unseen speakers.

"Welcome to Casa Crisa," Reynold said. "We created this place as a haven for our kind. There are so few places where we can gather, socialize, feel . . . well, somewhat normal. Of course, its existence is a well-kept secret. Only the locals, those we know and trust, are aware of it."

Topaz nodded, and slid onto a stool in front of the bar, running her fingers over the copper surface. It was old.

"Why don't you tell me what brings you here?" Reynold asked. "Clearly, you have a purpose."

"What makes you think so?" Seth asked.

"Our kind don't usually seek out places with an abundance of sunshine, my friend. Those who come to Mexico usually come for a reason." He eyed Topaz. "And I sense the reason, in this case, is yours. Tell me what you're looking for, and maybe I can help."

She nodded. "I'm looking for Mirabella DuFrane."

He frowned hard, then turned toward one of the refrigerators in the back and opened it. "You mean the famous actress?" he asked. He was inserting a tap into a plastic bag with the Red Cross logo on it. He filled three glasses and set them on the bar. "Here, on the house."

Seth and Vixen slid onto stools flanking Topaz.

"Thank you," she said. "And yes, I do mean the actress. Everyone believes she was killed, but I know she wasn't. She was transformed. Brought over. She's one of us."

"And how do you know that, child? Gossip? Tabloids?"

Topaz sipped from her glass. "I know it because she transformed me, ten years ago."

She took another long drink, the blood soothing and empowering her. Her comrades had already drained their glasses, she noticed.

The reed-thin vampire frowned hard, clearly not believing her claim.

"And before she brought me into *this* life, she brought me into the other one," Topaz went on, starting to feel as if she really were sitting at an ordinary bar, drinking alcohol. The thought took her back. A tiny, not unpleasant buzz was beginning to take hold. "The original one."

"I don't follow," Reynold said.

"She was," Topaz said, "*is* . . . my mother. And I want her. I want my mother." Tears welled in her voice, and her throat went tight. And just as she realized something was very wrong and lowered her gaze to stare at her now empty glass, Seth's head clunked down onto the bar on her left. Vixen slid in slow motion off the stool on Topaz's right, sinking to the floor. She lifted her head and sent Topaz a goofy smile before she closed her eyes.

Topaz faced Reynold again, blinking at him as he swam in her vision. "What did you put in our drinks?"

"We protect our Bella," he said softly. "And you aren't the only ones out there looking for her. So until we know for sure what you want, we have to take . . . precautions."

The woman who opened the door in response to Jack's knocking was beautiful, with dark hair and eyes like a Gypsy's. She wore a low-cut black halter dress that hugged her all the way to the floor. She was tiny in stature, with an innocence about her eyes, and a youthful aura that suggested she wasn't any older than Jack himself.

"What can I do for you two fine vampires tonight?" she asked, her voice sultry and suggestive as she stood in the doorway and stared them up and down.

Jack looked at Reaper. Reaper looked back, then frowned and turned his gaze past the woman to scan the inside of the house. Jack followed his line of sight. It was quiet inside. Beautiful mortal women lounged around here and there in revealing clothes, their skin abnormally pale, their throats bearing the telltale marks that would disappear with the touch of the sun, so long as they were alive to see it when it rose.

"They work for you?" Reaper asked.

The woman nodded. "My name is Rosa. This is my place." Her accent was thick. "You can wipe those judgmental expressions from your faces. The women are here of their own free will, and they are *very* well compensated. And well pleasured, besides. At Rosa's place, everyone wins."

Jack frowned and nudged Reaper. "I'm not getting it."

"It's a whorehouse, Jack," Reaper said. "Mortal women service the needs of vampires. Blood, body, whatever, for a price."

"Obviously you did not know that before you arrived," Rosa said. "So tell me just what it is you *do* want, *señor.* Why have you come here?"

"We're looking for someone," Jack said softly. "Mirabella DuFrane."

The woman's eyes widened, and she turned and shot her gaze around the room. The women who'd been lounging around got up and hurried away — down hallways, up stairs, through doors that closed behind them. From above came the sound of footsteps rushing around.

His voice would have carried to any vampire within range, of course, Jack thought.

Rosa looked past them into the darkness of the yard. Reaper and Jack turned, as well, and saw several vampires, mostly men, but one or two females, sailing downward from second-floor windows to land easily on the grassy lawn, then speeding away. Rosa pulled the two of them inside and closed the door.

Jack looked around in surprise. The place seemed abandoned now. Oh, there were still mortals around, quivering in their rooms, but every vampire had left the building, except for the one who stood before them.

Rosa rolled her eyes. "There goes one of the most profitable nights I was ever going to have. Thanks to you. *Dios,* what is the matter with you, mentioning that name? Are you loco?"

"I didn't know it would cause such a stir," Jack said, and if he sounded a bit defensive, it was because that was how he felt. She acted as if he'd committed a cardinal sin.

She frowned. "You are not from around here, yes?"

"No."

"Then why have you come?"

"Look," he said, irritated that he had to repeat himself. "I'm here because I need to find Mirabella DuFrane before someone else does. Someone who might be dangerous to her."

She lifted her perfectly arched, raven-black brows and studied him. "How do I know you are not the ones who are dangerous to her?"

Jack started to assure her of that, but Reaper held up a hand. "Then you do know where she is," he said, cutting straight to the chase, as usual.

"I know she is near. But she has friends, vampires, who protect her beyond all reason. No one gets near her. She does not go out to feed. They bring sustenance to her instead. If she grows bored, they smuggle her out into the countryside, or sometimes even out of the country, going to elaborate lengths to disguise her. They adore her as if she is a goddess. And when anyone comes around asking questions about her . . ."

She stopped there, lowering her gaze.

"What? Does this gang of hers do something to them?" Jack demanded. "Are they killers, Rosa? Are they rogues?"

She shrugged. "I have never seen any bodies. I only know that those who ask questions, and those who answer those questions, tend to vanish. Most have never been heard from again."

"Most?" Jack repeated.

She lifted her head, met his eyes. "All." Her lips pulled into a smile. "And that is why it is imperative you leave here right now. I have no doubt at least one of my clients this evening is lurking, waiting to see how long you stay. I must not give the impression I have told you anything, even the tiny amount I have."

"Where can we find her?" Reaper asked.

"I do not know." She opened the door, shoved them out and shouted, "I do not know what you are talking about, I tell you. Get out! Already you have ruined my evening's profits."

What about this gang of hers? Where can we find them? Jack sent the message to her mind alone, blocking out the probing intellects he felt lurking, listening in.

Casa Crisa.

She slammed the door in their faces, and they looked at one another, shook their heads in frustration and headed back to the car. *You drive,* Reaper said, targeting Jack alone. *I want to scan . . . Yeah, as I thought. She was right, there are at least three vampires lurking in those woods.*

I thought I felt someone trying to read our thoughts.

Reaper nodded. *Think she's being paranoid?*

Yes, and I think maybe she has reason to be.

"What the hell is Casa Crisa?" Reaper asked, when they were far enough away that eavesdroppers were no longer a problem.

"That's the name of the place where we

sent the others."

Reaper swung his head around fast. "Shit."

"I couldn't have said it better." Then he stepped on the gas and prayed.

12

"Lock them up," Reynold ordered. And as the other vampires who'd been lurking about the place surrounded the three fallen strangers without a question or a pause, he took Crisa by the hand. "Come, little one. We have to go."

"Where are we going, Rey-Rey?" She grinned broadly as she asked the question. "Are we going to Bella? Are we going to see Bella?"

"Yes, child."

She clapped her hands and bounced excitedly. Then she raced behind the bar and returned to his side, a blindfold in her hands, which she immediately tied around her own face. "I remember the rules. See?"

"I do see. You're a very good girl, Crisa."

"I *am* good," she assured him.

Smiling, Reynold took the innocent by one arm and led her out of the establishment, his haven and theirs, and into the night. They had one vehicle, which they shared. A hybrid they'd pooled their resources to buy. He put Crisa into the passenger seat and fastened her safety belt, then he got behind the wheel and drove.

She didn't fuss about the blindfold, didn't fight, or try to peek or cheat or take it off. A normal vampire would, he thought, be able to find the place again by sensing it, by feeling the way the car moved and memorizing the directions, or by recognizing the sounds, both of the road and the air around them, and the smells and the feel of the place. But Crisa wasn't a normal vampire. She was impaired in some way. He didn't know whether she'd been that way in life, or whether something had happened since she'd been brought over, or perhaps during the transformation process. She had never told him. He wasn't sure how to ask, much less whether she would understand what it was he was asking. He wasn't even sure if she knew why she was the way she was. Sometimes he didn't think she was even aware of her own differences.

So he left it be. It didn't matter how she'd gotten to be this way — she was, that was all. It couldn't be changed by picking it apart or analyzing it. And he loved her as much for her innocence as for anything else.

He drove over the winding back roads, one and then another, until he should have been hopelessly lost. He wasn't, though. He knew this place. Knew it well.

Finally he stopped alongside a rambling fence in the middle of nowhere, got out and moved a pile of deadfall aside, revealing the gate it had hidden. He opened the gate, drove the car through, then stopped to get out again, close the gate and hide it once more.

Back behind the wheel, he took the winding path-like road to the miniature castle that was home to the legendary Mirabella DuFrane. He pulled the car, a boxy hatchback, to a halt in front of the stone structure. "You can take the blindfold off now, Crisa," he said.

She did, and, as always, she gazed in ever-new wonder at Mirabella's home. It was truly one of a kind, this place. It looked like a castle but was no larger than an ordinary house. Its exterior was composed of hand-hewn stone, imported from a real castle in Europe. It boasted a pair of towers, one on either side of a square, two-story center structure.

Reynold didn't make use of the giant brass lion's head knocker on the arch-topped front door. Instead, he turned to the tiny keypad tucked to one side, hidden by the leaves of a potted fern, and went to punch in the pass numbers. But he hesitated, fingers poised, free hand pushing fronds aside, as he noted the green light, glowing steadily. It was supposed to be red.

The door was already unlocked, the system disarmed.

"Bella?" he asked. A shiver worked its way down his spine as he moved closer to the door, closed his hand around the knob and pushed it open.

"Where is she?" Crisa asked, her innocent voice devoid of any hint of concern.

"I don't know, love." He stepped into the foyer, which spread wide, with curving staircases at either side leading up to the bedrooms, one in each tower, and one along the hallway in between. "Bella?"

"That's not right," Crisa whispered. She rubbed her arms as if she were chilled and stared off to the right.

Reynold followed her gaze and noticed then that a small table was cockeyed, the embroidered doily dangling off one side, and the lamp balanced precariously on a corner, ready to tip off at the least instigation.

He frowned and moved farther inside, straightening the lamp on his way, his eyes scanning now, as were his senses.

"Something happened here!" Crisa cried, just as Reynold's senses began telling him the same thing. "The air here is angry. Can't you feel it?"

He could. There had been a surge of emotions. Fear, anger, resistance, rage. There had been violence. As he walked the length of the place, he found more signs of struggle, a clear path of it from the front entry through the long hallways to the back door. Paintings hanging crookedly on the walls; a broken vase, with water and fresh flowers, had been dashed to the floor; an umbrella stand was tipped over; and the back door was standing wide open, with the doormat half in and half out. And as he inspected the damage, he could visualize what had happened here. In his mind, he saw Bella being held, dragged, forced, clinging to everything she passed in an effort to keep from being taken. The portraits. The umbrella stand. Her feet dragged the doormat half out with her, and there, in the paint, were the marks of her fingernails in the wall and in the woodwork around the back door.

"Someone has taken her," he muttered. Then he moved through the back door and down two steps to the ground below, where he saw tire tracks. He opened himself up to feelings, impressions, and knew it had been a while since everyone had left. "They're gone," he told Crisa. "They've been gone more than an hour, maybe close to two."

"But who would do that? Who would take our Bella?"

"I don't know. But I have a good idea." His anger built, and he gripped Crisa by the arm, then led her back through the house and out the front door to where they had left the car. "Come on, love. We need to ask a few questions of our *guests*."

Casa Crisa was abandoned. Empty. Jack sensed it before he even pulled to a stop beside Seth's ill-gained and much beloved classic Mustang. He dove out of the car, his mind scanning the surroundings, his senses probing deep, his gut calling out for Topaz.

But there was no reply.

"Jesus, they're gone! All three of them. Gone!" Arms out at his sides, he turned in a slow circle, stopping when he faced Reaper.

The Grim One's face was a study in concentration. He almost seemed to be sniffing the very air for clues.

"What the hell do we do now?" Jack asked.

"What we don't do is panic." Reaper's

tone was calm and cold, and he looked at the ground, then walked a few steps and stared off into the distance. "There are tire tracks here. Lots of them, but they mostly head off in the same direction."

"Mostly?"

"If we can get our hands on anyone who was here tonight, I can make them tell us what they know. I guarantee you that much," Reaper said. "If the CIA taught me anything, it was how to extract information."

Jack suppressed a shiver, because Reaper's tone made it pretty clear this was the kind of thing he'd had to do before — something he knew he could do well. And that was chilling.

And yet, Jack knew he wouldn't hesitate to resort to torture if it meant getting Topaz back alive. Torture, hell. He wouldn't balk at murder. Or worse. God only knew what was happening to her right now. He remembered her time in Gregor's hands, the torture she'd withstood, before he'd managed to intervene. What if . . . ?

Reaper clapped him on the shoulder. "Stop imagining the worst. It isn't going to help matters."

Jack nodded. "If they hurt her —"

"If they hurt her, or Seth or Vixen, they're

going to die slow. We agree on that, Jack."

"Good."

"Let's go inside, see if we can find any clues." Reaper glanced at the sky. "We have six hours till sunrise. Let's make use of them."

"They've been gone an awfully long time," Roxy said.

She was lounging in a chair on the wide deck of the bungalow, facing the ocean, watching the waves roll in beneath the night sky. The sea breeze blew over her face, and she could taste the salt with every breath.

"Do you think they're in some kind of trouble?" Ilyana asked.

"I don't know. I've opened my mind as much as I know how, even called out to them. But I'm no vampire. My skills in that area aren't anywhere near what theirs are."

Ilyana, who sat in another chair, lounging just as Roxy was doing, was dressed in one of Roxy's gorgeous saris. They'd each chosen one from the collection Roxy had brought along. Both were silk, straight from India, and handmade. Roxy wore ruby and black; Ilyana was in multitoned green. They resembled, Roxy thought, royalty.

"We could ask *her,*" Ilyana said with a

glance back toward the house.

Roxy followed her gaze upward to the second-story window of Briar's bedroom. Beyond it, the dark vampiress moped. She was moody, lethargic, all but silent, and as isolated from the rest of the group as she could manage to be while still being with them. It was as if she'd walled herself off in every imaginable way.

"She's not as bad as you think she is, you know," Roxy said.

"No one could be as bad as I think she is."

Roxy closed her eyes and deliberated before speaking. "She was tortured. Brutally. By the man she believed loved her."

Ilyana sat silent for a long moment. So long, in fact, that Roxy didn't think she was going to respond at all. But then, at last, she did. She said, "So was I. By the man who fathered my son."

"Fathered your — You have a son? With *Gregor?*"

Ilyana met Roxy's eyes. "He's like us. One of . . . the Chosen."

"And where is he now?"

"Gregor has him. That's why I need to find him, and why I'm so frustrated by this delay. And if you tell any of *them* about this, Roxy, I swear —"

"But, Ilyana, they might know something. Jack, Vixen — God, Briar was there, with Gregor, in that mansion of his. Surely if there were a child there, one of them would have seen him."

Ilyana met her eyes. "*I* was there with him. They never saw *me*."

"But —"

"It's my secret to keep, Roxy. Respect this. We're kin, you and I, in some way I don't fully understand. It's in our blood, our bond. You're the only person I've trusted with this information. Please don't betray me."

Roxy nodded slowly. "All right. I won't tell them. Or anyone. Even though I think you're making a mistake."

"Thank you." Ilyana sat up in the chair, put her feet on the floor. "If you think it will help speed things up, then I think we should go to Briar and ask for her assistance. If she rips out our jugulars for our trouble, well, I'll just hope she goes for yours first."

"Lucky for both of you, I've already eaten."

Both women gasped and turned sharply to see Briar standing in the pitch darkness of the bungalow's back door. They could barely make out her black silhouette. The screen door's hinges creaked as she pushed it open and stepped out onto the back porch.

"Don't look so shocked. You two have been calling out for Reaper and the others for an hour now. It's not like I could keep from hearing you. I just hope no unfriendly undead did the same. Now, what is it you want?"

Ilyana shot Roxy a look, and Roxy knew exactly what she was wondering. Just how much of Ilyana's secret had Briar heard?

Clearing her throat and facing Briar, trying to keep thoughts of Ilyana's son from her mind, Roxy said, "We're concerned about them. They've been gone longer than they should have been."

"They're fine."

"I would believe that if one group had made it back by now. But the fact that both groups are late seems to suggest that something's happened."

"You worry like a mortal, Roxy."

"I *am* a mortal, Briar."

The dark bitch closed her eyes briefly, as if exasperated. "Just what do you expect me to do about this, anyway? Jump on a white horse and go charging to the rescue? Have you got some armor you want me to put on? A sword you want me to swing? Do I

271

look like fucking Joan of Arc to you?"

Roxy bit back the retort that leapt to her lips, took a deep breath and counted to three because she didn't have time to go all the way to ten. Then she spoke. "I want you to contact them mentally and find out what's gone wrong. Would you do that for me, Briar?"

Briar rolled her eyes, but she nodded. "Fine."

Then she turned to face the direction of the road and focused on the others. She was quiet for a long moment, and Roxy watched every expression that crossed her face. Her brows rose in surprise, then lowered in what looked a lot like worry, though they all knew Briar too well to suspect she would ever waste a moment's worry on anyone besides herself.

Finally Briar drew a breath and turned to face the two mortal women once more. Ilyana was tense as a cat. She was petrified of Briar, more so, even, than Vixen was.

"Well?" Roxy asked. "Did you reach them?"

Briar nodded. "Much as I hate to admit it, mortal, you were right. Seth, Vixen and Topaz have vanished from the establishment they went to check out — a place called Casa Crisa. In fact, there's no one there at all, though their car is still in the parking lot."

"Oh, no," Ilyana whispered.

"Reaper said a vampire named Rosa at some sort of vampire whorehouse —"

"Vampire whorehouse?" Ilyana repeated, interrupting, and earning her a glare from Briar, who went on without explaining or answering Ilyana's unasked but obvious question.

"This Rosa told Reaper that the vamps at Casa Crisa are Bella's protectors. Kind of a rogue gang of their own. And that people who show up asking questions about her generally disappear."

"He thinks this gang has taken them?" Roxy asked.

"Looks that way," Briar said, as if she really didn't care. "And now I suppose we're going to have to rescue them, or we'll never get back on Gregor's trail."

"You're right about that," Ilyana said.

Briar shot her a look that was slightly surprised. "Agreeing with me? Even though you think I might . . . How did you put that again? Rip out your jugular?"

Ilyana's jaw tightened. "I'm sorry about that."

"You shouldn't be," Briar said. "I might. Not tonight, though. Tonight I suppose we need to get to Casa Crisa to help search for the missing misfits."

"I'll get Shirley," Roxy said, running inside for the keys to her oddly-named, customized conversion van. "Meet me around front."

Reaper had been stunned to hear Briar calling out to him mentally. He and Seth were searching Casa Crisa and, so far, finding nothing of use, when he felt her summons.

Reaper. Answer me.

He'd paused in what he was doing and focused only on the sound of her voice, a voice that played up and down his nerve endings like a bow over taut violin strings. It made him hum and vibrate inside.

I'm surprised to hear from you, Briar. Is something wrong?

Your mortal bitches are worried about you. Asked me to make contact.

And you agreed? Interesting. She never did anything unless it benefited her.

Seemed the quickest way to shut them up. Has anything gone wrong?

He wanted to think that Briar, too, had been concerned. That Briar, too, wanted to make sure nothing had gone wrong. He wanted to see something in her that would justify his feelings toward her. Something that gave a hint she might have a shadow of a soul, or even a trace of a heart.

But what he wanted to see tended to shade what was truly there, at least where she was concerned. Reading between the lines with Briar was nothing more than an exercise in self-delusion. She was what she was. Evil. Selfish. Shallow. Cruel.

He told her what had happened, what he'd learned from the madam, Rosa, and that he and Jack had arrived to find their three friends missing. But her final message had surprised him.

Do you sense that they've been harmed? she asked.

Frowning, he bit back the sarcastic reply that sprang to his lips. The one that asked her if she would care. *No. I don't sense any pain or fear. What worries me is that they haven't called out to us. If they were able to, they would.*

Briar replied, *Gregor found a way to block mental communications between the vampires inside his fortress and those beyond its walls. Perhaps these vampires have done the same.*

He shook his head, though she couldn't see it. *They don't strike me as geniuses, Briar. I haven't met them, of course, but the essence they left behind at this place suggests rather ordinary mental capacity. No hint of a brilliant mind.*

There was a brief pause, and then Briar told him, *I'm bringing the mortals. They'll only drive me insane if I don't. We'll be there to help you search as fast as that ludicrous van Roxy insists on calling Shirley can carry us.*

There was no more.

"Reaper! Look at this!"

Reaper snapped back to the world, drawing his focus from Briar, and extending his attention instead to Jack and the matter at hand.

Jack held an envelope in one hand. It had been opened, but its contents remained. It appeared to be a utility bill — electricity, perhaps. Reaper frowned.

"An electric bill?"

"Yeah, but not for this address," Jack said. He handed the envelope over.

Reaper examined it. "We need to find this place," he said. "Are there any maps around here?"

"Yeah, top desk drawer. Over there." He pointed toward a small office opening off the east wall.

Together they went to the desk, unfolded the maps they found there and began searching for the address on the bill.

■ ■ ■ ■

Topaz groaned as she opened her eyes. Whatever they'd used to knock her out, it hadn't been the tranquilizer with which she was familiar, the only one known to be effective against the undead. No, it must have been something far weaker, far more common. But an ordinary drug should only have been effective for a few minutes on a vampire. And surely more time than that had passed.

She looked around and tried to get her bearings. She was dizzy, her vision hazy, but even so, it was clear that she was no longer in Casa Crisa. She was in a white room. White ceiling. White walls. No windows. She was lying on a hard table of some kind, covered in a white sheet.

Beside her, there was an IV pole.

That, more than anything, sent a rush of adrenaline surging, and she sat up fast, only to sway and nearly tumble from the table.

A woman gripped her shoulders, brown hair as crazy as the look in her eyes. "Easy. It's okay. No one's gonna hurt you."

Topaz lowered her head and pressed the heel of one hand to her brow, remembering the girl. Crisa. The one who wasn't quite right. "What the hell did you people give me?"

"Just some Thorazine. Big dose." She nodded at the pole. "It wouldn't have kept you out long enough, but as soon as you went down, I put in the IV to keep you out until we had you settled in. And now it's okay for you to wake up."

Topaz lifted her head slowly, looking suspiciously at the woman-child. "*You* put in the IV?"

"I'm a nurse. Or I was."

And now you're a nutcase, Topaz thought. She heard a moan and turned to see Seth sitting up slowly on a gurney nearby, and kitty-corner from him, she saw Vixen, also beginning to stir.

"They're fine, too," Crisa said.

"Why are we here?"

"Because you asked about Bella. We don't like people asking about Bella." She looked around the place, smiling. "Do you like our clinic? We set it up to help injured vampires. It happens sometimes. You need a private place, lots of blood, and plenty of —"

"What the hell's going on?" Seth growled, sitting up, holding his head just as Topaz had, shocked by the throbbing, no doubt. "Aaaah, hell. Where are we? What did you give us? What's —"

Give me a minute here, Seth. I'm getting what I can from her.

He glanced toward Topaz as she sent her thoughts to him, then to Vixen, and Topaz knew the shifter had received the message, as well. Seth struggled to his feet, glancing down at the bandage on his forearm and the IV pole nearby. Shaking his head, he landed on the floor, and shuffled slowly and unsteadily over to Vixen.

"Don't fall down," Crisa warned. "You won't be very steady for a little while yet. Another hour or so. Then you'll be fine." She turned back to Topaz and reached toward her.

Topaz pulled back instinctively, but the little thing was only trying to touch her hair. Her fingers made contact, ran along one strand, then retreated. "I love your hair," Crisa said. "I wish mine were long like that."

She was definitely a few nails short of a full coffin, this one, Topaz thought. "Thank you. I . . . like yours, too."

Crisa smiled shyly. "I have to go get Rey-Rey. He said to tell him when you all woke up."

"In a minute," Topaz said. "I was dying to hear more about what you were saying. You don't like people asking questions about . . . who was it again? Bella? Do you mean

279

Mirabella DuFrane?"

Crisa lowered her eyes to hide whatever was in them, but she was painfully easy to read. That was exactly who she meant.

"So she's alive, then?"

"I have to go get Rey-Rey."

"Crisa, wait. You don't understand. Mirabella is my mother. I've been searching for her. My friends have been trying to help me find her. She wouldn't want you to drug me and hold me captive this way. She would want you to tell her about me. Couldn't you just do that? Just tell her I've come, and see for yourself what she wants you to do."

Blinking rapidly, her eyes welling, Crisa said, "That's what we were going to do. But she was gone. And we don't know where."

Topaz felt something slam into her chest with the velocity of a wrecking ball. "Gone? What do you mean, gone?"

"Rey-Rey thinks someone took her."

Topaz closed her eyes and shouted mentally, knowing the message would be weak, even though she put everything she had into it. *Jack! Jack, can you hear me? I need your help.*

The door to the small room crashed open then, and three men, mortals, wearing suits that were nearly identical, surged inside, aimed their weapons and fired, even as

Crisa spun around in surprise.

The tranq darts hissed. Crisa jerked as one hit her, smashing into a covered window, shattering the glass with one flailing arm, then sinking to her knees. Topaz scrambled off the far side of her gurney. She should have been faster. Would have been, at full strength, but there were narcotics poisoning her veins. She wasn't as fast as she normally would have been, and she wasn't certain her call to Jack had been heard. She only knew she was in trouble.

And these three mortal idiots were dead meat.

She saw a dart hit Seth as he launched himself at them, intent on attack. Then another hit Vixen as she ran to his aid, and Topaz felt one sink deeply into her own belly at the same moment.

As she sank to the floor, she saw beyond the men, through the open door and into the hallway, where Reynold lay unconscious. And then her line of sight was blocked by a dark-suited man with steely hair to match his eyes, a man she vowed would be dead before another night passed.

"Take this one," he called to his cohorts. "Leave the others. She's been dying to meet her mother anyway, right? We're doing her a favor."

"Jack did good after all, didn't he?" said the man who scooped her up and turned to carry her out of the room.

"Yeah, I guess he did."

Jack? No. No, please, God, not Jack, Topaz thought. He can't be responsible for this. Not this!

The pain that exploded in her heart then was so crippling, so intense, that it buckled her body. She bent forward on a sob that nearly broke her spine. And the man carrying her looked down in surprise as she jerked in his arms.

"Hey, I think this one's having some kind of reaction to the drug," he said.

The other one glanced her way. She was aware of his perusal even through the gray haze of her pain and the dulling impact of the tranquilizer.

"She's crying, that's all. Damn, she's *really* crying. Hang on to her. Don't drop her, for God's sake."

"Shit, she's damn near convulsing. *You* try holding her!" The man's arms tightened around her.

She closed her eyes and fought it, but the shakes continued, and the tears flowed freely.

"They really do feel things more than we do, don't they?" the third man said.

"Pretty thing, isn't she?" The one holding her bent his head close to her face. "It's okay, you'll be asleep in a minute. Just let it go. Let it go, okay?"

"Yeah, why don't you read her a bedtime story and tuck her in, asswipe? She's a *vampire*."

"Doesn't mean she doesn't have feelings."

"Get her the hell out of here. Now."

Her captor nodded, and carried her through the door and into the hallway. "You're gonna be okay," he told her. "I promise."

"Never. I'll never be okay again," she managed to whisper. She saw his eyes when they met hers. Blue, and even compassionate. And then they faded from her vision.

She was glad the tranquilizer finally kicked in and stole her consciousness away. She hoped, in that final moment, that she would never wake up again.

13

Jack heard Topaz cry out to him, but it was vague, and weak, and then there was nothing.

"Which direction is that address?" he asked Reaper.

Reaper looked up from the map he had unfolded on the hood of the car, met Jack's eyes, and then scanned the horizon. He pointed east. "That way."

"That's where she is, then."

Reaper's brows rose.

"She called out to me just now, but it was very weak. I think they've been drugged. We have to get to her, Reaper. Now."

Headlights came trundling up the drive, and the canary-yellow van with the sunflowers on the sides and the customized plates bearing its name bounded closer. It stopped abruptly, and the three women jumped out of it. They were all armed, cocking their weapons as they came.

Jack thought briefly of *Charlie's Angels*. Only these were more like Hells Angels. One ageless mortal who never wanted to be a vampire but was already, he suspected, more vampire than human in many ways, her fiery red curls halfway down her back, bouncing as she walked. One blond enigma, tall and stick-thin, with a pixie cut and a face that reminded him of a supermodel whose name he couldn't recall. And one dark demoness straight from the depths of hell itself. Briar, with her black eyes, black hair and black heart.

She looked pissed.

Jack would have smiled to himself about that if he hadn't been so sick with dread for Topaz.

"Any clues?" Briar asked.

"Just one. Follow us," Jack said.

Briar nodded, then hesitated. "Is there a key for the Mustang? It would be better to take all three cars, just in case."

"Seth keeps a spare under the floor mat, rear passenger side," Reaper told her. "Just pray he left it unlocked," he added, as he and Jack headed for the Porsche.

With a nod, Briar headed for the muscle car. "I'm driving alone," she called out to Roxy. "Bring the van."

■ ■ ■ ■

The house where they ended up looked abandoned, decrepit. Its sagging roof had patches of rich green moss growing from its shingles. The wooden siding was unpainted, and had weathered to varying shades of gray in some places and near black in others. Some of the old boards were broken or split. Others hung loosely. There were once-green shutters here and there. Some hung by only one hinge, and most had slats missing. The entry door's peeling paint had been white. Now it was all but nonexistent. The knob, though, was out of place. It was shiny, not rusted or tarnished.

Jack shut off the Porsche's purring motor, got out and moved closer to the place. And then he sensed something that made his stomach clench and his throat tighten as panic swirled like a whirlwind in his soul. Death.

Reaper was out of the car, standing beside him, sensing it, too, and he clapped his hand firmly onto Jack's shoulder. "Steady."

"Fuck steady." Jack sprinted toward the door, and without trying the knob, he kicked it open. It smashed wide, and he lunged inside, his gaze swinging from left to right, his heart in his throat. "Topaz!"

No answer.

"What the hell *is* this place?" someone muttered.

Vaguely, Jack acknowledged that Briar had spoken. She'd come inside, with Roxy and Ilyana on her heels. And he noted, too, that the inside of this place didn't come close to matching the outside. It was clean, in perfect repair and spotlessly white. There were a few pieces of furniture around, also in good shape. The place was immaculate but, he felt, rarely used. And that was all his mind managed to process as he made his way down a hall, flinging open the first door he came to and moving through it, as the women kept going to check out the other doors. His heart was in his throat as he scanned the room, terrified of seeing Topaz lying dead on the floor.

It was another spotless white room. It contained a series of gurneys with white sheets, IV poles. A stainless steel tray and some instruments lay on the tiled floor. And so did several bodies.

"Topaz!" Jack shouted, and leapt forward, but he didn't see her.

"This one's dead," Reaper muttered from the hall.

Jack turned to see him bending over a

dead male vamp, one he'd barely registered as he'd passed and certainly never met. His gaze returned to the room he was in and landed on another — and frighteningly familiar — form. "Vixen!" Jack crossed the room in a blur of speed and gently rolled Vixen's body over, leaning close, feeling for her life force, her essence. It was there, but weak. Very weak.

Someone groaned from beyond one of the gurneys, and Seth dragged himself into sight, across the floor. He was trying to speak and failing, and still too weak to communicate mentally. But his eyes said it all as they stared from Vixen's lax, beautiful face to Jack's.

"She's alive," Jack assured him. "What in the name of God happened here, Seth?"

Reaper rushed into the room to bend over Seth. He gripped the fledgling under both arms and hauled him to his feet. As he did so, he spotted the tranq dart in Seth's arm, jerked it out and held it up. "They've been darted. Whoever did it must have given that poor bastard in the hall too much and killed him." He glanced at Jack. "How's Vixen?"

"I think she'll live." He stared at Seth, who was now on a gurney, sitting upright, barely, with Reaper supporting him and his head bowed forward. "Where is Topaz?" Jack demanded, even as he rose, picking Vixen up and then lowering her gently onto another gurney.

"They . . . took her."

"Who?" Jack left Vixen in the bed and went to Seth, vaguely noticing the women entering and spreading out through the room. He gripped the young vamp's shirtfront. "Who took her, Seth?"

Seth's head wobbled. "Men. Mortals."

"Reaper?" Briar called from the far end of the room, near a shattered window. As both men turned, they saw her standing there with a tiny, odd-looking female vampire in her arms. "This one's circling the drain."

The woman she carried had a bloody cut on her forearm and was clearly in danger of bleeding out.

"Put her down over there and deal with her," Reaper snapped, indicating the gurney next to him. Then he returned his full attention to Seth, shaking him. "Seth, you've got to give us more than that. Who the hell took Topaz?"

"And where?" Jack demanded. "How many were there? Did they say anything, *anything,* that might be a clue?"

Seth's head had fallen forward again, his chin sagging nearly to his chest. Jack gripped his hair and lifted his face up, only to see that he was out cold.

"Jack . . . ?"

The voice was quiet, soft, new to him. Jack turned to see the one Briar had brought over peering at him. Roxy was bending over her wounded arm, pinching the edges of the jagged cut together in an effort to stop the bleeding.

He moved closer. "I'm Jack."

"Crisa," she muttered weakly.

"Crisa? That's your name?"

She tried to nod, but it was more than she could manage, and she stopped. "There's . . . a message . . ." Her eyes closed.

"What? You have a message? For me?" He bent closer and gripped her shoulders. Briar's ice-cold hand closed on the back of his neck and jerked him away so hard he nearly lost his footing.

"Where's Ilyana with that first aid kit?" she snapped.

"Here," Ilyana said, rushing into the room with the kit in her hand. "Right here." She joined Roxy at Crisa's side, opening the case and handing her items as Roxy asked for them. Silk thread and curved needles. Roxy was nothing if not prepared.

Jack moved forward to question the little oddball again, but Briar put a hand on his chest and leaned in herself. "Tell me, if you

290

can, Crisa. What were you supposed to tell Jack?"

Crisa's eyelashes fluttered, and her eyes widened briefly as Roxy put in the first stitch, and even Jack winced, knowing what kind of pain she was feeling.

Crisa grunted, then clenched her jaw and moved her lips. Even with his vampiric senses, Jack couldn't hear what she said. But Briar bent closer, her ear very close to the girl's mouth.

When she straightened again, she was holding a piece of paper she'd pulled from Crisa's clenched hand, and staring at Jack with mingled disgust and surprise in her eyes. "Jack, now we have something you want," she read aloud. "What do you suppose that could mean?"

He knew exactly what it meant. It meant that it was his fault Topaz had been abducted by dangerous men. And probably her mother, as well. It meant she probably knew by now that he'd been dealing with the CIA.

It meant she could die. Because of him.

"So help me, if you betrayed us, Jack," she went on in a low, steady voice, "I'll kill you myself."

Topaz came awake all at once, her head

snapping up, body going taut and pulling against the handcuffs around her wrists, holding her arms behind the straight-backed chair in which she sat. It felt as if she'd nearly pulled her shoulders from their sockets.

She grunted in pain, closing her eyes briefly, then flashing them open again to try to assess the situation. She'd been kidnapped by vampires, then kidnapped from the kidnappers by a trio of death-wish-bearing mortals in the most boring cheap suits she'd ever seen. That much she knew.

She was in the bedroom of a hotel suite. She could tell by the predictable furniture and the fire escape plan tacked to the inside of the door. The windows were covered in black plastic. There were two beds, and someone lay in one of them, dead to the world, and covered in blankets and shadow, so the face was invisible to her. Vampire, she sensed, but one so drugged, so far from consciousness, that barely a vibe emanated from her. There were a television, desk and phone nearby. Through a doorway she could see a small sofa, and a pair of feet, shiny black shoes intact, resting on a glass-topped coffee table. She could hear newspaper pages being turned. And she could smell mortal blood.

She would be tasting it soon.

"Didn't they teach you in goon school that a vampire can snap handcuffs like tooth-picks?" she called.

The feet on the table moved, landed on the floor, and then a man came into view. One of the three who'd attacked them, drugged them and taken her captive. He stepped into the open doorway and stared at her. He had a face like chiseled granite, hard, and gray with the beginnings of a beard. Not a deliberate growth, just the suggestion that he hadn't shaved in a while. He had brush-cut dark gray hair with silver highlights. There were bags under his eyes.

"Not for a while, you can't," he told her. "The tranq takes time to wear off."

She sent him a look that should have wilted him like lettuce in the desert, then focused her mind and called out — but not to Jack. Never again would she call out to him. Not with her voice or her mind or, God forbid, her heart. Not in need, and never in passion. He'd betrayed her, betrayed them all.

Reaper. I've been abducted by what I think are CIA agents. I'm being held in a hotel suite, with one other vampire.

There was no reply. And the shouts of her mind felt muffled, as if contained within the echoing walls of a hollow cave.

Reaper!

"I know what you're doing."

"I couldn't care less what you know."

The man shrugged. "You're wasting your energy. First of all, you're still under the influence of the tranq. But even if you weren't, we've taken . . . precautions."

She narrowed her eyes. "Like the ones Gregor took? The way he made that house of his impervious to mental communication with anyone beyond its walls?"

"Where do you think he learned it?"

"You know you're going to die for this, right?"

He shrugged, came in farther, pulled up another chair and turned it backwards in front of hers. Then he sat down, straddling it.

"Where's Reaper?" he asked.

"Oh, here we go again. Where are your hot poker and bucket of coals? Huh? Where are your sharpened blades?"

He frowned, studying her for a moment. Then his brows rose. "You think I'm going to torture you?"

"Gregor did. Where would I think he learned it?"

The man sighed, shaking his head. "Gregor is out of control. We'll deal with him. What he did wasn't sanctioned."

"And what about Jack? Was everything *he* did 'sanctioned'?"

"Jack's become more liability than asset, I'm afraid."

"What the hell is that supposed to mean?"

He met her eyes, shook his head. "It's not anything you need to know about. All you need to know is that you're not going to be harmed. All we want is Reaper. And now that we have the two of you, we have every expectation that Jack will hand him over."

"Me and . . . who? That half-insane fledgling? What makes you think Jack would cross the street for either one of us?"

"He will."

"Dream on, Columbo."

He said nothing. Just studied her.

"Where are my friends? The ones you drugged back at that clinic from hell?"

"Still there, I imagine. Unless Reaper and Jack have found them by now. In which case Jack knows we have you, and we should be hearing from him soon." He looked at his watch. "Or not. It's getting close to dawn. Ah, well. Maybe tonight."

He got off the chair, standing up. "You sure you don't want to tell me where Reaper is? It would make things go a lot faster. You two could get out of here sooner."

"I've got nothing pressing, pal. You're the one on borrowed time here, not me."

He shrugged. "If you say so." Then he turned to go. But as he reached the doorway, he turned and glanced at the vampire who lay in the bed. "By the way, that's not the half-insane fledgling in the bed over there. We left *her* behind, too."

Topaz frowned. "Well then, who is it?"

He nodded toward the bed. "You can thank me later," he said. "After all, you've been waiting a long time for this." He stepped out of the bedroom and closed the door most of the way, leaving it open just enough for him to keep an eye on her.

Topaz's heart seemed to clench in her chest as she stared at the blanket-draped form in the bed. She began moving, chair and all, hitching it across the carpet in fits and starts, moving it to the side of the bed, then scooting it bit by bit, higher, toward the pillows. She saw her captor look in at her, then shrug and walk away.

And then she was staring at the face of the most beautiful woman who'd ever lived, and choking on tears as she whispered, "Mother?"

There was no answer.

For a long while Topaz sat beside the bed, staring down at the woman who lay there, unconscious. There was no mistaking the face that had been one of the most beloved ever to grace the silver screen. The face that had been on billboards and in tabloids the world over. The face of Mirabella DuFrane. Simply Mirabella to most. The way Elvis was just Elvis, Cher was just Cher, and Madonna . . .

To Topaz, though, she was more. To her, she was Mother.

The sculpted, delicate jaw, the high, accentuated cheekbones, the milky white skin. It was more porcelain now than bronze, as it had been in life. And more beautiful. Her mink-brown hair was held by a white headband that couldn't quite keep the careless curls from falling in soft waves around her face. Here and there it gleamed with deep shades of auburn. All natural, her hair had never been chemically touched. It was more like an elaborate headpiece made of satin ribbons than ordinary hair.

Topaz stared at her, and her entire body filled with emotion. It choked her so that she couldn't speak, held her so that she couldn't move, leaked out only through her eyes in the form of tears she'd been waiting far too long to shed. And those fell slowly, uncertainly, still hesitant. They rolled down her cheeks one by one, burning all the way.

"Mother," she whispered again. Mirabella had abandoned her before she'd even been old enough to have uttered her first "mama," so Topaz had grown up thinking of the glamorous starlet whose photographs littered her memory, and whose films filled a shelf in her mansion, formally, as "Mother."

Yet looking at her now, it was difficult to think of her that way. She didn't appear any older than Topaz herself. Might even have been younger. Vampires didn't age once they were transformed. Topaz tried to count backwards, but the logical part of her mind wasn't functioning. Mirabella had been, she thought, twenty-seven when she'd been killed. Only, she hadn't been killed at all. She'd been made over, given the dark gift. By whom? Topaz wondered. And why?

Topaz had been twenty-five when she'd been turned, and she had been a vampiress for a decade now. So yes, technically, her mother was older. Two years older, by mortal calculations. And even after ten years undead, that fact seemed surreal to Topaz. It made her slightly queasy, slightly dizzy, because it flew in the face of the reality she had spent most of her life knowing.

There was no such thing as knowing, though. There was only believing. Convincing yourself of a fact because you believed it so strongly. Seeing it contradicted after that was like looking at the impossible. But there was no such thing as impossible, either, was there? There was only belief.

For so many years she'd believed her mother was dead, but now, here she was, undead and well, though drugged at the moment.

Emotion rose in her, and she pulled at the handcuffs until the chain snapped in two. Then she rose from the chair and moved closer to the bed. Battling tears, Topaz reached out a hand that trembled and let it hover for a moment above her mother's smooth cheek. She almost couldn't bring herself to touch the sleeping beauty. Almost couldn't bear to feel the proof that this was no illusion, no dream, but real.

And then she did. She lowered her hand, her jaw and spine so stiff they should have cracked. Her fingertips touched her mother's smooth, cool skin, then gently pushed back a long lock of wavy hair that felt like satin.

Thick-lashed eyes twitched, muscles tightening, then relaxing, and then her lashes fluttered a few times.

Topaz sucked in a breath and jerked her hand away in response. She sat back, her gaze riveted to the woman's face, as slowly, slowly, Mirabella's eyes came open. She blinked a few times, seeming to bring her vision into focus with an effort. One elegant hand rose unsteadily to the side of her head. And then her brows drew together, and she closed her eyes again.

"I've had this dream before."

"Vampires don't dream," Topaz whispered.

"Untrue. I dream. Only during those brief twilight moments just before the day sleep takes me, or just as I'm waking at sunset, but I dream."

"Of me?" Topaz asked.

"Who else?"

Topaz sighed. "Do you even know who I am?"

The woman's eyes came open again. She studied Topaz, perhaps beginning to realize that this was no dream. "I've always known. I've watched over you for your entire life, Tanya."

"Then you know how miserable I was. How unhappy. How utterly unloved."

Mirabella pressed her palms to the mattress on either side of her and pushed herself up into a sitting position. "I know. I'm sorry."

"I needed you. You abandoned me." Topaz

turned away from the bed and paced the room, unable to look at her mother as she asked the question, then awaited the answer she'd been seeking for so long. "Why?"

"Not by choice, my child. I swear that to you."

Topaz didn't turn to look back at her mother. Quietly, with a voice gone cold, she asked again, "Why?"

Mirabella sighed. Topaz heard the movements of her body on the mattress as she slid around and got to her feet. She moved closer, coming up behind Topaz, lowering a hand to her shoulder. "I was having an affair with a married man."

"Wayne Duncan?" Topaz asked.

"Yes. His wife . . . Lucia . . . she tried to kill me. Did kill me, for all intents and purposes. There was no way I could have survived the gunshot wounds she inflicted that night."

"And yet, you didn't die?" Topaz asked.

"No. I didn't die. I had a friend, a vampiress. Her name is Sarafina. She is an ancestor of ours. Call her an aunt, it's as close as you'll ever come. She was there when it happened. And she managed to get to me in the hospital before I expired, and that's where she did it."

Topaz said nothing.

"It's what happened," her mother said. "Why do I get the feeling you don't believe me?"

"Because I have your letter. And I've talked to your manager, Rebecca Murphy. You were planning this. Oh, Rebecca thought you were going to commit suicide. She believes the shooter was a hit man you hired to do the job for you. But your letter to me is all the proof I need. You planned this. To fake your own death and leave your infant daughter behind as if she'd never even existed."

Mirabella sighed, lowered her head, and turned away. And that, more than anything, gave Topaz the strength to turn around and face her again, even though she was only facing her mother's back. Then Mirabella turned again, as well, and met Topaz's eyes.

"It's true, Sarafina and I were planning it. But before we could carry out our plan, that bitch shot me. It was too late then."

"And I was on my own. You might as well have tossed me into shark-filled waters and left me to sink, swim or be devoured, Mother. It amounted to the same thing."

"I was going to make better arrangements for you. I didn't want you raised by uncaring, money-hungry —"

"Then why the hell didn't you?" Topaz

shouted, not caring that the man in the next room was bound to hear. Her voice had taken on a gravelly quality, and the tears were choking her now. "Why did you leave me alone? You could have taken me with you! There had to be a way!"

"Oh, baby . . ."

Mirabella moved closer, reaching out to touch Topaz's face, but Topaz jerked away before she could make contact. "No. Don't. Don't play the caring mother now, not after all this."

Mirabella froze with her hand in midair and blinked rapidly, as if she, too, were close to tears. "You've become hard, Tanya. Cold."

"You made sure I would. You left me not knowing who my father was. You left the courts in charge of deciding who would raise me. You left me in the care of a man who never wanted anything other than my money."

"I know. I know, baby."

"You didn't love me enough to stay, he didn't love me at all, and then I fell in love with a man I thought did. I really believed he loved me. But it turned out he was only using me, too."

"Jack," her mother whispered. "I know. I'm so sorry."

Topaz's head came up swiftly. "How do you know his name?"

"I told you, I've been watching over you. And I know how deeply he hurt you, and I'm sorry."

Topaz's heart ached in her chest at the very mention of Jack's name. "The stupidest thing of all is that I let him. I mean, just the fact that he refused to tell me he loved me for so long should have been enough to warn me off. But it wasn't. I held on, tried to make myself believe. And then, when he came back for more, I bought into it all over again."

"And for good reason," her mother said.

"No. It turns out he's been using me all over again. Working for these CIA idiots, planning to turn in one of my best friends, all for money. At least it's not my money this time, but I was a means to an end for him. Just as I've always been."

Her mother was silent. Appearing to be deep in thought.

"What?" Topaz asked.

"I just . . . I don't believe that. I've seen him — from a distance, of course — but I've seen him. Seen the way he looks at you."

"Yeah, well, he's the greatest actor since Olivier. But believe me, that's all it was. An act. Hell, he's the reason we're here with these assholes."

Her mother frowned, and shot a quick look toward the nearly-closed bedroom door. "Where are we, exactly?"

"What do you remember?" Topaz asked her.

Mirabella pressed a hand to her head. It was a perfect hand. Smooth, silky. Manicured nails, though the polish was chipped. "Not much. I was in my house, and I heard something, so I went to the window to look. And then the window smashed inward, and there was something stabbing me in the stomach. I thought I'd been shot."

"Tranquilizer dart," Topaz guessed.

"Yes. I looked down and saw this thing sticking into me, and there was blood around it, staining my dress." She looked down as she said it. The dress was a summery halter dress, floor-length, white, with a pattern of big green loops, reminiscent of the seventies. She had that white band around her hair, and white shoes that looked impossibly high, and yet she walked without a wobble.

Mirabella touched the single red stain in the front of her dress, confirming her own memory. Then she lifted her gaze and met Topaz's eyes again. "I passed out, I think. I don't remember anything else until I opened my eyes just now and saw you sitting beside my bed, and thought it was a dream." She searched Topaz's face. "Tanya, what's going on?"

Topaz sighed. There was so much she wanted to say to her mother. So many things she wanted to ask her. But mostly, she wanted the starlet to convince her that she really had loved her daughter. That she really had been given no choice but to leave her behind. She wanted to be convinced.

But she wasn't. Not even a little bit. Her mother was just the first in a long line of people who were *supposed* to love her but had fallen far short. The first in a long line of those who had put their own needs ahead of hers, only to walk away when she needed them most.

Her mother had set the pattern that her entire life had followed. And Topaz wanted to hate her for it. Instead, she hated herself for being unable to.

She decided to let all that rest for now. Her mother was right. The focus now had to be on their situation and on their options.

"I've become good friends with a vampire named Reaper."

Her mother nodded. "I know. I was very worried about it, at first, but I —"

"You know about Reaper?" Topaz interrupted, staring at her mother with a frown.

"I told you, love, I've kept careful track of your life. Always. *Always,* Tanya."

"It's Topaz now."

"It's Tanya to me and always will be."

Topaz sniffed skeptically but went on with her story. "Reaper used to work for the CIA. They did some stuff to him. Brainwashed him. And now they can control him with nothing more than a couple of trigger words."

"Control him? In what way?"

Topaz drew a breath and decided to tell her the truth. After all, Mirabella's life was on the line now. She deserved to know why. Well, maybe "deserved" was too strong a word. She likely *deserved* to be drawn and quartered for abandoning her baby to the wolves the way she had. But she at least had a right to know.

"Reaper was an assassin for the CIA. Now he does the same job for the undead, taking out rogues when the need arises. The CIA wants him back. When they use his first trigger word, he becomes enraged, mindlessly violent. He'll destroy anyone in his path until and unless the second word is uttered. And we don't know what that second word is."

Her mother's eyes grew wider as she listened.

"The CIA wants him back in their control. A vampire hit man, one entirely under their power, is too valuable a prize not to try to reclaim." Topaz met her mother's eyes squarely. "They plan to use us to get him."

"Jack will bring him in to save your life," her mother guessed.

"Jack wouldn't cross the street to save my life." Topaz wondered why those words rang so false to her, even as she uttered them. And yet, she told herself, they were true. "But Reaper would. He'll hand himself over to them for our sakes." She put a hand on her mother's arm. "We can't let that happen."

Her mother met her eyes, so much emotion swirling in her own that Topaz couldn't begin to interpret her feelings. "Then we won't," she said. "But we're going to have to work together to get through this, Tanya. We're going to have to trust each other."

Topaz stared at her and thought that trusting the woman who'd abandoned her was going to be a hurdle. But she would try.

14

Briar hit him.

Jack hadn't been expecting it, hadn't been ready for it, and didn't even sense it coming. But when it did, he sure as hell knew it. She delivered a powerful uppercut to his jaw that snapped his head back, lifted him off the floor and sent him down again flat on his back. It hurt like hell, and surprised him even more than it hurt him.

He sat up slowly, shaking the stars from his eyes and glancing up to ask her just what the hell her problem was, but the words died on his lips when he saw the way she was struggling to get free of Reaper, who stood behind her with a solid grip around her waist.

"Dammit, let go of me!" she shouted.

Reaper stood calmly and showed no intention of complying with her demand. "You don't know the whole story."

"I know all I need to know. That asshole's

been ratting us out to the feds this whole time."

"Ratting *me* out, Briar. And while I appreciate you getting this angry on my behalf — even while I fail to understand it — it's not necessary. I promise you that."

She calmed marginally. "On your behalf, my ass. I was on the run with you, don't forget. Dodging spooks, seeing them show up almost before we caught a minute's rest anywhere we went. Your behalf? Shit. I don't act on anyone's behalf but my own."

"I've known what Jack was doing the entire time," Reaper said.

Briar went stone silent and stopped struggling. Reaper loosened his grip on her, and she turned to face him, her eyes widening. Jack pushed himself slowly up off the floor, sensing it was safe now. Behind him, Seth and Vixen were coming slowly forward, both of them looking every bit as stunned as Briar apparently was by Reaper's unanticipated revelation.

"At first I thought Jack was putting me at risk by keeping the agents informed of my whereabouts in exchange for money. I later realized he was giving them information, but he was giving it to them late. Keeping them a step or two behind me." He glanced at Briar. "Us," he corrected. "Still later I learned he wasn't doing it for money at all, but in exchange for information that might help him track down Topaz's mother. It was a closely guarded secret, what really became of her."

"I thought they found that out on their own," Vixen said. "When Topaz got that letter her mother left for her and compared it with the one her creator wrote."

Roxy gathered Crisa off the bed. "Argue amongst yourselves. I'm taking this one to the van. We need to get her somewhere safe, feed her something, or she's not going to make it." She carried Crisa out of the room, Ilyana rushing ahead of her to open the door.

Jack was straightening now, brushing off the back of his jeans. "Unfortunately," he said, "these agents are as good at running a game as I am. Maybe better. They gave me information damn near as useless as what I'd been feeding them. Until we got here, at least. Once they knew we'd learned the truth about Mirabella on our own, they threatened to harm her unless I drugged Reaper and turned him over to them."

Reaper nodded. "And he told me all about it," he said to the others. "Jack hasn't done anything behind my back. Well, at first, but even then, no harm was intended."

"Unfortunately, good intentions or not," Seth snapped, "those bastards have Topaz *and* Mirabella now."

"So what the hell do we do now?" Briar asked.

Seth sighed heavily, still battling the slowly fading effects of the drug. "You guys keeping shit from the rest of us is totally responsible for all of this. You both realize that, right?" He was shifting his angry gaze from Jack to Reaper and back again. "The only thing we can do now is find out where these agents are holding Topaz and Mirabella, bust in, kick ass and rescue them."

"Won't work. They know how to secure a house and block mental communication, just like Gregor did." Jack stood with his head lowered, his stomach in knots. The thought of Topaz in danger . . . the fear of the thoughts that might be running through her head right now. What she might be thinking. What those agents might have told her. She undoubtedly believed the same thing Briar had. What must she be going through right now?

Dammit, he should have told her the truth.

"Then what the hell do you suggest we do?" Seth barked.

A familiar "owwwwuuugaaa" sounded

from outside. Shirley's distinctive horn. "I suggest," Jack said, "that you all go out and take care of Crisa, and leave me to take care of the problem my actions created."

"It's not your problem, Jack." Reaper met his eyes. "I'm the one they're after. I'm the one who let all of you hook up with me, putting every one of you at risk."

"And I'm the one who chose to deal with the devil to get what I wanted," Jack said.

Reaper sighed. "Let's get out to the cars. We'll head back to the cabins, take care of Crisa, and try to figure a way out of this mess."

As they retraced their steps out through the front hall, Jack noticed a cell phone sitting suspiciously in plain sight on the floor just to the right of the door. Something told him it wasn't there by accident, so he picked it up and slipped it in his pocket, wondering just when and how this particular chicken was going to come home to roost.

Crisa was, Briar thought as she opened the van's sliding door and climbed in, *exactly* what this band of misfits needed. Something about her wasn't right. And not in the same fish-out-of-water way Vixen had been a little off. This one was mental.

Crisa lay across the rear seat, eyes closed, shivering visibly. Ilyana, the unreadable skinny blonde, knelt on the floor, holding her hands, palms down, on either side of the wound in Crisa's arm, head bowed, eyes closed. Roxy was behind the wheel, and the engine was running.

Briar took everything in with one swift gaze, then went to the middle seat and sat down sideways, arm resting on the seat's back, eyes focused on the nut job, though her words were for the blonde. "You get the bleeding stopped?"

Without looking up, Ilyana said, "Between the patch-up job, Roxy's witchcraft and my Reiki healing, we've got it mostly stanched. But not completely."

"She's not gonna make it without blood," Roxy said. "And I'm not convinced that cold mortal shit in the plastic bags is going to be potent enough to save her."

Briar looked forward at the image of Roxy's eyes in the rearview mirror, and Roxy looked back at her, even though she couldn't possibly see her, since Briar cast no reflection.

Still, the look Roxy sent her told her *exactly* what she was suggesting.

Briar glanced out the van's windows, only to see Seth and Vixen pulling away in the

Mustang, following Jack and Reaper in the Carrera. She should never have surrendered the Mustang to Seth, and agreed to ride back in the van with the damned mortals and the wounded loon. But it was too late now. They were in a mad fucking rush to get back to their base — and if there was a more unlikely headquarters for a band of night walkers than a pair of beachfront cottages, she couldn't think of one — none of them aware the little nut wasn't going to last long enough to get there.

Briar didn't doubt Roxy's intuition on that score.

She focused on Reaper as the van bounded along the barely paved road. *Roxy says the whack job isn't going to make it back without a shot of vampire blood, pal. You'd best pull over and switch vehicles.*

His reply was quick and firm. *Why would I waste time on that when you're right there with her already?*

Because I'm not doing it.

There was a pause. Then, *We have to get to shelter before sunrise. We're already going to have to do eighty or better all the way to make it. No. We can't stop. You'll have to take care of it.*

I'm not fucking doing it.

She felt his frustration. *Then she's going*

315

to die. Your call, Briar.

Briar stared at the screwed-up woman on the backseat. And even as she did, the girl's eyes opened and met hers head-on. They were unfocused and rather dopey, although Briar suspected that their usual state wasn't much different.

"Is Rey-Rey in one of the other cars?" Crisa asked in that childlike way she had that set Briar's teeth on edge.

"Would he be the skinny one who was with you at that hospital from hell?"

Crisa nodded, eyes drooping, then widening again. "I don't know why I feel so cold. I never feel cold."

"You never feel cold because you're a vampire," Briar told her. "We don't feel it the way mortals do. Didn't your precious Rey-Rey ever explain that to you?"

She shook her head. "So why do I feel it now?"

"Because you're dying."

Ilyana gasped and sent Briar a look. Briar ignored it, got up, moved into the rear of the van and nudged Ilyana. "Give me some space, okay?"

Ilyana didn't need to be asked twice. She was still petrified of Briar. As well she should be, Briar thought, since she would just as soon eat the other woman as

316

look at her.

Briar knelt on the floor beside Crisa. "Your friend Rey-Rey is already dead. If you'd prefer to go with him, I totally get it. Been close to suicide myself a few times, and I'll tell you right now, my only regret is that I didn't do it. Life stinks on ice, as far as I can see, and I'll probably off myself sooner or later. Would have by now, I imagine, except I'm kind of curious to see how this mess turns out. So if you wanna die, I'll let you. Go with my blessings. But if you don't, I can take care of that, too. It's really no skin off my nose either way. Totally your call. So what do you say?"

Tears had been pooling in the dying woman's eyes ever since the first sentence of Briar's little diatribe, and now they spilled over, running down her cheeks and sinking into the cloth seat, making dark blotches in the fabric.

"Rey-Rey is dead?" she rasped.

"Yeah. Sorry, kid. It's a tough break."

"B-but he's a *v-vampire.*"

"And vampires can die. Though I don't imagine he explained that to you either, did he? Yeah, we can die. Just like you're going to in another couple of minutes."

"He took care of me." A full-body shudder worked through her. Or maybe it was some kind of spasm. One of those death throes you heard about, Briar thought. Crisa jerked all over, and then she stopped, her body limp, her eyes closed.

For a second Briar thought she was dead.

But then the girl pried those crazy eyes of hers open a little bit and said, "I'm too young to die."

"I was afraid you'd say something like that." Briar shook her head, but at the same time she rolled back her sleeve. She tripped the trigger in her ring that made the tiny blade flash out of its center and jabbed it into her left wrist. Then she held the cut to Crisa's lips. "Drink, then."

Jack answered the cell phone on the first ring, even though he was driving. He'd told Reaper about finding the phone, and they'd both been expecting the call. He didn't say "Hello." He didn't say his name. He said only, "If you hurt her, you'll die. If you even raise your voice in her general direction, you'll die. And it'll be slow."

"Wow," the man on the other end said. "So it's safe to say she's mistaken in her assumption that you wouldn't — how did she put that again? Oh, yeah, 'cross the street to save her life.' "

"Why would she think that?"

"Probably hit her around the same time she learned you've been working for us."

"You bastards."

"Hell, Jack, it's not our job to fix your love life. You can take care of that yourself as soon as you get her back. Then you can start worrying about mother-in-law problems, just like the rest of us."

Jack met Reaper's eyes, took the phone away from his ear long enough to hit the speaker button, then laid it on the seat between them. He was fairly certain Reaper could have overheard the conversation anyway, but he did it as a gesture. He needed Reaper to know that he'd told him the truth. "You've got me over a barrel, Magnarelli. Just tell me how you want to do this."

"I'll tell you *exactly* how I want to do it. And you're going to do it that way. No changes. No adlibbing. No deals. This is a take-it-or-leave-it offer, Jack. You say yes to every term, or they both die. All right?"

"Depends on what you have to say."

"I want Rivera. I want him delivered in broad daylight."

"And just how the hell do you suggest I do that without both of us becoming toast?"

"Tranq him before sunrise. Stuff him in a body bag — I've left one for you in a strategic location. It's sun-proof."

"Can you guarantee that?"

"It's been tested."

Jack felt a chill go up his spine. "How many body bags failed the test before you found one that passed?"

"Sixteen. And yes, we used live subjects. You have a problem with that, Jack?"

Jack didn't bother to answer. His gut was churning as he glanced at Reaper and saw a similar reaction. Raw fury.

"So I drug him, put him into a body bag, and . . . ?"

"And leave him where I tell you. I have a nice spot in the desert picked out. Once the sun comes up, so I know he can't go off on me or try anything, and the rest of you can't ambush me, I'll pick him up. You'll find your women waiting in the same spot, in the same type of bag. You leave him and take them, and we're done. By the time your so-called Reaper wakes up, he'll be in CIA custody."

"You've really covered every base, haven't you?"

"I like to think so. So that's how it's going to be. Naturally, there's not enough time tonight for you to retrieve the body bag, drug Rivera and drop him in the desert, and it'll take a solid hour to get out there. The sun will be up in fifteen minutes. But I'll tell you what. I'll keep your women safe and comfy with me while they lie around completely oblivious and utterly defenseless all day. And I'll call you right after sundown, and let you know where to find the body bag and where to leave Rivera. How's that sound?"

"If you touch them while they sleep, they *will* wake, Magnarelli. And they will wake in a rage that makes the one you people managed to plant in Reaper's mind look like a child's game."

"That's the first time I've heard *that* bit of vampire trivia. Are you sure you're not just making it up, Jack?"

"Are you sure I *am?* Go ahead. Risk it. If I don't hear from you tomorrow night, I'll know you're dead. Drained to a lifeless husk and left to rot somewhere. It's no less than you deserve."

Jack felt the fear rippling from the other man. Not a lot of it, and not for more than an instant. But it had been there, and it had been real. Jack met Reaper's eyes and saw him nod in silent approval of the blatant lie.

"I'll call you after sundown tomorrow," the CIA man snapped. "Be near the phone." And then he was gone.

■ ■ ■ ■

Topaz and her mother sat staring at one another. They'd taken stock of the entire room. They'd sized up the men in the next room and decided they could take them, if they rushed them. But they were exceedingly low on time — sunrise was right around the corner. They might not have time to find shelter elsewhere, safe from any other agents who came calling, and even if they did, it would be so close at hand that they would probably be found in short order.

So for today, they would sleep here in the care of the CIA, not so much because they trusted these liars to keep them safe — they would be stupid to do that — but because they both realized that they had no viable choice but to stay and take their chances.

But at sundown? At sundown they would make their move.

They'd had their entire conversation mentally, without the men in the next room being any the wiser.

And then one of them entered. The blue-eyed one who'd carried Topaz after she'd been darted. "About time you two turned in," he said. "Sunup in five."

"Your concern is touching," Mirabella said.

"I'm going to rip out your jugular at sunset, you know," Topaz told him. "I tend to wake up ravenous and slightly cranky."

He blinked. Of the three, he seemed the only one with at least some semblance of a heart beating in his chest. The others were far less human. But she hated them all.

"You'll be happy to know that Jack has agreed to do as he's been told. You'll only have to be with us one more night."

"Why one more night? Why not make the exchange right after sundown, when we rise?"

"I'm not at liberty to discuss that with you. I just thought you'd want to know. Is there anything you need before you . . . er . . . retire?" He glanced beyond her, and Topaz knew it was because he couldn't look her in the eye, even though he made it seem as if he were checking the room for anything that might be lacking.

"Your heart on a plate, with ketchup," Topaz said.

He shot her a look. "I'm being as nice as I can here."

"Yeah, I just love kidnappers with manners," she said.

He backed out of the room. "Good night."

323

Then he closed the doors. She heard the lock turn, and she called, "If you think that mortal lock could keep us in here against our will, my friend, you are sadly mistaken. When we're ready to leave here, believe me, we'll —"

Tanya, stop!

The harsh tone of her mother's thoughts stunned her. And wounded her, too, though she told herself that was utterly stupid.

There's no point in giving away everything we've got. If they don't know we can beat that lock, for example, why tip them off? We could easily wake up to a new lock, one we can't break.

Hell, Topaz thought back at her. *It's a miracle I ever survived without you, isn't it? These guys are experts on our kind. I'm not telling them anything they don't already know. Though I do appreciate the motherly advice.*

Sarcasm isn't an attractive quality, Tanya.

It's Topaz. And I'll be as sarcastic as I want. You think I've been searching all over the country for you just so you could start mothering me now? Keep it, Mirabella. I don't fucking want it.

Her mother's face was stricken. She went to the bed where she'd slept earlier and sank onto it, her back to Topaz. "I'm sorry, you know. I'm sorry. I know it doesn't change how you feel, but it's true, and I'll keep saying it until you believe me. If I had thought I had any other choice, I would have taken it. I swear it on my soul."

"Even if you had no choice when it . . . happened, *Mother,* even if you couldn't see yourself raising a mortal child, there have been a lot of years in between. You could have contacted me once I was an adult. And you *certainly* could have stuck around and told me the truth the night you changed me over. You can make up all the reasons you want to for abandoning me as an infant, but there just aren't any excuses that explain why you did it all over again the night I was reborn as a vampire."

Mirabella was silent as she pulled back her covers and stripped off the gown she wore, revealing the black lacy slip beneath it. Then she lay down in the bed.

Topaz stripped off her jeans, removed her bra from beneath her shirt without taking the shirt off, and then she crawled into the other bed.

The sun was rising. Topaz felt it, the weight of it, the tug of sleep — of death, really — pulling at her.

"You're right," her mother said at last. "There is no excuse. I was ashamed. I was afraid to face you. I was afraid of the very condemnation you've now delivered. I didn't want to feel your anger, much less your hatred. But I'm sorry, Topaz. I'm so sorry."

I never hated you, Topaz thought, even as she drifted into sleep. *And it's Tanya.*

"I have an idea. A germ of an idea," Reaper said as Jack drove. And then he focused his mind, leaving it open to Jack's, to keep him in the loop.

Rhiannon. Can you hear me? Rhiannon. It's Reaper, and it's urgent.

Moments ticked past. Moments during which Jack was unsure Reaper would receive an answer. "Where is this Rhiannon you're trying to reach?" he asked.

"In the States. I'm not sure exactly where."

Jack gaped at him, then clamped his jaw closed when he realized what he was doing. "Surely even your mind isn't powerful enough to reach that far," he said.

"She's my maker. And one of the most powerful vampires alive. She'll hear me."

And she did, Jack realized with awe when she finally replied.

For the love of the gods, darling, if I wanted to be bothered, I would have called you. What is it?

Reaper smiled, something Jack had seen rarely enough to notice it with a touch of surprise. *Your friend Eric Marquand, the vampire scientist . . .*

Yes, yes, my dear Roland's best friend. What about him?

I heard a rumor that he created a formula several years back that would allow a vampire to remain awake by day. Is it true?

Jack snapped to attention, surprise echoing in his mind. Not only had he never heard of such a formula, he could feel the vampiress's reaction, and it wasn't a good one.

It's true. But Roland nearly killed me when he tried it. It makes us violent, Reaper. It's dangerously flawed.

That's a chance I'm going to have to take. Can you get it for me — and get it to me — before tomorrow night is out?

Why? Why would you need something so volatile?

Lives are at risk. I can't go into detail, though I'll tell you the rest when I see you. Trust me when I tell you it's vital. Can you do this for me?

I can.

In time?

I have a private jet.

Will you?

There was a pause, and then, finally, *Yes. I will. Tell me where you are.*

By the time they arrived back at the bungalows, Reaper and Jack had a plan worked out. They still hadn't agreed on which of them was going to be taking up space in that body bag twenty-four hours from now, but Jack thought he would win that argument in the end.

It wasn't foolproof, their plan. It was going to take the help of every last member of their gang. Even the mortal ones. But it could work.

Hell, it *had to* work. Jack had no intention of letting Topaz die thinking he had played her yet again. It was killing him to know she thought it now, even for a little while. He had to get to her. He had to tell her the truth. And then it occurred to him that he might die himself before he got the chance. This plan was risky at best. Suicidal at worst.

He put a hand on Reaper's arm as he pulled into the driveway that led to the beach houses.

Reaper looked at him.

"If anything happens to me . . ." Jack began.

"I'll tell her the truth," Reaper said. "Just

like I told the rest of them. She'll know you weren't running a con this time, Jack. You have my word on that."

"She has to know something else, too," Jack said. "That I . . . that I . . ." He closed his mouth, unable to say the words that had always come so hard to him. "Just tell her it was real this time."

"Hell, Jack, are you just figuring that out? Roxy's known it from the day she met you."

Jack shot him a surprised look as he braked to a stop and cut the engine. Reaper only smiled at him, and then they jumped from their vehicle, just as Vixen and Seth got out of the Mustang. The four stood watching as Roxy's van bounded along the driveway and came to a stop in front of the first little beach house.

She opened the driver's door, got out and blinked at the eastern sky. "It's starting to pale. Come on, get inside, all of you. Hurry."

The van's side door slid open, and Briar stepped down, carrying Crisa in her arms. Reaper rushed toward her. "I'll take her," he said, reaching for the wounded girl.

But as Reaper tried to take her away, Crisa's arms snapped around Briar's neck, and she buried her face there, clinging.

Briar rolled her eyes, then met his. "Great. Now she thinks I'm her mommy. I hate you for making me do this, Reaper." Then she carried Crisa up the front steps and into the bungalow.

15

The jet landed on one side of the border, while Reaper waited on the other. Before he knew what she intended, Rhiannon had raced toward him, her powerful body moving far too fast to be visible to the human eye, even if anyone had been looking. For the most part, the border patrol were more concerned about keeping people from coming into the U.S. than they were about keeping them from leaving it. Still, the jet might have drawn some attention, Jack thought worriedly.

Too late to worry about that. The jet she'd left behind was taxiing across the expanse of naked desert and taking off again seconds after she'd debarked.

And then she was standing in front of him.

"Rhiannon," he began, a warning note in his tone. "Why did you send the plane away without you?"

"Oh, please," she said. "Don't waste time

on worn-out arguments, Reaper. I'm here, I'm your maker, and I'm staying. So shut the hell up and let's get on with this."

He held her gaze for one long moment, then sighed. "All right."

"Glad to see you can be sensible."

He thought about Briar. About Rhiannon meeting Briar. Rhiannon *hating* Briar. Rhiannon and Briar ripping each other's hair out.

Hell, this mission had better go off as planned, not to mention as fast as humanly possible.

Topaz woke quickly and completely. One instant she was in the depths of her death-like slumber, and the next, her eyes and her senses were wide open, scanning. She sat upright in the bed and virtually sniffed the air for signs the room had been entered while they'd been asleep, but she saw none. More importantly she *felt* none. Her bed was exactly as it been when she'd fallen asleep. The door was still closed. She didn't feel as if she'd been touched while she'd rested, and she thought that if she had been, she would know it.

With a sigh of relief, she let the tension ease from her body and turned to see her mother coming awake more slowly. Mirabella woke like a cat, gradually, eyes opening a bit at a time, then closing again, as if sleep were too blissful to leave behind just yet. Then they opened again, a little wider this time, and finally she stretched her arms above her, arched her back and tipped up her chin. Then she rolled onto her side, facing Topaz with a bright smile. "Good morning."

"It's evening."

"Then . . . *good evening.*" She said it the way Bela Lugosi would have said it, her accent ridiculously overblown.

Topaz fought back a smile and kept her expression serious. "This is no time for joking around, Mother. Our lives are on the line here."

"What better time will there be, then?"

"We have to get out of here before Reaper gets himself killed trying to rescue us."

Mirabella's cheerful expression faded. "Are you so sure it won't be Jack doing that?"

Topaz averted her eyes. "I believed in him once, and he betrayed me and broke my heart. I was stupid enough to give him another chance, and he did it all over again. There's no way I'll ever trust him again."

"Or me, either, I imagine," Mirabella said softly. "And for exactly the same reasons. I walked away from you . . . not once, but twice. And it doesn't matter that I've regretted it ever since, does it, Tanya?"

Topaz didn't answer.

"Jack might be having regrets of his own by now. I mean, he *must* be. He must have felt something for you. You're too intelligent and too perceptive and far too wary to be completely fooled, even by him."

"I believed what I wanted to believe. I fooled myself far more than he ever could have."

"So it's yourself you don't trust?"

"I don't trust anyone. Myself included."

Mirabella nodded slowly. "You know, even in baseball, you get three strikes."

"This is life, not baseball," Topaz said, turning her back on her mother and everything she was saying.

"And what if you're wrong?" Mirabella asked. "You said you don't trust yourself, that you fooled yourself into believing something. But what if you're wrong about being wrong? What if you're judging him, judging *me,* according to how you *think* we feel, how we made *you* feel, without even knowing how either of us truly feels? You're judging us by the mistakes we've made in the past, without caring how different we might be in the present. If you'd give us a chance, Tanya, you might find out that you're completely wrong. You're so convinced that no one will ever love you that you wouldn't see it if it were staring you right in the face. You can't even see that you've been loved all along. By me, at least. And maybe by Jack, as well."

Topaz still had her face averted. She had to keep it that way, because her eyes were wet, and that was something she didn't want her mother to see. In a tight voice, she said, "Please don't try to make me start hoping for that. It only leads to heartbreak — every single time."

"Why did you spend so much effort searching for me, Tanya?" her mother asked. "Was it only to condemn me for my actions, show me your anger, vent it a little and then walk away?"

Topaz blinked her eyes dry and faced her mother. "I honestly don't know. I think I just wanted to ask you why you walked away."

"The first time, necessity. The second time, shame. And I'm sorry, but those are the only answers I have to give."

"They're not good enough." Topaz paced the room. "Let's get on with this."

"All right." Her mother got out of bed finally, and pulled on the white-and-green halter dress she'd been wearing the night before. "I wish we had time for a shower."

"If we hang around too long, they're liable to decide to drug us again. Besides, I wouldn't trust those three enough to shower here." Topaz put on her shoes as she said it.

Her mother shrugged. "They couldn't do more than peek, and that wouldn't kill us."

"Neither will skipping a shower. Come on."

Sighing, Mirabella slipped on her shoes. High heels, open toes, spotlessly white. She came to stand beside Topaz, right at the bedroom's closed door.

"I'll see where they are first," Topaz said. "Then we'll rush them, no holds barred. We can move faster than they can see us coming."

"It's as good a plan as any," her mother said.

They stood, silent and ready, on either side of the door. Topaz reached for the handle, gripped it — and then went rigid as a bolt of electricity hammered through her body. The blow was like a wrecking ball to the chest, and it sent her flying backward. She hit the foot of a bed and crumpled to the floor, shaking all over.

"Tanya!" Her mother was beside her instantly, kneeling on the floor, her hands cupping Topaz's head, her eyes searching and wide with fear. "What . . . ?"

Behind them, from beyond the closed double doors, a voice spoke, loudly enough for them to hear. "Sorry about the electricity, ladies. You try the window, you'll find the same precautions have been taken."

Topaz looked toward the window, and though her eyes were less than focused, she could see that the glass had been lined with a metallic screen from the inside. Had it been there all along, or had someone been inside this room last night after all?

"I'm afraid you're confined to your room for tonight," their captor said. "No point in fighting it."

Still lying limp and trembling on the floor, Topaz lifted her head slightly. "I'm *so* going to kill them," she whispered, her body still vibrating with the effects of the jolt it had taken. Her every muscle felt stretched and torn, and the pain of that was debilitating. Even so, she was absurdly glad she had been the one to grab the door handle, not her mother.

To her shock and surprise, her mother no longer looked worried or frightened. Her face now wore an expression of raw fury. She turned her head toward the door. "You will pay for that stunt, gentlemen. You will pay *dearly,* mark my words."

"Relax," the man said in reply. "It won't kill her. And don't try anything so foolish again. Any part of the door you touch is going to give you the same results. Bide your time, and by nightfall tomorrow you'll wake amongst your little gang again. All of them but one, that is."

Topaz released a pent-up breath, and it came out in stutters. "We can't let them take Reaper."

"I'm not sure what we can do to stop them. Not yet, anyway. You need to get your strength back first."

Topaz nodded and steadied herself. Her body was slowly relaxing, muscles uncoiling. "Sounds like we have all night. Somehow they've set the exchange to take place by day, though I can't imagine how."

Her mother slid her arms beneath Topaz and lifted her. She carried her to the bed and lowered her onto it. "Rest. Get your strength back. We'll deal with them once you've recovered."

"It's ridiculous to keep arguing about this," Jack said.

"I agree," Reaper replied. "So stop arguing. Rhiannon, give me the injection."

They were all gathered in the first of the

bungalows. Night had long since fallen, and the bastards' phone call had come right on schedule. Seth and Vixen had made the trip, to an abandoned gas station fifteen miles away, where they'd found the body bag waiting, as promised. With it came a note with further instructions.

Reaper was to be tranquilized before dawn and taken to a spot in the desert. Rather than written directions, Magnarelli had left a GPS device, pre-programmed to guide them from the site where the body bag had been to the place in the desert where they were supposed to leave Reaper. It had been rigged with a timer and wouldn't boot up until a couple of hours before dawn. Jack imagined that not knowing the exact location ahead of time was supposed to make it more difficult for them to set up some kind of an ambush. As if they could, by day. Magnarelli had specified the time they were to leave Reaper in the desert, promising dire repercussions to Topaz and Mirabella should they arrive one minute earlier. They would barely have time to reclaim the women and make it back to the bungalows before sunrise. Which was exactly what the bastard must have intended.

Rhiannon hadn't moved from her spot, resting queen-like in a rattan chair with a fan-shaped back, her legs crossed, one of them exposed by her skintight gown's extensive slit. She and the others had been listening to the two men argue for the better part of an hour now, and Rhiannon was growing visibly tired of it.

Now she uncrossed her legs and rose slowly. "I'm afraid that I have to agree with Jack on this, my friend," she said to Reaper.

He stared at her as if she'd sprouted horns.

"They can control you," she went on. "They can utter that trigger word and send you into a murderous rage, and you know it. Adding this drug of Eric's to that mix could be disastrous. You could kill us all, including the captives. And for all we know, that might very well be what these jackals intend."

Seth had been pacing, aggravated and intense. He stopped then, and faced Reaper. "Much as I hate to be on his side in anything, Reap, I agree with Jack, too. He made this mess, anyway, so he needs to clean it up. He should be the one in that body bag when they pick it up in the desert."

The others nodded. Even Roxy, to Jack's surprise. She nearly always took Reaper's side. But it seemed everyone agreed with him on this. All but Crisa, of course, who hovered very close to the chair where Briar sat, and offered no opinion one way or the other.

"And just what do you think is going to happen when they realize it's not me in that bag?" Reaper demanded. "What do you think they'll do when they find out they've been double-crossed?"

Briar said, "They want you alive. They won't unzip the bag in the desert in full daylight. You'd go up in flames. They'll have to get you back to shelter before they do that."

"And by then," Roxy added, "Ilyana and I will have Topaz and her mother safely out of their reach. It'll be too late for them to come to harm."

"But what about Jack?" Vixen asked.

Of them all, she was the only one who had taken the time to consider that, Jack thought. Besides him, at least.

"If this drug Rhiannon brought does what it's supposed to —" Jack began.

"It does," Rhiannon interrupted.

"Then I'll be fully conscious when they open that bag to check its contents. And I intend to come out swinging." He shrugged. "I'll kill all three of the bastards. The rest is simple. I find some shelter until dark, and then meet up with the rest of you."

"They'll have more than three agents,"

Reaper said. "You've only seen three, Jack, but don't underestimate these guys. They'll have backup, and they'll have tranq darts ready. And you'll be facing them alone." He shook his head. "I don't like this." He paced the floor. "No. No, I can't let you do it, Jack."

Jack stepped into his path and faced him squarely. "Do you not get that it *has* to be me?" He lowered his head, then searched for words. "Do you know what I've put her through? Do you have any idea how much pain I've caused her in the past — how much I'm still causing her, now that she believes it was all just another con, that I've played her all over again? It *has* to be *me*, Reaper. I'll either die in the effort or I won't, but either way, she'll know the truth. She won't be able to doubt it anymore. She won't have to spend the rest of her life believing that no one ever really . . ."

"Loved her," Roxy whispered, when Jack couldn't go on. She dropped her head and blinked her eyes, which had become suspiciously damp. Then she faced Reaper. "You have to let him do it, Raphael. It's not about danger, and it's not about whose fault this is. It's about love. And really, what else matters?"

"God, I think I'm gonna puke," Briar

muttered, and she shot Jack an accusing look, as if he'd somehow betrayed her.

Maybe he had, in a way. The two of them had been alike — both outcasts among this tightly woven group of friends. Both formerly on the wrong side in battle. Both swearing love was nothing but a lie, an illusion used to anesthetize the masses to the reality that life sucked.

He used to believe that. He didn't anymore.

"All right," Reaper said. "All right, we'll do this your way. But if you get your ass killed, Jack . . ."

"I'll do my best not to."

Reaper clapped him on the shoulder, then turned to Rhiannon. "Is it time, then?"

She glanced at the clock on the wall and nodded. "Yes. If we inject him now, the effect should last all day. Unless they tranquilize him."

"And what would happen then?" Jack asked.

Rhiannon held his gaze. "We have no idea what effect mixing this drug with the tranquilizer would have on a vampire. It's never been tried. So don't let them tranquilize you."

He thought that was far easier said than done, and she knew it.

Rhiannon unzipped the small black pouch she'd brought with her, and took out a syringe and a glass vial filled with clear fluid. After poking the needle through the vial's rubber stopper, she pulled back the plunger. Then she put the vial, still two-thirds full, back into the pouch, where he glimpsed a few other cellophane-wrapped syringes. She zipped up the pouch and dropped it into the chair where she'd been sitting.

Jack shivered a little and wondered just what the day ahead would bring. And then he squared his shoulders and knew it would be worth it, whatever the outcome. He moved toward Rhiannon as she tipped the syringe, needle end up, flicked it with her forefinger, and squirted a bit of the drug out the tip.

Vixen ran forward and flung her arms around Jack's neck. He was stunned by the surge of emotion that welled up in him at her gesture, and he hugged the odd little creature in return.

"I knew you were good inside. I knew it all along."

"You're pretty smart, then, because I didn't," he told her.

Seth came up beside her as she released Jack. He gripped Jack's hand hard. "Good luck, Jack."

"Thanks."

"I have ice packs chilling in the freezer," Roxy said. "I'll put them in the body bag with you. There's no telling how long they'll let you lie there in the desert sun before they come to get you. It might help some."

"Thanks, Roxy." Jack glanced at Briar. "What, no tearful goodbye from you?"

"If you get dead, it's your own idiotic fault," she snapped. Then her lips thinned, and she sighed. "Try not to."

Ilyana said nothing, and Crisa just watched everything with her eyes wide. Jack wasn't sure if she fully understood what was happening or not.

Rhiannon, for her part, pretended to be unmoved, but Jack thought he saw emotion in her eyes. "As touching as this is," she said, "if we don't get started, we're not going to make it to the appointed place on time. And we don't want to be even a minute late or we'll never make it back here. They've given us little enough time before sunrise as it is."

Nodding, Jack faced her and extended his arm. "Do it."

Rhiannon sank the needle into his flesh.

■ ■ ■ ■

"Better?"

Topaz came to slowly, to find a glass being held to her lips. She drank deeply and tried to sit up as her mother set the glass aside. "I passed out?" she asked.

"Yeah."

"And the barbarians brought me sustenance?"

Her mother set the empty glass aside and shook her head. "No. I provided that." She held up a hand to reveal her forearm, which had a strip of cloth bound tightly around it. "You were too weak to take it on your own. I've been feeding you from a glass. How are you feeling?"

Topaz took stock, felt the power flowing through her, the healing, rejuvenative power of vampiric blood. "I feel stronger. How long have I been out?"

"Most of the night. But there's still time. And I have a plan."

"What is it?"

"Uncomplicated and straight to the point. I smash through the door, you take them out. Simple."

"Not simple at all," Topaz said. "You'll get jolted and be useless to help us escape."

"I have a feeling you can handle the three of them on your own."

"You have more confidence in my fighting skills than I do, then."

"You can do it," Mirabella said. "And once you do, you just get me out of here and find us shelter before sunrise."

"It could kill you, Mother."

Mirabella shook her head. "Dawn is only an hour away. You grabbed the handle and survived it. I think I can manage a much briefer contact without dying from the shock."

Topaz nodded, because the logic of that made sense. "I still don't like it. But I don't think we have any other option." She got to her feet, smoothed her clothes, glanced at her mother again. "You took a shower, didn't you?"

"Didn't have any other plans. Are you ready?"

"I'd better be. We can't wait much longer and have any hope of success." Topaz moved closer to the door and tipped her head to one side. "I don't feel them out there. But I hear the television blaring."

"They've probably blocked mental contact between rooms to keep us unaware of their comings and goings," Mirabella suggested.

"Yeah. That's probably it." Topaz positioned herself slightly to one side of the door, crouched and ready to spring on the unsuspecting mortals beyond it. Her mother backed all the way to the farthest end of the room, paused a moment to gather her energy and then launched into motion.

By the time she hit the door she was moving quickly. Not at full speed — there wasn't enough space for that — but fast enough. She hit the door bodily, and it flew open with a crash. Mirabella surged through, then collapsed to the floor on the other side, even as Topaz lunged into motion herself, leaping her fallen mother, and preparing to snap the neck of the first mortal she saw.

Except there were none.

Frowning, Topaz stood, poised for battle, and scanned the room, all senses searching. But there was no one there. She checked the bathroom, the closets. Nothing. No one.

Turning, she spotted her mother, trembling on the floor just as Topaz had been several hours earlier. "They're gone," she told her, moving closer, crouching beside Mirabella. "We're alone here."

Blinking against her pain, Mirabella said, "They've gone to make the exchange."

"But it's *not* an exchange if they didn't take us with them."

"No," Mirabella said. "It's a trick. A trap.

Your friends are in danger, Topaz."

Topaz rose from her mother's side and went to the door to peer through the peephole. She pursed her lips and sighed, then went back to her mother again. "There are guards outside the door."

"They didn't hear that crash?"

Topaz shrugged. "Maybe the TV blocked it."

"How many?" Mirabella asked. Her voice was weak, but she was struggling to stay focused.

"Four that I can see. There could be more. I can't sense anything beyond this room."

"Is the window in this room rigged with electricity, like the one in the bedroom was?"

Topaz went to the window, yanked open the drapes, and saw only clear glass. "It doesn't look like it." Then she glanced down. "But it's way too far to jump, even for us. At least twenty-three stories. Maybe twenty-four. And it doesn't look possible to climb down."

"We're going to have to try."

"You're too weak, Mom. I can give you blood —"

"Don't be ridiculous. It's the only thing keeping you as strong as you are right now. One of us has to be able to handle this, baby. And I'm afraid it's going to have to be you. Open the window."

"I don't even know if it opens." Topaz checked and found that it did, then fumbled the safety grate away and dragged it into the room. Then she turned to find that her mother had pulled herself to her feet and was making her way weakly across the room. She had torn her skirt off at midthigh, to give herself more freedom of movement.

"Turn around, hon," Mirabella instructed. "You're going to have to carry me."

"I don't know if we can do this."

"What's the worst that can happen?"

Topaz shuddered to think. But she turned. Mirabella wrapped her arms around Topaz's neck, her legs around her waist. And then Topaz climbed out the window, hung by her hands from the edge, eyed the next ledge below her and let go. They plummeted, but she kept her hands touching the building's side, and when she felt the next ledge, she gripped it for all she was worth. And somehow she caught it and held on. She dangled there, terrified and yet exhilarated.

"We did it! It worked." She smiled in spite of herself. "We can do this. Just drop from ledge to ledge until we're close enough to jump to the ground. Hold on, here we go."

She released her hold on the second ledge,

and again they fell. But this time, when her fingers hit the next ledge down and she tried to grip it, the cement crumbled in her hands and they kept right on falling.

16

They piled into the van, all of them, their plan in place. Jack's one goal was to ensure that Topaz got out of this mess alive. His own safety didn't matter as much to him, though he would give ten years of his undead life for one more night holding her in his arms. He didn't know why the hell it had taken him so long to realize that his feelings for her were real and not just part of a con game too convincingly played. It reassured him to know that Reaper would tell her the truth, if worse came to worst. But he would much prefer to be able to do it himself. And not just tell her, but show her, convince her, love her until she could never doubt his feelings again.

The hell of it was, he might never get that chance. The suit-monkeys were going to be pretty pissed off once they realized they'd been played.

Roxy pulled the van to a stop on the

shoulder of an abandoned stretch of desert and turned around in her seat. "This is it. The GPS says the drop's a mile, due east, straight into the desert."

Jack drew a breath. "Well, grab the body bag and let's go, then."

He gripped the side door, started to open it, but Reaper stopped him with a hand on his arm. "They could be watching and you're — *I'm* supposed to be drugged and inside the bag at this point. We don't want to tip them off too soon. Not until we get Topaz and her mother safely out of harm's way."

Sighing, Jack released his grip on the door. "So you're gonna haul my ass all the way out there in a body bag?"

"I have to stay out of sight. Seth, Rhiannon, you take him out there. It'll take both of you to bring the women back here. And the way they've set this up, there's barely time to do it and get home before sunrise, so you'll have to be fast."

It was far from a perfect plan, but they had precautions in place. Jack picked up the body bag and handed it to Seth. "Sorry about this, kid."

"It'll be worth it if it works." Seth opened the side door and took the body bag out, then unfolded it on the ground and un-

353

zipped it.

Jack sat down on the van's floor with his back to the door. Seth gripped him under the arms and tugged him out as Jack let his head fall forward, feigning unconsciousness. He let Seth do all the work, lifting him, positioning his body in the open bag and closing the zipper completely. He was careful, tugging it tight to be sure no sunlight could leak through.

Freaking cowards, afraid to face him by night, Jack thought. He felt frustrated and murderous. Every cell in his body rebelled against lying still, and in a far different way from anything he'd ever felt before. It must be part of the drug's effects.

He felt himself lifted, bag and all, then tossed over Seth's shoulder and carried into the desert to meet his fate.

A short while later, Seth lowered him to the desert floor. Jack listened to the conversation going on around him and fought with himself the entire time in his effort to remain perfectly still while everything in him was straining to move, to act, to fight.

"Where are they?" Rhiannon asked. "I don't see any other body bags lying here waiting, as promised."

Jack tensed, waiting, wanting to tear through the bag and find Topaz himself.

"There's a note," Seth said. "There, pinned to that cactus."

Jack heard the paper rattle and tear a bit as Seth read aloud. "You'll find your women three miles further, due east. Good luck beating the sun."

"Damn them for this," Rhiannon muttered. "If you're out there watching, you men should get your affairs in order — soon!"

Sorry, pal, but we've gotta run, Seth told Jack mentally.

Go. Just get them back safely. That's all that matters.

Reaper waited as the sun got closer to rising. He'd taken precautions of his own, precautions none of the others were aware of. He'd slipped that little black pouch of Rhiannon's into a pocket when no one was looking, and he had a syringe full of the drug prepared and ready. He did not intend to sleep through this while his friends risked their lives.

"They're taking longer than they should have," Roxy said. They had all gathered beside the van, except for Ilyana, who stayed in the front seat, and Reaper. He remained in the back, staring through the side window toward the paling sky above the desert.

"Roxy," he said, "open the hidden compartment in the back. We need to get everyone into shelter. We can't wait any longer, and we're clearly not going to make it back to the bungalows before dawn."

Roxy reached into the van and hit a button. The rear seat folded back as the floor slid open, revealing a comfortably padded bed hidden beneath it. As soon as it was open, Briar ran around to the rear and opened the back doors.

"Good," Reaper said from the front seat. "Briar, you, Crisa and Vixen get in."

"What about the rest of you?" Vixen asked. "There's not room for five of you to rest up there." She voiced her concern even as she obeyed Reaper's orders, climbing under the floor and crowding as far to one side of the hidden bed as she possibly could.

"We can fit. We won't be able to lie down, but we can fit."

"But the sun —"

"Show her, Roxy."

Roxy hit another button, and a black barrier slid upward, separating the front seats from the rest of the van. Other screens slid upward, as well, blocking the side and rear windows. Then she got out of the van, walked around to the back and joined the others.

"You see?" she said with a smile. "Once we close these doors, the entire back of the van is completely safe. Everyone will be fine." Worriedly, she looked again at the sky and added, "If they hurry up and get their asses back here, that is."

"Leave the back doors open, Roxy." Mentally, Reaper called out to his friends. *Seth, Rhiannon. Where the hell are you? The sun's about to rise!*

They left the women farther away, Reap, Seth replied. *We've got them, and we're running for all we're worth, man, but —*

Are they all right? Reaper interrupted.

Drugged, I think. We didn't have time to check, had to grab them and run. I don't know if we're going to make it, Reap.

We'll make it, Rhiannon put in. *Just have some damned shelter waiting when we get there.*

Dive into the van. The back doors will be open and waiting. And hurry, dammit.

Thanks so much for that bit of wisdom, my friend. Rhiannon's tone dripped with sarcasm. *And here I was thinking of taking my sweet time.*

"The sun," Roxy said. She was pointing, and Reaper could see its orange rays beginning to paint the sky far on the eastern horizon.

"Briar, Crisa, get in there," he commanded. "There's no more time."

Briar climbed in, but Crisa backed away. "I'm afraid!"

Reaching for her hand, Briar said, "It'll be okay. You'll be right beside me. I promise, it'll be okay. We'll . . . we'll talk until the sleep takes us. Come on, Crisa. Trust me."

Reaper blinked, shocked at the warmth in her tone — something he'd never heard coming from Briar in the time he'd known her. He assumed it was false, put there to soothe Crisa so she didn't get them all killed. Then again, Briar had shared blood with the childlike vampiress. Perhaps the bond it had created had softened Briar's icy heart.

He pretended to pace away in worry, but in truth he only needed a private moment. Taking the needle from his pocket, he quickly injected himself, then pulled his sleeve down over the site and tossed the spent hypodermic into some desert sage before returning to the van.

Crisa took Briar's hand, then climbed in on the makeshift bed, sitting upright.

"Good," Briar said. "Now just lie back."

Roxy was already racing around to the front of the van, and the moment Briar said,

"Close it up, Roxy," she hit the button and the floor slid slowly closed over the three women. He could hear Crisa sniffling as it did, and he could also hear Briar's voice, soothing and soft, as she tried to comfort her.

Then Roxy was beside him again. "Get in. Get as far toward the front as you can. I'll wait here and close the doors as soon as the others are inside."

"Not a minute before, Roxy," he said. "If they roast, I roast with them. Understood?"

She held his eyes.

"And if that happens," he went on, "remember that Topaz and Mirabella should still be safe, in those body bags. It'll be up to you and Ilyana to get them back to safety on your own."

"I understand," she told him.

He climbed in, but he didn't move away from the doors.

"Dammit," Roxy said, looking skyward again. "The sun is cresting the —"

"Faster, dammit!" Rhiannon's voice boomed.

And then she was there, hurling the heavy body bag from her shoulder into the back of the van. Reaper grabbed it and pulled it as far in as he could, then reached for Rhiannon's hand. But she was turning, racing

359

back the other way.

Reaper sprang from the van and followed. Seth came into view then, running full bore, but he wasn't nearly as strong or as fast as Rhiannon and Reaper were. Rhiannon yanked the body bag off his shoulder as his hair began to smoulder. Reaper grabbed the younger man and jerked him right off his feet, and then they raced for the van as he felt his skin beginning to blister.

At last they were there, hurling their cargo into the blessed darkness and clambering in behind them.

Roxy slammed the van's rear doors closed. Reaper fought off the pain of being seared by the first and weakest rays of the slowly rising sun, and wished he could count on the day sleep to alleviate it and heal him. But the day sleep wasn't coming. Not for him.

He watched as Seth, his back against the wall, his knees drawn up to his chest, fell into slumber. Rhiannon sat near Reaper himself, leaning against his shoulder, body relaxed, eyes closed. And Reaper stayed awake, becoming more so with each moment that passed.

As Roxy put the van into motion, he eased Rhiannon's weight from his shoulder, leaning her against the closed door, then moved on hands and knees to the two body bags that rested on the van's floor. He wanted to make sure the women were all right. He unzipped the first bag.

A dead man lay inside. Mortal, not vampire. A neat bullet hole marked the center of his forehead. His skin was blue-gray and cold to the touch. Swearing under his breath, Reaper yanked at the zipper of the second bag and found the very same thing. Another dead male mortal lay inside.

"Roxy!" he bellowed.

Ilyana released an alarmed squeak as the van veered wildly. Then brakes squealed, and the van came to a bumpy stop on the road's shoulder.

"Reaper?" Roxy called from the front seat. "What are you — how — hell, you used that drug of Rhiannon's on yourself, didn't you?"

"Of course he did," Rhiannon replied, the sound of her voice making Reaper jump. "As did I."

He stared at her, blinking in shock. She'd been feigning her sleep! "Rhiannon, why would you . . . ?"

"Because I know you very, very well, Reaper. And I wasn't about to let you face all this alone."

He shook his head slowly, processing their

new situation. "Roxy," he said, "there are bodies in these bags. *Human* bodies. Men, both of them. Looks as if they were killed execution style. Single shot to the head. The CIA didn't keep their end of the bargain."

"Why am I not surprised?" Roxy said. "So what the hell are we going to do now?"

"I'm damned if I know," Reaper said.

"Well, I do." Rhiannon closed the zippers on the two bags as she spoke. She probably didn't like looking at the dead men inside, he thought. "Turn the van around. Go back to the site by the desert. Find a place to park where we won't be readily seen," Rhiannon said. "We sit there, and we watch for those bastards to come for the body bag we left them. Then we follow them back to wherever it is they're holding Topaz and her mother."

"If it's not already too late," Reaper put in, even as Roxy turned the van around and floored it.

"It isn't," Rhiannon said. "The sun only just rose. They're too cowardly to risk facing you before daylight, in case you might not be tranquilized as promised. By daylight, as far as they know, there's no chance of you reviving and giving them what they so richly deserve. So they wouldn't have gone after you until dawn. And it'll take them a

362

lot longer to walk that distance than it took us. They'll still be there." She tapped the barrier between the back and front of the van. "As soon as they leave, follow them. Carefully."

"You bet I will," Roxy promised.

An ambulance pulled up to the hospital just before dawn, and the attendants rolled two sheet-draped gurneys out the back and in through the automatic doors.

"Crying shame," one paramedic said, speaking in Spanish to his partner. "Even with their faces all busted up, you can tell they were beautiful, and so young. Sisters, it looks like. Why would they jump to their deaths like that?"

"No telling," his partner said. "I just wish we could've done . . . I don't know, something."

"You saw how broken they were," said the first. "Hell, they were already stone cold."

"I don't get that, either. The witnesses said they'd only seen 'em hit the ground a few minutes before we got there."

"It's a traumatic thing to witness. People get confused. Look, let's just get 'em inside. Shift was over ten minutes ago."

"Yeah."

They rolled the gurneys into the building,

then took an elevator down to the basement and the hospital morgue.

Jack managed to lie still, though keeping his body relaxed was an effort almost beyond endurance, the way he felt just then. Impatience clawed at his insides like a rat at a rotting wall, and the urge for action was impossible to ignore, so he simply fought to quiet it, to bide his time.

He felt the heat of the rising sun, and wondered whether Seth and Rhiannon had found Topaz yet, whether they'd made it back to Roxy's super-van in time. He prayed they had. If anything happened to Topaz — if he lost her now — God, he didn't think he could bear it. And then it occurred to him that this must have been exactly how she'd felt when he'd left her. She'd loved him. God, she'd loved him like no one else in his entire life had ever loved him or ever would. She'd poured her heart and soul out to him, and he'd repaid her by taking all she had to offer and walking away. She must have been feeling just the way he was right now. Facing the loss of the one you loved, certain you could never bear it.

How could he have hurt her that way? A woman who deserved it less than any he'd ever known?

Even as the heat from the rising sun made his situation nearly unbearable, making him feel as if he were being baked from the outside, he heard footsteps, sensed movement, heard an odd creaking sound. And then voices, one of which he recognized as belonging to that bastard Magnarelli.

"No dawdling. We just take him and go."

"How can we be sure it's Rivera in there?" a second agent asked. One of the two others Jack sensed out there. He had rarely, if ever, heard either of them utter a word. "How do we know they didn't pull the same —"

"It doesn't matter. If it's him, we're golden. If it's not, we still have all the leverage we need. For now, we just do what we came here to do." There was a pause, then, "There it is."

Seconds later, he felt himself being lifted, one man holding either end of the body bag. And a little while later he was dropped onto a hard surface. He landed with a thud and bit his lip to keep from grunting at the impact.

"I don't know why we couldn't have rented a couple of ATVs or something. It's a mile back to the road, and that's hell in this heat." That was the third man entering the conversation.

"Because the noise would make it too easy for someone to notice us, maybe get curious, wonder what we're up to," Magnarelli said, his tone suggesting that his underling must be some kind of moron to even suggest what he had. "Do you really want to explain to a truckload of *Federales* why three CIA agents are dragging a body out of the Mexican desert, pal?"

Number three sighed. "I guess you're right."

"Damn straight, I'm right. We want to get him back across the border without a fuss, not cause an international incident."

"It's hotter than hell." That was underling number one again.

"It's the desert. It's *supposed* to be hot. And it's only a mile. So quit your whining and pull your weight."

Jack tried to relax as he was trundled across the desert on some sort of cart with two creaking wheels at the rear, near his head. The three men took turns pulling him along, and he bumped and bounced over the terrain. He almost smiled as he thought of how difficult it must be for the mortals to drag the cart through sand. And he hoped it was as hot and uncomfortable for them as it was for him, because he was utterly roasting and miserable despite Roxy's ice packs. With everything in him, he wanted to tear through the leather bag and attack the trio. But even a small opening in his prison would spell his death. And then he would never know for sure what had become of Topaz. Suddenly something one of the underling agents had said had every alarm bell in Jack's head going off, full volume. *How do we know they didn't pull the same . . .*

Pull the same what? Trick? Stunt? What the hell had the man meant?

He thought back and tried to reconstruct the conversation. The younger agent had been wondering if Reaper were really the one in the bag. Wondering if the vampires had pulled the same . . . something. And that had Jack worried as hell. Did these bastards still have Topaz and her mother in their brutal hands? Had they played some kind of trick by putting someone or something else in the body bags that were supposed to hold them? And would he, working on his own, be strong enough to save them?

Eventually his ride through the desert ended. He felt the ground beneath him change to something smooth. Then he heard a vehicle's doors opening, and he was unceremoniously lifted and dumped again. The sound of the trunk slamming closed was unmistakable.

"Let's crank the AC," one of the lesser agents said, and then the car doors closed and he was once again in motion.

"That has to be them," Roxy said, pulling the van to a stop. "It's a black Lincoln."

"That's them. Make sure they can't see you, Roxy," Reaper instructed.

"I'm not an idiot, you know." She waited, no motion, no words. Then, "Yes, there they are. They have Jack. They're putting him into the trunk. *Damn!*"

"What?" Reaper demanded.

"They tossed him in there like a bag of feed. That *had* to hurt."

"Jack's tough. He can take it."

"I'd hate to be those two when he comes out of that bag, though," Roxy said. "I think they just managed to piss him off even more than they already had, if that's even possible." She paused, then went on. "You should speak to him, Reaper. Tell him we're following."

"No," he replied instantly. "He'd want to know about Topaz, and I'd have a hard time lying to him about that. He'd sense it. And if he finds out, he won't wait to tear out of that bag."

"With that drug in his system, he'd tear

them to bits," Rhiannon promised.

Roxy said, "No. He'd get himself killed trying, though." Then she started to drive, keeping a safe distance.

They followed the agents for better than an hour. Then the car stopped at a cantina, and the three cold-hearted operatives went inside for what must have been a hearty brunch, given the time it took them to come out again. The sun was at its zenith by the time they exited, rubbing their bellies and grunting about how good the food had been. One of them lit a cigarette and went to lean on the car as he smoked it, only to jerk his hand away from the scorching-hot metal.

Roxy reported everything to Reaper and Rhiannon as she observed it from a safe distance.

"Jack must be baking alive in that trunk," Rhiannon said. "Maybe this wasn't such a great plan after all, Reaper. We'll be lucky if he survives this much time in such extreme heat. I have no idea what effect that would have on one of our kind."

"He'll survive it." Reaper sounded more confident than he felt. The truth was, he was worried about Jack. He'd started out hating and mistrusting the cocky young con artist, but he'd seen something in Jack

Heart as all this unfolded. He'd seen courage, raw and reckless, but real courage all the same, and a deep feeling for Topaz that didn't even bear doubting. It was real. *He* was real. And decent, too, deep down, Reaper sensed. Vixen had been right about that, and he probably should have trusted her instincts. Jack was decent. He might not even know it himself, but he was.

"Okay, they're moving again," Roxy said.

"Keep following, Roxy," Reaper said.

And Rhiannon added, "Just don't let them see this monstrosity of a van. It's too loud not to be remembered, and if they see it a second time, they'll know we're tailing them."

"Shirley is not a monstrosity. In fact, her special features have kept you and the rest of the gang from being barbecued today. You should be on your knees thanking her."

"We'll all be on our knees thanking *you* if this works," Reaper said quickly, soothing her ruffled feathers.

"Well, that's an acceptable alternative," she said, sounding placated.

The van rolled into motion again, and silence reigned as Roxy negotiated the narrow, winding roads.

The agents made several more stops. Once for gas and cold drinks. Once for a bathroom break. That time they lingered outside the facility, with Magnarelli talking on his cell phone for a while. And then they got back into the Lincoln and drove some more.

"Have to stop here," Roxy said at length.

"Why?"

"They've turned into a gated drive. It winds up to a freaking *hacienda* like you've never seen. It's huge, Raphael. Gorgeous, too. Full-length veranda with columns, wide flagstone steps, tropical plants everywhere you look, giant windows everywhere. Hell, there's even a fountain."

"Someone important must live there," Ilyana said. She'd been oddly silent for most of the trip, so it startled Reaper to hear her quiet, serious tones. He'd nearly forgotten her presence. "Someone influential."

"You're right. It'll be either a government official or a drug lord," Reaper said. "Or both. The place will be well guarded. Do you see anyone standing around outside?"

"No," Roxy said. "But there's the gate. They stopped by it for a sec, and then it swung open. Someone must be operating it from somewhere."

"Or there's a code and they knew it." Reaper wished to God he could look around for himself. "Are there any other vehicles in sight?"

"No," Roxy said.

"There are outbuildings, though," Ilyana put in. "One of them has to be a garage."

Rhiannon whispered, "I sense only three mortals nearby, plus Jack." She frowned. "I don't pick up any sense of other vampires. Topaz and her mother aren't here."

Reaper frowned, not wanting to believe that. "Maybe the place is shielded. And they wouldn't be putting out much of an essence by day, Rhiannon. It could be that you just can't pick up on them while they're —"

She sent him a look so quelling that he stopped in midsentence. "Do you *know* how old I am?

How powerful?"

"Of course I do, but —"

"I am Rhiannon, daughter of Pharaoh, princess of Egypt."

"I know, but —"

"Goddess incarnate, priestess of Isis, practitioner of the ancient arts."

"I *know*, Rhiannon."

"Desired by men, envied by women, both worshipped and feared by all who encounter me."

"Okay. Okay."

"I am more than three thousand years old, Reaper. I am the third most powerful vampire in existence, created by Dracula himself. He and the great Gilgamesh, the first of us all, Damian Namtar, are the only two older, or with blood more powerful than mine. Do not doubt my ability to detect a pair of relative fledglings, Reaper. Not awake or asleep. Not alive or dead. Not —"

"You didn't detect that they weren't in those body bags, though, did you, Princess?"

Rhiannon bit her lip. "I was too busy trying to keep from being toasted, thanks to your asinine plan! Had I bothered to sense for them, I would have known. And if, after all I've done for you, you would still doubt me —"

He held up a hand. "I would never doubt you. I trust you, Rhiannon. I just . . . I don't *want* you to be right this time. Because if Topaz and Mirabella weren't in those body bags, and they aren't in this *hacienda,* then — then, Jesus, where the hell *are* they?"

"We're not going to find out until after dark," Roxy said. "We can't get to that place for a closer look until then."

"We have to," Reaper said.

He heard Roxy's frustrated sigh, but it was Ilyana who picked up the argument. "We can't drive up. We'd be seen. And you two can't walk up before sunset without being roasted. Roxy and I could, but what chance would we have against three well-trained, well-armed agents? There are video cameras mounted all over the place. I can count five of them just from here."

"We're going to have to wait, Reaper," Roxy said again. "I'm sorry."

It was at that precise moment that Reaper heard Jack's agonized screams begin.

17

"Ready?" one agent said to the other two.

Jack no longer cared who was speaking. It didn't matter. His muscles were practically itching to move, to spring, to attack. His body was finally being taken from the suffocating heat of the car's trunk and carried into blissful coolness. He smelled the airconditioning and began to feel its relief within a moment or two, as the leather bag cooled and his body followed suit. Short of being ablaze, Jack didn't think any vampire had ever been this hot and survived.

He was suspended between two of the men as they carried him, and he knew he was inside, but nothing beyond that. He was within a structure, and it was cool. He sensed only the three agents, Magnarelli and his two sidekicks. He couldn't detect the presence of any others. No drones or armed soldiers were waiting to back them up. Good.

The way he felt right now, they wouldn't stand a chance against him without help.

Finally he was slung onto a hard surface. And almost before he could anticipate what would come next, the zipper was being yanked open. Every cell in him tensed as he prepared to spring. And the moment the leather was pulled open, he did, coming out of the body bag in a fury, springing first onto his haunches and then launching himself over the heads of the three men, flipping in the air and landing behind them.

They spun, their faces expressing shock and disbelief, and Jack lunged at the first one, landing a kick to the man's chest that sent him smashing headfirst into the wall so hard that he crumpled. Spinning to the left, he delivered a roundhouse to the second man's jaw. That agent careened and teetered, then went down. But at almost that same instant, Jack felt the sting of a dart in his shoulder. He turned toward Magnarelli, who'd fired a tranq gun, and lunged at the bastard, but a second dart plunged into his chest, and then a third, in the neck, all in quick succession.

Jack's muscles slowed, his senses slowly went numb, and yet he tried to reach for Magnarelli, even as he sank to his knees. His last thought was of the words he'd heard Rhiannon say earlier. "We have no idea what effect mixing this drug with the tranquilizer would have on a vampire. It's never been tried. So don't let them tranquilize you."

Don't let them tranquilize you.

Shit.

He soon found out what the results would be — at least the initial ones — as Frank Magnarelli, a lone mortal no stronger than most, lifted him up off the floor, slammed him into a chair and handcuffed him to it. Jack's efforts at resistance didn't even slow the guy down. Eric Marquand's version of No-doz kept the tranq from knocking him out, but the tranq kept him too weak to do much in the way of fighting for his life.

"There are things I want to know, Jack," Magnarelli said, standing in front of him. "And you know I'm not going to go easy on you. I'm pretty angry with you right now."

"I imagine you are," Jack said.

Magnarelli punched him in the face, a dead-on blow that knocked him over onto his back, chair and all. It felt as if it had crushed his nose and split his lip, and landing on his cuffed hands hurt almost as much as the punch had.

Bending, Magnarelli gripped Jack's shirt-front and lifted him upright again. "So how is it you're awake during the day, Jack?"

Jack shrugged, licked his lip, tasted blood, and hoped it wasn't too much. He didn't think it was. It hurt like hell, but he didn't feel as if it were pouring out of him. Yet. "I don't know. It's some kind of fluke. Maybe something to do with how hot it got inside that body bag while you drove me all over hell and gone in your damned trunk."

The agent didn't believe him. "I suppose we can get that information later. It's not like you're ever going to taste freedom again."

"No?"

"You don't fuck with the CIA, pal. So let's not make this tougher than it has to be. Where is Rivera?"

"Who?"

"Raphael Rivera."

"Come again?"

Magnarelli hit him again, in the gut this time. The chair skidded backward but stayed upright, as Jack doubled over as much as the cuffs would allow, mouth agape.

"Reaper," the agent said. "And you can stop playing stupid with me, Jack. You know his name."

When he could form words again, Jack said, "I know his name. But I don't know where he is. I only agreed to your plan to get Topaz and Mirabella back. I never knew where Reaper was. You're wasting your time."

"We'll see about that."

The other two, who'd been lying flat out from Jack's attack, began stirring now. One of them got up, and Magnarelli said, "Grab your partner and go get the women. He'll talk faster if they're the ones suffering for his silence." He took note of Jack's stunned expression. "That's right. We still have them. You're not the only one who can pull off a con, Jack."

Jack had figured he could handle any torture this jerk could dish out. But if he were hurting Topaz, Jack knew he would talk in short order. He also knew Reaper would want him to.

"While they're gone," Magnarelli said, "we're going to see just how much pain you can take, Jack." He walked to a corner and picked up a bag. "We can't cut you, or you'll bleed out, so maybe we can come up with some creative alternatives." From the bag, he took out a hammer, and a pair of pliers.

Jack closed his eyes. Surely the pain would knock him out sooner or later.

Or maybe it wouldn't.

■ ■ ■ ■

Topaz woke with a scream ringing in her head, in her mind. *Jack's* scream. She sat up fast, her eyes opening wide as she swung her head, searching for him, ready to do serious harm to whoever might be hurting him. The reaction was instinctive and gut level. But in an instant she realized his scream had been mental. Jack wasn't here. And in that same instant she understood just where *here* was. There were sheet-draped bodies on gurneys all around her. Their feet were exposed, and tags hung from their toes.

Solemn-faced, she slid her gaze to her own exposed feet and saw a tag attached to her own big toe, as well. With a growl of impatience, she leaned forward and yanked it off.

The morgue was unmanned, as far as she could tell, as she slid off the cold metal and onto the bare floor to begin peering under the other sheets in search of her mother. She was still wearing her clothes, though they were torn, stained with dirt and blood, and even some street tar. Whatever injuries she'd sustained from the fall had been healed by the miraculous power of the day sleep. And that was little more than sheer luck — she could just have easily expired before the day sleep arrived to heal her. She could have bled out. She could have lain there a bit too long and been exposed to the rising sun. Anything could have happened.

She hoped her mother had been as lucky.

Finally she tugged back a sheet and saw her mother's face. It was unmarked. Her dress was tattered as hell, though. She must have been badly injured, Topaz thought. Maybe too badly.

She touched her mother's face. "Are you alive?"

Her mother didn't respond. A little knot of fear formed in Topaz's stomach, but she quickly reminded herself how slow her mother was to wake. The way she took her time about it, waking only by degrees, as if surfacing from some deep ocean crevasse.

And then she heard Jack screaming again, and everything in her body jerked to attention. It tied her heart in knots. Yes, he'd lied to her, used her, broken her heart to mere bits, but none of that had made her stop loving him. Oh, it had made her *want* to stop, but it hadn't killed the feeling. She didn't think anything ever would. And she would be *damned* before she would allow some sorry son of a pig to hurt him.

"Mother!" She gripped her mother's shoulders, shaking her gently. "Mother, come on. Wake up, we have to hurry."

Mirabella moaned softly and began her routine, stretching her arms above her, arching her back in her catlike way.

Topaz removed the toe tag and begged, "Mom, wake up. We don't have time for stretching and yawning and basking. We have to move."

With a soft "mmmm," Bella stopped stretching and opened her eyes.

"Someone has Jack," Topaz told her. "He's being tortured. Right now, as we speak." To herself, she added, "I'll freaking kill them."

Those loving eyes went icy cold, and Mirabella swung her legs to the side, sitting up and then standing all in one fluid motion. "Where?"

Topaz took her mother's hand, and the two of them moved through the dismal underworld, inhabited only by the dead, in search of an exit. When they found one, it led into a hallway, and after briefly searching that, Topaz found a sign marked *Salida* with an arrow that pointed up a flight of stairs.

They took the stairs at a run, not caring whether they might be seen. No one would stop them — they might try, but they wouldn't succeed. At the top there was a wide door with a push bar on the inside. Topaz hit it, and it swung open wide, revealing a parking lot, some shrubs.

She lunged through the doorway and let it close behind her, then stood for a moment, listening, *sensing.*

It didn't take long before the scream came again, but this time a coherent stream of thought came with it. *If they hurt Topaz, I'll kill them. I'll kill them or die trying. I swear to God, I will.*

She blinked and sent a look at her mother.

Mirabella nodded. "Yes, I heard it, too. I told you he loves you."

"Just because he doesn't want me hurt, that doesn't mean he loves me."

"He went after you. He's in those bastards' hands because of it. He risked himself to save you."

"You don't know that."

"Who else would be torturing him?"

Topaz shrugged and turned to face east. "He's this way."

"Then let's go."

They began to run, racing at top speed, until Topaz heard her mother's plea, delivered mentally. *Stop, darling.*

There was pain in that plea, a sensation of

weakness flowing into Topaz as clearly as the words. It was so heartrending that she came to a halt immediately, and her mother did, too. As soon as she stopped moving, Bella sank to her knees, and fell forward, palms to the earth.

"Mother, what is it?" Topaz shouted, dropping to her knees beside her. But even as she asked the question, she knew. Her mother had been electrocuted, then taken a fall that would have killed a mortal ten times over. She was older than Topaz, and therefore more powerful, but also much more susceptible to the debilitating weakness brought on by pain and blood loss. Furthermore, she'd given Topaz her own blood, then imbibed nothing to complete her own healing. The day sleep could heal, yes, and it had. But to restore Bella's strength, she needed blood. Topaz helped her into the concealing shelter of a grove of trees.

"I can't go on," Mirabella said softly. "I'll just rest here awhile. You have to continue on without me, Tanya."

Topaz stared down at her mother. "Those agents are still after us, I'm sure of it. I can't leave you alone."

"Send someone back for me. No doubt the others are on their way to help Jack, as well. Send one of them. Until then, I'll be fine."

"But, Mother —"

Her mother pressed a palm to Topaz's cheek. "Go, darling. I know you won't believe me, but this . . . this is worth anything. *Anything.* This kind of love, the love you feel for him . . . it's once in a lifetime, Topaz. Believe me. I know. Go find him. Do it now."

Topaz nodded, knowing her mother was right. What she felt for Jack *was* once in a lifetime. She only wished what he felt for her was a fraction of that. Or that he felt anything real for her at all.

But she couldn't control his feelings any more than she could control her own. She loved him, good or bad. No matter how much and how deeply he hurt her, she loved him. And as lousy as he'd treated her, Topaz thought, there wasn't a person on this planet who was going to get away with hurting the man she loved.

"No way in hell," she said aloud, and she pressed a kiss to her mother's cheek, then straightened away from her. As she strode forward, launching into a run once more, she held Jack's image in her mind, and her heart seemed to swell to bursting. She realized it didn't matter what he'd done to her. She loved him, flaws and all. She loved him, as cold and uncaring as he had been toward her. She loved him unconditionally. And it was all right if he didn't feel the same. She could live with that, because she was a strong, incredible woman. If they couldn't be together, so be it. She would manage to go on. But she would go on loving him. Always.

What she wouldn't be able to live with, she knew, would be her own guilt if she allowed anything bad to happen to him.

"Well?" Magnarelli said, when his sidekicks returned. "Where are they?"

"I don't know, sir."

Underling number one, Jack thought. Interested, despite the intensity of his pain, he managed to lift his head. He tried to see the men, but his eyes were so swollen that only the merest slits remained open, and what he could make out through them was blurry and unfocused.

Three blobs, vaguely man-shaped. Movement now and then.

"What the hell do you *mean,* you don't know?"

"The bedroom door was smashed to bits. The electric barriers had shorted themselves out. The living room window was open."

"And the guards posted outside saw nothing? *Heard* nothing?"

"They only heard the TV, they said."

Magnarelli swore, and Jack thought it looked as if he turned a small circle and pushed a hand through his hair. At least, his arm went up. He might also have been waving a fly away or knocking down a cobweb.

"That window's too high. Even a vampire couldn't survive a jump like that."

"They didn't." The second underling was speaking now. The first seemed to have used up all his courage in bringing bad news to his boss.

Magnarelli spun around fast.

"The doorman says two women jumped to their deaths just before dawn. They were pronounced dead at the scene."

"And taken where?" Magnarelli asked in a monotone.

"I don't know. A morgue somewhere, I imagine."

Magnarelli gripped the underling by the front of his shirt and jerked him forward. "Find out, dammit. Get back there and find out where they were taken, and exactly what time, and whether they're still there now. Do you understand?"

"But . . . but . . ."

"Do it. Now."

He released the younger agent, who stumbled a few steps backward.

Jack let his head relax again, feigning unconsciousness, though he didn't have to fake it much. He would have been unconscious right now if not for that damnable drug of Rhiannon's. Hell, he was like a walking corpse.

He started to laugh, because that was what he was anyway, right? Undead. A walking corpse.

"What the hell are you laughing at?" Magnarelli asked. One of his rookies remained there with him. The other one had already scurried away to do his master's bidding.

"My girl," Jack said, though his mouth was swollen, lips puffy and split, and his voice sounded as if he were talking around a mouthful of marbles. "She outsmarted you."

"Not if she's dead on a slab in the morgue, she didn't," Magnarelli said. "And if that's the case, I'll be the one laughing. Believe me. I wouldn't be one bit sorry to see that pain-in-the-ass bitch dead and buried."

Jack lunged forward, picking the chair up with him. Bent over, he charged the bastard, head plowing into his stomach before he knew what was coming. Magnarelli doubled over, then fell to the floor, and Jack spun around fast, so the legs of the chair would smash into his head.

But the agent ducked, then gripped one of the chair legs and swung it, so that Jack hit the wall face-first, chair and all. His cheek was razed by rough-surfaced bricks. His already broken nose mashed against them. He sank to the floor, the rush of pain incapacitating him. But rather than passing out, as he should have done, he just lay there, trembling in unbearable agony.

Reaper managed to wait until sundown, but just barely. He and Rhiannon were cranky and angry and impatient. He had the floor opened up before the others were even awake, and Briar, Crisa and Vixen were out of the compartment almost before Seth had stirred.

He opened the rear doors of the van, eager to get out, stretch his legs, move a bit and get a look at the *hacienda* where Jack was being tortured.

The others climbed out and surrounded him, Roxy and Ilyana coming around to the back, as well.

"What's the situation?" Seth asked.

Reaper pointed toward the sprawling white mansion. "Jack's being held in there by three agents. They've been torturing him for about two hours now."

Vixen turned her head quickly, her hand flying to her mouth. Crisa clutched Briar's arm tighter, while Briar swore under her breath.

"How the hell did three mortals manage to get the best of him?" Briar asked. "Didn't the drug work? Was he asleep when they opened the bag?"

"They tranquilized him," Rhiannon said softly, her eyes cast downward.

"I thought you said no one knew what kind of reaction the two drugs would cause when they were combined?" Vixen asked.

"No one does," Rhiannon said. "Or rather, no one did. I imagine by now your Jack has a fairly decent idea."

"Well? What the hell are we waiting for?" Briar demanded. "Let's go after him."

"Topaz is on her way. She's asked that we send someone back for her mother, who's apparently in a weakened state and needed to stay behind." Reaper looked at the group. "Roxy, I'd like you to take Crisa and Ilyana, and go back for her. Topaz says she needs sustenance. Badly."

Roxy nodded. "We'd need the van for that."

"I know. Unload the medical kit, a few

pints of blood and most of the weapons before you leave. We'll need them. When you get back here with Mirabella, park somewhere safe, and we'll meet you there once this is over."

"There's a dirt road off this one, a mile back. I'll head up there a few miles and pull off into a secluded spot."

"We'll find you," Reaper promised. "Meanwhile —"

Something rushed past him in a blur. He caught the essence of fury, of rage — and of Topaz.

"Hell, she's not waiting. Let's go. *Now!*" Reaper ordered.

Briar, Seth and Vixen joined him in racing full bore toward the house.

Topaz leapt the gate, then raced up the drive and hit the *hacienda's* huge double doors so hard that one of them split as they crashed open. She crouched just inside the door, looked left and right, sensed for Jack's essence and was speeding closer to him again, all in the space of a single heartbeat. Every door that blocked her way was demolished. Every piece of furniture that stood in her path was obliterated. She was a fury, and nothing was going to stop her.

When she reached the basement room and

saw him, bound to a chair that lay cockeyed on the floor with two of its legs broken off, his face so swollen she wouldn't have recognized him if she couldn't feel him, she went still for no more than an instant.

But that instant was enough. She was jolted with enough electricity to put her on her knees. A stun gun.

One agent cuffed her hands behind her back, even as the second returned to his spot behind the door with that stun gun, awaiting the others, whose thundering feet were within Topaz's earshot even then. But not within earshot of the mortals. She thought wildly toward them, *Stop! Wait! It's a trap!*

She sensed their retreat instantly and sighed in relief, then lifted her head as the agent grabbed her by her arms and plunked her down in a chair, applying shackles before she regained enough strength to fight him off.

"I should have known it was a trap. You didn't seal off the house the way you did the hotel room. You wanted me to hear Jack's pain. You knew I would come for him."

"We wanted Reaper to come for him. We thought we'd left you safe and sound in our suite. What happened? You decide to check out early?"

"You're the one who's going to check out. Permanently." She nodded at the stun gun. "What happened? You run out of tranquilizer darts?"

"Not at all. We just wanted you conscious for a while. Torture isn't very effective when the subject is unconscious."

She shot a look at Jack. He was in anguish. "Doesn't look like it's very effective on conscious subjects, either, or you would already know everything you could possibly want to."

"Oh, hell, he doesn't give a shit about his own suffering. But yours — I think that'll be a whole different matter."

"Bring it on, bastard," she said.

"No."

Jack's voice was strained, weak. Her heart broke on hearing it. She could barely stand to look at him, to see him so badly beaten. And yet, even when she wasn't looking at him, she could feel his pain.

"Don't . . . hurt her. I'll tell you everything."

"Like you were supposed to be doing all along, right, pal? Instead of feeding us useless crumbs? Now you see what you get when you try to double-cross the CIA."

Reaper. Topaz sent the message urgently.

We're in a basement room. One way in and out. Two men here. One is waiting just inside the door with a stun gun.

"Go throw the switch, activate the silent-zone around this room," the lead agent ordered the other. "And turn on the electricity."

The other walked to the far side of the room, toward a large metallic box, with several switches and levers attached.

They're about to activate that force field, Reaper, Topaz thought rapidly. *We'll be unable to communicate soon. And they're electrifying the doors. If you touch them —*

Got it. You should know that I knew what Jack was doing the whole time, Topaz. He was playing them, not us, to get information on your mother for you.

Topaz couldn't believe it. She gasped and then stared at Jack, and her heart broke for the pain he was in. The agent threw one switch, then another.

Why the hell didn't he tell me? Topaz thought toward Reaper.

Nothing. Dead silence. Like speaking into an empty room. The subordinate agent returned to his position, and Topaz asked Jack, *Why didn't you tell me?*

He met her eyes, though she doubted he could see her through the puffy purple grapes that were his own. *Didn't think you'd believe me. Didn't want to lose you.*

He bent forward as far as he could, and started to cough and choke, not stopping until he threw up blood.

Topaz loved him with her entire being. She would have died just then, to give him the tiniest bit of relief. Lifting her head, she said, "Let Jack go. I'll tell you what you want if you'll just let him go."

"Don't . . . bother," Jack managed. He did his best to wipe his chin on his shirtfront. "I won't leave her."

The head agent rolled his eyes. The underling had to avert his. "I'm not letting anyone go, and I don't have any sympathy for your star-crossed love story. Either Reaper turns himself in within the hour, or you both die. It's that simple." He picked up a tranq gun from a table and handed it to his partner. "If they move, tranq them." Then he eyed the two vampires once again. "Be aware, my friends, that the dosages in that gun are enough to kill you this time." He focused on Jack. "And yes, it's been tested."

"There will be no need for that," Reaper said softly. His voice came from just beyond the closed, locked and electrified door to the room where they were being held. Mental voices wouldn't penetrate, but normal spoken words did.

"You've got me, Magnarelli. Let them go."

The lead agent, the one Reaper had identified as Magnarelli, went warily to the door. "You'd better come in alone, Rivera. We've got our tranq guns loaded with enough of that shit to kill the strongest vampire known. And we *will* use it — on these two if you pull anything, and on anyone else who tries to enter with you."

"Understood," Reaper replied.

Magnarelli nodded to his cohort. Topaz noticed it was the one she'd thought had some semblance of a conscience, the one with the deep blue eyes. "Cut the power," Magnarelli told him. "Be ready to turn it right back on the second I tell you."

Blue Eyes returned to the breaker box and lowered a lever. Magnarelli watched him, and as soon as it was done, he unlocked and opened the door, glancing past Reaper nervously before ushering him quickly inside and slamming the door closed behind him. "Reactivate the power," he ordered.

The other one threw the switch again.

"Now get over here and cuff him!" Magnarelli shouted. As the younger one rushed to obey, Reaper turned, obedient and nonthreatening. He put his hands behind him and allowed himself to be hand-cuffed.

"These cuffs are not vampire tested," Magnarelli said. "They won't hold you."

"You think?" Reaper asked.

"I know. But if you try to break free, we'll kill your friends. And we have a contingent of agents, heavily armed, highly trained, on their way here to transport you back to the States. There won't be any more of your nonsense, *Reaper*."

"I wasn't planning any," he said, and he took a seat, as if he planned to sit there calmly for however long it took to await his transportation home.

"Why don't you just tranquilize me now so you can quit worrying about what I might do?"

"I will if I have to," Magnarelli promised. "But I was asked to keep you conscious until you could be questioned."

"By whom?" Reaper asked.

"You'll find out when he gets here."

"Has to be Dwyer. My former boss. Well, it'll be great to catch up," Reaper said.

Topaz noticed something moving inside his shirt, though, and frowned, wondering, What the hell?

Get their attention off me for a second, Reaper thought.

Topaz stared at him but didn't bother questioning him. The big guy was up to something, and she didn't much care what it was, as long as it would get them out of this mess and get Jack some relief, and soon. She wasn't sure how much longer he could last in this much anguish.

She rose, picking up her chair with her and, shrieking like the proverbial banshee, she charged the wall, smashing the chair against it, then backing up and preparing to do it again, her attention focused on Reaper the entire time.

The two agents rushed her, as she'd hoped they would do instead of shooting a lethal dose of tranquilizer into her, seeing as she was only hurting herself, not going after them. And even as they tackled her to the floor, she saw the small red fox squeeze up out of Reaper's shirt, leap lightly to the floor and race across the basement room to where the breaker box was. Neither of the agents had seen it. The fox curled up on itself and lay still, tail curling over its tiny brown nose.

Vixen. And she was going to shift back at any moment. They would spot her fast, but it wouldn't take long. Even now, the others must be gathering beyond this door. Waiting.

Topaz drew her eyes from the little fox,

who was beginning to squirm and writhe now, to the men who'd taken her to the floor. They were threatening violence if she didn't calm down. She decided to go for hysteria. She cried, she screamed, she shouted the walls down. "You have to let us go! You said you would. I can't be in here any longer! I can't. Let me out, let me out, let me ouuuuut!"

One backhand to the jaw silenced her, but even as her head snapped back, she saw Vixen shifting. She couldn't give up her act, not yet.

"There's no need to strike her!" Reaper shouted.

"Don't," Jack muttered. He was oblivious to what was up with Vixen, his attention only on her. "Please, baby, don't give them . . . a reason . . ."

But she kept on screaming and crying, thrashing and twisting in their arms, until one of them pointed the tranq gun at her.

"It's enough to kill. You want to die?"

She looked at Jack. "If you don't get him some help, he *will* die, you idiots! And if he does, yeah, that's exactly what I want. But not until I can take the two of you with me."

Vixen rose from the floor, stark naked and utterly beautiful, and threw the switch.

"Now!" Reaper shouted at the top of his voice.

Instantly the door burst open, and vampires swarmed inside, an imposing and unfamiliar vampiress leading the way. The agent with the tranq gun turned to fire at her, and Topaz sprang, hitting his arm with her head as hard as she could. The dart went wide, and then the woman was on him, and Briar was on the other one. The two vampiresses met each other's eyes, and almost as one, snapped the necks of the men they held. Seth was running toward Vixen, while Mirabella rushed to Topaz, bending over and trying to release her from the cuffs, but she was too weak from everything she'd been through to snap them on her own.

"The older one has the keys," Topaz said. "Hurry."

Briar dug in a pocket, found the keys and handed them to Crisa before letting the man's limp body sink to the floor. Crisa ran the keys back over to Bella, who freed Topaz. "Are you all right, darling?"

"Yeah. Fine." Topaz turned, ran to Jack and fell to her knees close to him. Carefully she moved him just enough so that she could unfasten the cuffs that held him. Then she bent close to him, sliced her own arm and pressed it to his lips.

He drank only a little before pulling away. "Don't. You need it."

"Not as badly as you do."

He shook his head, then looked into her eyes. "I meant it this time, Topaz. I meant it. I'd have died for you."

"You nearly did, Jack. You very nearly did."

"I love you, Topaz. I think I have all along, only I just didn't know it. Didn't believe in it, so I didn't see it as even the most remote possibility. But I couldn't keep your money. I regretted taking it. I've missed you and ached for you every minute that we were apart. And I swear, I'll never lie to you again. I love you."

"You're damn right you'll never lie to me again," she said, but she said it through rivers of tears that were streaming down her face.

"That's not what I'm waiting to hear," he told her weakly.

She smiled through her tears. "I love you, too, Jack. I always have. Always will."

She kissed him very gently.

"We need to move," Reaper said. He'd been going through the dead agents' pockets and had extracted several items. "They have a goon squad on the way to pick me up. Besides, we need to get our con man here to someplace where Roxy can patch him up

401

and see to it he survives until dawn."

"Nothing could do me in, Reaper," Jack said. "Not now." And his eyes were on Topaz.

Those eyes. Those eyes of his that had told her all she needed to know right from the start. She could see the same thing in them now that she'd seen before. She'd thought it was part of the con, but now she knew better. His eyes had been saying "I love you" from the day they'd first kissed.

And she had a feeling they would keep on saying it for a long, long time.

ABOUT THE AUTHOR

Tasty, tension packed, haunting, bewitching and better than chocolate are just a few of the ways *New York Times* bestselling author **Maggie Shayne** and her award-winning novels have been described by critics and colleagues alike. Shayne is one of the hottest and most beloved authors ever to pen a paranormal romance. Her works are ever-fresh, cutting-edge and young, just like her characters, and much like the author herself. Maggie lives in a restored and happily haunted century-old farmhouse in the wilds of Cortland County, New York. For more information visit www.maggieshayne.com.